Relatively
Rainey

R. E. BRADSHAW

Titles from R. E. Bradshaw Books

Rainey Bell Thriller Series:
Relatively Rainey (2015)
Colde & Rainey (2014)
The Rainey Season (2013) Lambda Literary Awards Finalist
Rainey's Christmas Miracle (2011) (Short Story: E-book only)
Rainey Nights (2011) Lambda Literary Awards Finalist
Rainey Days (2010)

The Adventures of Decky and Charlie Series:
Out on the Panhandle (2012)
Out on the Sound (2010)

Molly: House on Fire (2012)
Lambda Literary Awards Finalist

Before It Stains (2011)

Waking Up Gray (2011)

Sweet Carolina Girls (2010)

The Girl Back Home (2010)

Relatively Rainey

A Rainey Bell Thriller

R. E. BRADSHAW

Published by
R. E. BRADSHAW BOOKS

USA

●R.E.B.BOOKS●

Relatively Rainey
By R. E. Bradshaw

Website: http://www.rebradshawbooks.com
Facebook: https://www.facebook.com/rebradshawbooks
Twitter @rebradshawbooks
Blog: http://rebradshawbooks.blogspot.com
For information contact rebradshawbooks@gmail.com

Acknowledgments

To my family and friends who know just how long this year has been, thank you for standing with me when I had a hard time standing by myself. To the readers who waited patiently, thank you. Much love to you all.

About the book…

Terrors come during vulnerable moments in the night. While lost in sleep, demons arise to expose our deepest dreads. Happiness is not a deterrent to the treachery of memories and fears.

Having suffered a traumatic event nearly five years prior, Rainey has settled into contented family life. When a body tied to JW Wilson surfaces, the compartmentalization Rainey Bell practices proves to be her near undoing. As the buried demons of her past come to call in nearly nightly terror-filled dreams, self-doubt becomes a constant companion.

Rainey endeavors to juggle life as a devoted parent, a loving spouse, a big sister, and a successful entrepreneur. Currently, she is using her behavioral analysis skills for the multi-jurisdictional task force hunting a fetish burglar turned murderer while trying to resolve her resurfacing post-trauma issues before Katie sends her packing. Rainey is also attempting to keep the youthful enthusiasm of her half-sister, Durham Police Officer Wendy King, from torpedoing her young career and endangering her extended family.

REB

Dedicated to the woman whose hand rests gently in the small of my back—encouraging, sheltering, and sure.

Part I

PRELUDE TO A NIGHTMARE

"There are moments when even to the sober eye of reason, the world of our sad humanity may assume the semblance of Hell."
— *Edgar Allan Poe*

Relatively Rainey

CHAPTER ONE

7:00 PM, Monday, September 2, 2013
Chancery Court Subdivision
Durham County, NC

The small window screen in Dr. Kent Barker's hand puzzled him. His profound bewilderment drew the attention of his neighbor.

"What's the trouble there, Kent?"

"I'm sorry. What?" Kent, half listening, still tried to make sense of things.

The smiling neighbor pointed a dripping hose nozzle at the screen.

"You've been standing right there since I started watering this flowerbed. I was so caught up in watching you, I think I over-soaked it."

Kent looked at the perfectly maintained bed of flowers edging the driveway next door. The flowerbed exemplified the order in Kent's upper-middle class, manicured subdivision. The homeowners' association made sure everyone conformed to the neat and tidy rules. Upon returning an hour ago from a Labor Day weekend trip to the beach with family, the Thomas Kincaid-ness of his cul-de-sac struck him once more. The French country style homes formed a perfect jigsaw puzzle picture of the American dream. No matter how many times Kent made that corner, the image remained the same.

He remarked to Marilyn, his wife, "I could take a picture of this street every day, and it would only reflect the change in seasons." He smiled at his college freshman daughter's reflection in the rearview mirror, adding, "There is comfort in that sameness."

Hannah was almost on her own now, soon to relegate her time with the family to weekends when she could manage it. She was the last of the Barker brood to leave the nest. Kent had just turned fifty, and the slower pace of suburban living suited him. None of his medical school buddies would believe beer-bong champ Barker would prefer the mundane and routine in his later years. But after a long day of surgery, surprises were the last thing an anesthesiologist wanted. Spotting the screen out of place interrupted the solace Kent felt in his world of comfortable banality.

The neighbor persisted, "What happened? Did you get that off and now can't figure out how to put it back?"

Kent asked, "Reece, were you around this weekend?"

"Yes. Well, I was. Travis took his mother to see his brother on Sunday, but I was here all weekend. Why? What's wrong?"

Kent glanced back down at the screen and the basement window it should have been covering.

Shrugging, he answered, "I don't know. This screen was off, but the window was still locked on the inside, and the alarm was active. Marilyn says it just feels like someone was in the house, but we can't find anything missing."

"Now, that's disconcerting. I sure didn't see or hear anything. Is she sure?"

Nineteen-year-old Hannah came screaming out the front door with the answer.

"Daddy, some pervert went through my laundry and stole all my underwear—all of it, bras, and everything."

Hannah left her first week's worth of college laundry in the basement before joining the family for the beach holiday with her older siblings and their spouses. Kent knew this because he carried the bulging duffle bag down the stairs Friday afternoon.

2

Kent's wife fled the house close on Hannah's heels, phone to her ear and in mid-sentence, "...broke into our house and stole our teenage daughter's underwear. And if I'm not mistaken, there is some genetic material you need to come collect."

At that moment, everything in Kent's banal world changed.

#

10:00 PM, Friday, July 25, 2014
Buckhorn Road, Chatham County, NC

Arianna Wilde climbed into her grandmother's farmhouse canopy bed, sinking into the feather top and down pillows. A source of countless fond memories, she felt the bed cradle her as it had on those special occasions when she visited the farm. Snuggled under Nana Wilde's arm, Arianna would listen to her favorite books read aloud. Her war bride grandmother maintained her cultured British accent throughout her life, even after spending the last sixty-nine years of it near the banks of the Cape Fear River. Arianna believed a genuine appreciation for Alice in Wonderland and Peter Pan achievable only when the texts were read aloud by a British grandmother.

She inherited the farm and her grandmother's feather bed in January. After finalizing her divorce and the sale of the matrimonial home, Arianna moved into the farmhouse in May. The money from the settlement helped restore and modernize the old place. Having lived in Chapel Hill since her college days, the move twenty-five miles south to her family's ancestral country home was a welcomed one. Wherever her laptop received a signal became an office, and the solitude of country living appealed to her at this juncture in her life. Relocating seemed the answer to the question Peggy Lee sang over and over in her mind for the last few years, "Is that all there is?"

The intense stress of living on site during a remodel was well worth it. Arianna relearned the self-sufficiency of her youth after too many years of living dependent on the skills of others. Now in the final stages, she was down to the cosmetics of painting the interior and trying to get a handle on the overgrown grounds. Beating back nature to the wood line in the massive yard by day and painting the two-story interior by night, Arianna worked her body to its limits over the last few weeks. She had no spare moments to dally in the past. The work focused her and kept her old friends Regret and Dread at bay.

Arianna regretted she didn't love her husband. He was sweet and kind, but it wasn't enough. She regretted that she'd stuck it out for thirteen wasted years and dreaded the thought of dating again at forty-one. She regretted she hadn't spent more time with her aging grandmother. She dreaded the weekly phone calls from the ex, ostensibly to make sure she was all right, but it was more about propping him up.

He ended almost every conversation with some form of, "I could understand if it was someone else, but you just stopped loving me."

Arianna regretted having been honest with him about her feelings. She had contemplated telling him there was someone else, in hopes that he would move on with his life. She regretted that she didn't care enough to lie.

Today she added a new bit of remorse to the list. She thoroughly regretted saying, "How hard could this be," before turning the key on the old tiller and promptly sending it through the side of the barn.

"I should have remembered the tractor debacle," she said aloud, following it with chuckles.

Her muscles ached but were taut. Her body looked better than it had in years. She overcame many things since the move, learning something new about herself and the farm seemingly minute by minute. She had taken back her name and worked on taking back her life one day at a time. Regrets aside, Arianna had mastered her dread of a coming new day.

Tomorrow, I will conquer the tiller.

She reached for the bedside lamp. As she pulled the old chain, plunging the room into darkness, she said aloud, "Think happy thoughts." It was something her grandmother would say each night. Arianna thought of the happiest thing she could.

The new washer and dryer will be installed in the morning. Praise baby Jesus.

The lace curtains of the canopy bed swayed slightly with the light summer wind coming through the open windows. The heat and air would be installed once all the construction dust settled.

"No need to clog up a new system, ma'am," the installer informed her as he handed her a trip ticket with a much later installation date than she had hoped scribbled at the bottom.

The dust was the reason the wood-framed screens were removed downstairs and the large windows thrown open. Fans sat on sills, running day and night to dry paint and suck out the seemingly never-ending drywall dust. She cleaned and vacuumed every day, but the dust prevailed. Plastic covered the portal to the bedroom where she slept. With the door shut much of the time, the room stayed relatively free of contaminants, but the powder-fine gypsum dust still managed to slip through the tiniest cracks. She thought the hand-tatted canopy should come down before it was damaged, but it comforted her with the retained fragrance of her grandmother's perfume. Arianna's eyes fluttered shut as the night breeze tickled her nose with Nana Wilde's Chanel No. 5.

#

He knew she would be one of his girls the first time he saw her. He had twenty-five regularly visited targets, but was always ready to add a new one if the urge struck. He had jogged past the old Wilde farm the day she ran the tractor into the ditch by the road.

"Perhaps brush-hogging the front forty wasn't your wisest choice for a first outing," he had said to her.

"No kidding," she said, and then laughed before blowing strands of stray hair from her brow.

He had been obliged to stop, along with several other helpful country neighbors. That was the thing about people living in the county where they buried Mayberry's Sheriff Taylor's Aunt Bee. Down on the river, away from the suspicion and self-absorption of urban life, folks were there to help a neighbor in need. He needed Arianna Wilde from the moment she smiled in his direction.

He paid his first furtive visit to her that very night. He helped himself to a black bra and panties left hanging from a makeshift clothesline on the back porch and now treasured among the many items he removed during successive visits over the last eight weeks. It took him only a few minutes the next day to find out about the new resident on Buckhorn Road. He simply mentioned the activity around the Wilde place to the man at the feed store over in Brickhaven. What the old timer didn't know, his nosey wife filled in. A little more searching on the Internet and he had all the information needed on his new target, Arianna Wilde.

He watched her bedroom window as the amber glow of the bedside lamp went dark. It wouldn't be long now.

#

7:50 AM, Saturday, July 26, 2014
Arianna Wilde's Farmhouse

"What do you mean there wasn't anyone at home? I'm at home. I saw you drive away."

Arianna listened to the voice on her phone for only a second before unleashing a tirade.

"I think spending thousands of dollars with your company warrants more than a cursory knock. Flash Gordon could not have made it to the door before you decided no one was home."

The voice interrupted her rant, causing her to pause. Upon hearing the delivery driver's response, she sighed heavily.

"You want to know who Flash Gordon is? Oh, for the love of— Look, your office said the delivery would be between 8:00 and 9:00 this morning. It is just now 7:50. You turn that truck around this instant or return after I get off the phone with your boss, your boss's boss, and on up the chain of command until I have a washer and dryer installed and working in my home— today."

Arianna was halfway down the stairs when she hung up on the apologetic driver. The old washer was on its last legs and the dryer gave up the ghost years ago. Dogs or cats or some other creatures had been making off with her lingerie for weeks. She suspected the crow that hung out near the clothesline. He looked guilty and seemed always to be watching. Arianna laughed at the thought of a tree somewhere decorated with her bras and panties. She hated to think of the alternative—that one of the workers had a thing for ladies underwear. Her dirty clothes from the past week waited in a basket on the kitchen counter in anticipation of a new working washer and dryer and as a way to stem the tide of vanishings. She couldn't afford to hang any more underclothes on the line to dry. She had no time right now to shop for more.

Reaching the front door, she flung it open and stood there ready to speed dial the appliance store if its truck did not return in a timely fashion. Another bright July day had dawned on a clear blue Carolina sky. Sunrays shot through the open door, illuminating the dust she stirred on her way down the stairs. Arianna watched the particles dance in the sunbeams. The light revealed a floor and stairs she'd cleaned the evening before, cast again with a layer of powder-thin dust.

"When will this end?" she asked, with a palm raised to the invisible powers that be.

She saw the footprints at the same time the appliance truck slowed on the road in front of the house and began the turn into the driveway. Tracing the path of the footprints with her eyes, Arianna noted they approached from the back of the house, went up the stairs, and then returned the way they came.

"Carl, are you here already?"

Arianna called out to the handyman she'd hired to help with the finishing touches. Maybe he arrived early and realized she had not come out of her room yet. He was supposed to finish the tile repair on the upstairs bathroom today. No response came from Carl. He was probably out back, waiting for her to appear with coffee. The guys were getting out of the delivery truck, tools in hand. All was right with Arianna's world for a moment.

The euphoria was short-lived. As she led the installers through the kitchen to the laundry room at the back of the house, Arianna saw her dirty clothes dumped on the floor. The empty basket was left on the counter. As she reflexively picked up the clothes and returned them to the basket, she froze with her eyes on the footprints. She could see now they led up to her bedroom from the back door. Arianna's sense of security took a major hit. Her anxiety registered with the men now watching her.

"Are you okay?" one of them asked.

Her shaken state evident in the reply, Arianna answered, "I believe someone has just stolen all my underwear."

#

7:10 AM, Saturday, September 20, 2014
Chancery Court Subdivision,
Durham County, NC.

Kent Barker turned the last bend in the running trail, legs and lungs on fire. With the end in sight, he dug deeper, sprinting as fast as his fifty-one-year-old legs would allow. Crossing his imaginary finish line, Kent alternated between walking off the lactic acid surging through his near-cramping muscles and grabbing his knees, gasping for air.

"Nice sprint," a sheriff's deputy said from the edge of the woods.

He and two other deputies appeared to be searching the strip of land behind Kent's house that separated the running trail from the yards in the neighborhood.

"Thanks," Kent replied between gasps. "What's going on?"

The deputy approached, asking, "Do you live around here?"

"Yeah," Kent said, finally able to stand erect. "I live right there." He pointed to the back of his home.

The deputy pulled out a pad and pen. "Could I have your name, sir?"

"Dr. Kent Barker. What's going on? Has something happened to my wife?"

"Why would you ask that, sir?"

Kent became impatient. "Because you're standing in the woods behind my house asking me questions."

"Your wife is Marilyn Barker?"

"Yes. What's happened? Is she okay?" Kent demanded.

"May I have a look at the soles of your shoes, sir?"

Kent immediately showed the bottoms of his shoes to the deputy and began to panic, "Oh, my God. Marilyn. Tell me what's happened."

"Your wife is fine, Dr. Barker. Someone broke into the house two doors that way." The deputy pointed just a few hundred yards down the trail. "During the canvas this morning, we found tracks in the mud there and the same tracks here behind your home and more muddy prints on your back patio. They do not match your shoes. We spoke to your wife. We understand you reported a theft a little over a year ago. Is that right?"

"Yes. Did he come back?" Kent asked.

"The crimes seem to match the fetish burglaries we've had over the past twelve months, starting with your home last September, only this time the female was at home."

"The Tanners. That's who you're talking about, right? Is anyone hurt?"

"Tanner, yeah that's right. Do you know them?"

"Yes, we all know each other. It's a friendly neighborhood. You didn't answer me. Is everyone okay?"

"Yes, sir. No one was hurt. The teenager was home alone. She took a shower and when she came out, the clothes she left on the bathroom floor were gone along with the contents of her lingerie drawer."

"My God, he was in there with her. When did this happen?"

"Where were you around midnight last evening, Dr. Barker?"

Incensed that he was under suspicion, Kent responded, "What? You think I stole my own daughter's underwear and now I've moved on to the neighbor's?"

"We're asking these questions of everyone, Dr. Barker."

"I was home with my wife. Didn't you speak to her? Didn't she tell you that?"

9

The deputy smiled. "We have to ask, and yes she did. Did you see or hear anything unusual last night?"

Kent relaxed. "No, nothing. We went to bed around eleven. I take a sleeping aid, and I was out pretty quickly. I wouldn't have heard a thing for at least six hours. My wife says I'm like the living dead."

"In the last year, have additional personal items disappeared from your home?"

"Not that I'm aware of, but our daughter doesn't live here anymore. She shares a house with some friends a few miles away and closer to her school. The responding officers last year told us she was the target—that it was probably a teenager with issues."

"I think we're re-evaluating that assessment, Doctor. This is the eleventh reported fetish burglary in the last year."

"My God, I had no idea," Kent said, feeling sick to his stomach.

The deputy made a note and put the pad back in his pocket. "We might want to speak with you again. Keep your doors and windows locked, sir." He started to turn away but added, "You might lay off that sleeping aid for a bit. At least until we catch this guy."

#

4:56 AM, November 22, 2014
Arianna Wilde's Farmhouse
Buckhorn Road, Chatham County, NC

She watched the second hand on her grandmother's kitchen wall clock tick away the minutes in slow motion. The large red rooster with the clock in his belly had hung in that very spot as long as Arianna remembered. She'd been sure to rehang it as soon as the new paint dried. Mr. Rooster's clock hands said it was closing in on 5:00 a.m. Her attacker left her at 3:00, two hours ago. Two hours that crept by one tick at a time.

"Arianna, can you look straight ahead for me?"

The EMT's smile did not cover his concern as he focused a small flashlight in each of her eyes.

"Thank you," he said, clipping the penlight back inside his shirt pocket. He checked the bandage on her head, seemed satisfied, and asked, "Are you warm enough? Can I get you anything?"

Arianna pulled her grandmother's quilt tighter around her shoulders and resumed watching the seconds tick by.

"Are you sure we can't take you to the hospital?" a second EMT asked.

"I'm sorry, gentlemen. May we have a moment alone with Ms. Wilde?"

Arianna heard the voice of the female detective again, the one who tried to interview her before without much luck. The only words Arianna spoke in the last two hours were to the emergency operator. The details she gave were sparse. Her name, address, and the declaration "he raped me" were all she said before hanging up. The phone rang repeatedly in the long minutes she waited for the police to arrive. Arianna ignored it while she watched Mr. Rooster tick-tick-tick away the life she knew. Convinced this was punishment for walking out of her marriage, for trying to start over, for seeking the life of independence she craved, Arianna Wilde stopped talking because there was nothing left to say.

The flashlight-bearing EMT protested being asked to leave. "She needs medical attention," he argued.

"That's the goal, but right now what she needs is to process," the detective responded with authority.

"Well, if she starts showing signs of shock—"

A female voice unfamiliar to Arianna interrupted the EMT.

"I think what Ms. Wilde needs right now is a little quiet. If you will just wait outside in the hall, I'm sure she'll leave with you voluntarily when she's ready."

The room cleared of all but the detective and the other woman, the one with the calm, controlled tone. The moment the police arrived, the normally peaceful country night had filled with male voices and the sound of heavy footsteps. They attempted hushed communications, but Arianna could still hear them—and smell them. Or was that his odor lingering on her skin? She rubbed her nose in her grandmother's quilt, hoping for a whiff of Chanel No. 5, as quiet returned to the kitchen.

Arianna heard the refrigerator door open. She turned to see the calm voice belonged to a tall woman with short chestnut curls, dressed in a black, classic, long wool coat. At the moment, she was removing a carton of half and half from the shelf. Arianna became entranced with the woman who did not try to speak to her but went about making tea. A full five minutes of silence passed before the tall stranger sat down across from Arianna and slid a cup of tea in front of her. A little wisp of steam curled up between them.

"I hope I got it right," the darkly attractive woman said. "You look like you could use something warm. It's getting chilly in the early mornings, isn't it?"

Arianna nodded and reached for the cup. She pulled it close, wrapping both hands around it for the warmth. To her bones, she felt a chill that only seemed to turn colder as time wore on. Tea was exactly what she wanted, but she hadn't been able to articulate that to anyone. Arianna stared across the table into eyes that understood.

With eye contact made, the woman began to talk. Nothing in her voice registered the seriousness of the situation. She spoke as if they were sitting down for a casual tea, two strangers meeting for the first time.

"I'm a coffee drinker, but my spouse spent a summer in England during college. I've been told putting the milk in first and then adding the tea and water makes a better cup. Do you add your milk first?"

Arianna answered without thinking. "Yes, my grandmother was British and taught me to make it that way." She then took a sip of the tea and found it tailored to her taste. She smiled at the stranger. "It's perfect. How did you know?"

The woman returned the smile and replied nonchalantly, "You have half and half in the refrigerator. The used cup in the sink has a residue, giving me a clue as to the color I was shooting for. The sugar bowl, a few spilled granules, and the spoon on the paper towel by the hot water dispenser were a clue that you stirred a bit of sweetener into your tea. Since you are health conscious, according to your food choices, and appear to be in great shape, I guessed it was only a small amount, a guilty pleasure."

Arianna took another sip before asking, "Are you some kind of Sherlock Holmes?"

"In the way that Doyle explained the power of observation, I guess you could say I am a believer. My name is Rainey Bell. I'm a behavioral analyst by trade."

"Are you a detective, like her?" Arianna indicated the other woman standing silently by the kitchen sink.

"No, Detective Robertson and I go back to my days as an FBI agent, but I'm a consultant for local law enforcement now."

"Why are you here?" Arianna wanted to know.

"Sheila," Rainey said, giving a nod to Detective Robertson, "thought I might be uniquely qualified to help you."

"Why, because you have experience making victims talk?"

Rainey Bell leaned a little closer and locked her eyes on Arianna's. "No, because I've been exactly where you are. I know what this feels like, and I think I know what you need to hear."

"Oh yeah? And what is that?" Arianna asked with a bit of attitude, thinking this woman couldn't possibly know what to say to take away the self-blame. Could she have fought harder? Should she have fought him until he killed her? He would have— she was sure of that. And what was that feeling, nagging, pulling at her heart? Was it shame for choosing compliance over death?

The behavioral analyst kept her deep green eyes focused on Arianna as she explained, "Every assault is unique, but one thing remains the same. You did what you had to do to survive, and that is all that matters. You survived. Hang onto that. Hold it tight. It will help you in the days to come. When your brain starts telling you what you should have and could have done differently, simply remind yourself that you are alive to hear those doubts."

"He was going to kill me," Arianna said, and finally broke.

#

9:15 PM, Sunday, November 30, 2014
Long-term Parking, RDU Airport
Wake County, NC

"Park on the other side of that RV in the last row. The security cameras can't see this far back."

The older man laughed. "I see this isn't your first rodeo. How old are you, kid?"

The teenager turned to the man. "However old you need me to be to complete our business."

The man eased the car into the parking place and put the car in park.

The teenager instructed, "Turn it off. The security guard tools around here on a golf cart. He won't notice us if the car isn't running. Keep your foot off the brake."

"You come here often?"

The man's attempt at humor was lost on the teen. He replied to the joke, "Let's get this over with. Fifty bucks for the blow, like I said. If you want to touch me, that's going to cost you double. Money up front."

The man dug into his back pocket for his wallet. "I don't usually pay first."

"Well, you haven't been tossed out of a moving car by an asshole that didn't want to pay up."

The kid held out his hand for the money, unprepared for the cold steel that slapped around his wrist.

"You are under arrest for prostitu—"

The teenager didn't hesitate. He snatched his wrist free of the man's grasp, taking the handcuff with him. In an instant, he was out of the car and running toward the woods. There was no moon, and once he was out from under the parking lot lights, he was plunged into inky black darkness. His eyes took their time adjusting, but he didn't slow down. He heard footsteps and shouts coming fast on his heels.

"Stop! Police!"

"Fuck that," the boy said, and ran faster.

His heart pounded in his chest as his feet flew across the ground before he felt the earth drop out beneath him. A few seconds of hang-time later he plunged into the frigid water of the drainage pond.

"Dammit," he thought, "I forgot about the fucking pond."

He thrashed around in the cold water and finally found his footing. He stood up in the glare of multiple flashlights.

Silhouettes of officers shouted, "Show me your hands! Show me your hands!"

The teenager reached for the sky. A submerged tree branch caught on the handcuff still dangling from his wrist. It followed his hand into the air and slapped against his side.

"Jesus Christ," a voice behind a flashlight exclaimed.

"Don't shoot! Don't shoot!" the kid yelled before stumbling backward.

As he swung wildly to catch his balance, the branch swung around in front of him. That's when he saw it wasn't a branch at all. The teenage tough-guy turned into the little boy he truly was, screaming and falling on his back in the water as skeletal arms wrapped around him.

#

1:00 PM, Monday, December 1, 2014
Bell's Bail and Investigations
East Franklin Street
Chapel Hill, Orange County, NC

"Rainey Bell," she said into the phone.

"Ms. Bell, this is Detective March from the Wake County Sheriff's Office."

"Good afternoon, Detective. How can I help you?"

"Actually, I have some information for you," the detective replied. "It's about your assault case. I was told you should be informed of a recent finding."

"Okay, I'm listening," Rainey said and sat up straighter in her chair.

"We found three bodies in the drainage pond near a long-term parking lot at RDU. Two of the bodies haven't been there long enough to be JW Wilson's victims, but the third, a male, appears to be that of Dr. John Taylor. We don't have DNA evidence yet, but we did find his wallet and credit cards near the body. We aren't making this public knowledge until the test results come back, but things leak. You know how it is. We thought you should know before you read it in the paper."

"Thank you for that consideration, Detective. I appreciate it. You don't have to call the former Mrs. Wilson. I'll take care of that."

"You're welcome. Yeah, Detective Robertson, over in Durham, said you'd probably want to do the notification with Mrs. Wilson."

Rainey tensed and corrected him. "She's Mrs. Bell-Meyers now."

"Yeah, I guess she remarried. Anyway, we can put the case to bed. Wilson must have sunk the missing escorts out deep in the lake."

Rainey commented, "I guess we will know that when the bodies are discovered. Thank you again for calling. Is there anything else?"

The detective seemed confused by Rainey's dismissal. "Uh, no. I guess that's it. Have a good day, Ms. Bell."

"You too, detective," she hesitated, before sending him off with the truth. "By the way, Katie Meyers Wilson married me. She's my wife and the mother of our triplets. You can put that in the file before you close it. People should know there was a happy ending for us."

Rainey was pleasantly surprised at the detective's response, "I'll do that, Ms. Bell. That's good to hear. Congratulations."

She hung up the phone and stared at the wall.

Ernestine Womble, the office manager who came in only two days a week now, topped the stairs leading into Rainey's office. Known as Ernie by all who loved her, she was still as spry as ever, acting and looking much younger than her seventy-two years. She was semi-retired but kept an eye on things, as she had since Rainey's father opened the bail bond business back in the '70s.

"What crazed idiot does Wake County want you to help them catch this time?"

"That wasn't a consultation request," Rainey replied. "They found John Taylor's body—the veterinarian set up to take the fall for JW Wilson's crimes."

"Oh," came Ernie's one-word reply.

"I guess I better call Katie before the media leaks the story."

"You all right, kid?" Ernie asked.

Rainey would always be a kid to Ernie. She helped Rainey's dad, Billy, raise her and was more of a mother figure during her formative years than her biological mother. Ernie was giving Rainey the eye, the one that said, "Don't lie to me." Rainey knew better than to be anything but truthful.

"I think so. I'm not sure. Every time I get to a place where the memories of that time dissipate, something pops up to remind me. Here comes another round of nightmares." She added sarcastically, "Katie will be thrilled."

"He didn't win, you know," Ernie reminded her.

Rainey shook her head in response. "Yes, he did. He intended to scar me for life, and apparently he has. JW Wilson will just not go away."

Ernie would not abide self-pity. "He intended to kill your ass, how many, three times? He did not succeed and is dust in an urn as we speak. You're still here. You fill your head with that beautiful family of yours and evict that evil SOB from your mind. He's of no consequence to you now."

Rainey smiled at Ernie's simplification of a complicated neural process.

"That's not exactly how PTSD works. I can't control when the memories come. It doesn't matter how happy my life is. He comes again in the night with no warning. Each round of nightmares brings more detail than the last. I suppose until my mind processes the entire event, I'm going to be forced to witness the explorations of my repressed knowledge of that night." She paused before adding another truth with a sigh, "Ernie, I don't want to remember."

"Maybe that's the problem, Rainey. You need to talk it out. You never have. Your dad was the same way, kept everything tight to the vest. He wouldn't even talk to Mackie about the war for years. His demons came in the night, too, until he had to get help. Do you know when that was?"

"No, I just remember his nightmares, his screams, and barking orders."

"Oh, those were mild compared to the early years. He shot a hole through the sliding glass door in his bedroom once. He was dangerous in his sleep."

"I never knew that," Rainey said, wondering what else she did not know about her father. The first ten years of her life, she hadn't known he existed. She didn't come to live with him until she was fourteen. Parts of Billy Bell's life remained a mystery. Rainey had discovered only a few years ago that she had a half-sister.

"When you started coming to visit, Mackie and I told Billy he had to go to therapy or he might shoot you during one of his nightmares. He went every day for a while. He'd check in at the office in the morning and then head to the VA hospital over in Durham before beginning his day. It changed him for the better. He still had the dreams occasionally, but they were never as bad."

"I knew he spent a lot of time with vets, working through their PTSD battles."

"He was working on his own, as well, Rainey. You can't keep those horrid memories locked inside forever. At some point, they are going to come out. The question is, will it be on your terms or theirs?"

#

The house was finally quiet. After feeding, bathing, and tucking the triplets into their beds, Rainey read to them until the last little eye closed. She and Katie went to bed a few minutes later, exhausted from the trying day. The discovery of John Taylor's body had veiled the evening in somberness. Emotionally drained, they lay there quietly, each lost in thoughts of her own. Freddie, Rainey's cat, was comfortably curled at her feet. With Katie's head resting on Rainey's chest, they drifted off to sleep.

The movie in her dream began almost immediately. Rainey had experienced it many times before. Disconnected from her bound and gagged body, spread-eagle on the bed, she watched him rape her. Rainey saw him dig the scalpel into her flesh, as she floated above the scene, able to look on now without the heart-pounding panic of earlier viewings. Time had hardened her emotions toward the violence perpetrated against her body. The physical scars from those injuries had healed. It was the gaping wound to her psyche that had yet to close.

She had come to view this part of the dream as the prelude to the impending nightmare. If she were lucky Rainey could force herself awake, before being thrust into the helpless body on the bed and returned to the pain and panic of the attack as if it were happening for the first time. But that was not to be the case on this occasion.

He was at her ear, whispering, "You be a good girl now, or I will have to hurt her."

Rainey felt the plastic wrapped mattress beneath her body. She closed her eyes against the panic and the searing pain screaming through her body. She fought the bindings, flailing her head wildly from side to side.

"Look at her," he demanded.

Opening her eyes to see an unconscious Katie tied on the bed next to her, Rainey's guttural cries were muffled by the gag while the nightmare continued to veer from its normal course.

"What?" he asked, his eyes sparkling with delight behind the black mask concealing the rest of his face. "You don't want me to hurt her?"

Rainey glared at him through eyes nearly swollen shut, her breath fast and shallow, air puffing in and out of her gagged mouth. Her nose bled profusely, providing no access to more air

19

and threatened to drown her in her own blood, but still she fought him.

He raised the scalpel over Katie's chest. "She should have known, you know. She should have seen what I was. She wasn't paying attention. This is all her fault, right? She should pay for the pain she allowed me to inflict on you. Katie should have seen it all coming, don't you think?"

The blade glinted in the air. Rainey tried to scream and tore at the bindings, ripping skin as the rope dug deeper into her wrists. The small part of Rainey's brain that was conscious and horrified by what it saw began to beg.

Please God, start the siren.

Rainey's silent prayer was answered with the sweet sound of a distant whine blaring from a patrol car in route to save the day. It was an accident, a mistake that saved her life. The orders were to approach in silence. A rookie cop hit his siren and charged toward the scene before someone told him to turn it off. Mercifully, it sang out just long enough to warn her attacker.

The dream resumed its chilling retelling of the night JW Wilson nearly killed her. Katie's body disappeared. Rainey once again inhabited her private hell alone with JW, who bolted from the bed and scampered out of the room. Now came the moment when he paused at the door and looked back over his shoulder. Rainey could see his mouth move, but she could never make out what he said—until now.

She could only imagine he believed she wouldn't survive the overdose of narcotics he'd given her, or at least the amnesia-inducing effects would block her memories. Rainey didn't remember, but her subconscious had witnessed the entire attack and kept a record. It had been a long reveal, one painful disclosure at a time, but Rainey had now seen it all. Her mind finally played the last moments on the memory reel.

JW looked down at her. "I should have done that years ago."

The next and last second of the movie played in slow motion. It was the first time it had ever advanced this far. Rainey watched in disbelief.

Oh, my God!

20

"Rainey, wake up. Rainey! Wake the hell up!"

Rainey's eyes flew open. Katie was standing by the bed, cautiously hitting her with one of the decorator pillows from the chaise lounge by the window.

"Wake the hell—oh, there you are. Wow," Katie said, "that was a bad one. Sorry, I had to hit you. You were losing it. I didn't know what else to do."

Rainey sat up. "I'm sorry, honey. I wasn't loud, was I? I didn't wake the kids, did I?"

"No," Katie said, sitting down on the edge of the bed. "It was one of those where you're trying to talk, but it's all garbled in your throat. Are you okay, now? Did Freddie hurt you? He was biting your wrist."

Rainey blinked her eyes a few times and looked down at the tiny feline bite marks on her left wrist. She sighed deeply and then wrapped her arms around her wife. She buried her face in Katie's hair and whispered into her neck, "No, honey, I'm not. I need to call Danny. I need help."

CHAPTER TWO

6:30 AM, Sunday, December 14, 2014
Residence of Glena Sweet
Madras Lane, Orange County, NC

"The pace of his escalating violence is nearly unprecedented. I've not personally dealt with an offender like this," Rainey said, as she removed latex gloves from her hands, "but I've read about them, studied them. This is going to end very badly for a lot more women if he isn't stopped. He's just reaching his full potential."

Detective Sheila Robertson followed Rainey down the front steps of the two-story colonial revival home, after examining another in a series of crime scenes in perfectly manicured suburban neighborhoods.

"She should have been safe here," Sheila commented aloud what she was thinking.

"No one is safe, not from a predator like this. I would bring the BAU in if it were up to me."

Sheila, while crossing her arms in a defensive posture, responded, "That call is above either of our pay grades. The BAU is aware of the case and has thus far agreed with everything you've said. The task force saw no need to request BAU presence on the case just to reassure you that you are correct in your analysis. We are doing exactly what should be done."

"And yet, here we are on a Sunday morning, attending to another woman's broken life. Maybe I've missed something. More eyes and ears would be better."

Sheila dropped her crossed arms and led Rainey a bit further away from the law enforcement personnel swarming the scene and the gathering nosey neighbors. Once a safe distance from prying ears, she began to chastise Rainey for the display of insecurity.

"Self-doubt is not attractive on you, so don't start wearing a hair shirt yet. I don't think you've missed anything. The departments have all consulted their individual experts. There have been a ton of eyes on this material. They all say the same thing. He's escalating and we need to catch him, but no one seems to know how to do that."

Sheila paused to gain control of surfacing emotions. Rainey knew it for what it was. Seeing the depths of human depravity took its toll. The stress of being unable to solve a case could break the most seasoned of investigators, catching them unaware. Rainey was well aware of the pressure they were both under to solve this case. She waited for the deep breath Sheila needed to take hold. Once accomplished, Detective Robertson was ready to go back to work.

"So, our eyes and ears are going to have to be enough at the moment," she said. "Now, what went on in this house? That woman took one hell of a beating. From the looks of things, she fought hard for her life. Professor Sweet is lucky to be alive."

"Have you spoken to her?" Rainey asked.

"I stopped by the emergency room, but she's too injured to interview right now. They have to wire her jaw back together first."

"Did you see her, or has anyone noted her injuries for you?"

Sheila pulled out her phone and opened the photo file before handing it to Rainey.

"I took a few pictures in the exam room. The sexual assault nurse examiner will be more thorough."

Rainey used her fingers on the phone screen to manipulate the pictures until she was satisfied she'd seen enough.

24

"The pictures don't show it, but the doctor said the sexual assault was violent. She'll need some reparative surgery for those injuries," Sheila said in disgust.

Rainey returned the borrowed phone, saying, "He completed his transformation from power reassurance rapist to sadist pretty quickly. The first one, the assault on Mary Tweedy, showed inexperience with a live victim. He surprised her in her sleep and overpowered her almost immediately using only his size and strength. He hit her only once with his fist to quiet her. She stopped resisting. He showed concern for her comfort, tried to initiate personal conversations, and reassured her that she was pretty. He promised not to penetrate her, and he didn't, although he did please himself in other ways. He was not brutal, but he paralyzed her with fear so severely that she waited to call the police for a half an hour, as he had instructed."

"The second assault victim, Arianna Wilde—" Sheila began.

Rainey interrupted, "How's she doing, by the way?"

"She got her stitches out, put the farm up for sale, and bought a ticket to 'someplace warmer.' She left her ex-husband's phone number for contact information and said to call only if we caught the son of a bitch."

"I can't much blame her," Rainey commented. "She had a security system, just like the professor here, and he still got in. How safe could she ever feel in that house? The lingering effects of trauma cling to things and places as well as people. Recovery is different for every victim, if it happens at all."

Sheila turned her head to look at Rainey, a questioning look on her face, but she only said, "I hope she finds some peace."

Rainey agreed, "Me, too," before continuing the analysis. "He blitz-attacked Arianna. Hit her with a flashlight while she slept. That's immediate application of excessive force. Although his first assault had all the elements of a power reassurance rapist, there were anger indicators—the binding, the picture taking, the degrading posing. Mary Tweedy described his repeated ramping up of her fear only to return to casual conversation about the Halloween decorations in her yard. It's all about controlling her

25

fear, when she shows it and how much. The anger behaviors indicated evolution to a truer sadistic nature was inevitable."

"With Arianna," Sheila began, "he followed the blitz attack with forcefully binding her while she was still dazed. He cut her tee shirt and panties off with a knife. He teased it across her skin and slapped her when she screamed. He had no inflection during the assaults, she said. He calmly told her what to do and when to do it. But then he would speak to her as if they were old friends. That 'I love what you've done with the place' line was just creepy as hell."

"That was the sadist assuming his role as the torturer, whether in person or within the victim's mind. Mary Tweedy will never decorate for Halloween again. Arianna is selling the family home where she always dreamed she'd grow old. It's taunting with residual effects. He wants them to know he was watching and they never knew.

He plants the seed of doubt. The one that whispers, 'You will never be safe again. I will be watching.' Then he sits back and lets it take root. With or without return visits to his victims, he knows the mental terror he inflicted will stay with them long after he has gone. Again, that's about control and fear. Remember how Arianna said when she went limp, focused her mind elsewhere, he stopped raping her and put the knife to her throat again. He needed her terrified to complete his fantasy. That's the sadist, too."

Sheila paced the ground in front of Rainey while the crowd of neighbors grew outside the crime scene tape. She stopped to ask a question.

"But, remember, Arianna said when she fought him again, after the attack had been going on for some time, he hit her with the flashlight, knocked her out, and she awoke to him raping her again. She wasn't showing terror then. What does that tell you?"

"When she just checked out, she was ignoring him. That was unacceptable. An incapacitated victim, that's a whole other ballgame. Unconscious victims can represent to the offender the complete domination and subjugation, particularly one wrapped in sexual bindings unnecessary to prevent escape. It's part of his visual fantasy of the perfect victim. This guy is finding his sadist groove."

"So, what looks like Glena Sweet fighting for her life is him ramping up the violence."

Rainey nodded her head in agreement. "That's my assessment. I'd say with her slight stature and what the other two victims have said, he easily could have overpowered her and prevented much of the struggle. Look how this house sits further back in the woods than the others. At the end of the cul-de-sac and with this much spacing between houses, no one would have noticed her screams before he gagged her. That's another change to his methods with this one. He did not wait for her to go to sleep. He was probably in the house when she came home. For the first time, his victim saw him coming. He took her while the neighbors' houses were filled with the noise of family activities."

"That's what I can't figure out," Sheila said, shaking her head. "Why come when she's still awake? Why change what has been working?"

"He's hunting the rush. This behavior is more psychologically motivated than practical, making it part of his signature. Standing over them while they slept was thrilling. Seeing her fear when he surprised her in the basement laundry, that was orgasmic to this guy. He enjoyed the fight inside this house. The blood evidence shows he pummeled her repeatedly as he drove her up to the second-floor bedroom. I'm not so sure he meant to leave her alive. Her binding bruises looked the same as the others, but she's the first with finger marks on her throat. He probably tried manually strangling her and thought she was dead. It takes a long time to strangle someone to death with just your hands, about three minutes."

Sheila interjected, "So, maybe he doesn't know how to take a pulse. That rules out medical personnel."

"More than likely he blew his wad and lost his composure. This is just a guess, and I'll be interested to know what Professor Sweet has to say, but I'd be willing to bet he was assaulting her while attempting to squeeze the life out of her. He was seeking the ultimate act of domination, made even more sexually satisfying because of the death struggle of his victim. His timing was off on his first attempt, but he learned something."

Rainey looked back at the second story window where Glena Sweet had fought for her life.

"He didn't kill this one, but he'll kill the next one, and he'll do it soon. He'll bring something else to strangle her with—extra rope, a garrote, something to give him more control and leverage. He's an emerging sexual sadist serial killer. And we have a front row seat to his edification."

#

Monday, December 15, 2014
Press Release
Durham County Sheriff's Office

The Durham County Sheriff's Office Criminal Investigations Division and a Multi-Jurisdictional Task Force involving Wake, Chatham, Durham and Orange Counties are investigating a series of burglaries and sexual assaults, the majority of which have occurred within three miles on either side of a section of Highway 751 running south from I-40 in Durham County to the spillway bridge at Jordan Lake in Chatham County. These attacks appear to be connected to a series of voyeur reports and fetish thefts occurring in this area, as well as burglaries and a sexual assault that occurred in lower Chatham County, near Brickhaven. These crimes span from a burglary on September 2, 2013, to a violent sexual assault on December 13, 2014.

Early in the investigation, the majority of these crimes occurred inside single-family homes while the residents were away. Articles of clothing belonging to the female residents were taken. The suspect then began entering the homes of women living alone, while the women were at home and without their knowledge. On October 24, November 22, and December 13, 2014, the suspect escalated to violent sexual assault. In each of the assault cases, the female victim lived alone. The suspect

28

enters through locked or unlocked doors and windows and has used a device to disrupt wireless security systems in some cases.

The suspect is described as a white male, 35-45 years old, 6' to 6'3", well spoken, extremely strong, and physically fit. He may be an avid photographer. He is probably a runner and uses the greenways and running trails in the area for access to the crime scenes.

We are cautioning all single females living alone in the area to take extra measures for their safety. It may be wise to have a male friend or family member stay at the home. Other security measures include replacing outdoor lights with bright lamps and leaving them on. If possible install motion detector activated lighting at the back of property near any wooded areas, vary routines, place a stick in windows to prevent opening or install locks that bolt to the frame, install chain or swing-bar locks on entry doors.

Any female resident living in proximity to these crimes that believes she may have been a victim of a fetish burglary in the last two years is urged to come forward. The suspect has been known to return to scenes of his previous crimes. Persons with any information on these crimes should contact Detective Sheila Robertson, Durham County Sheriff's Department Criminal Investigations Division.

#

9:00 AM, Tuesday, December 16, 2014
Hardware Builder's Supply
Durham, NC

"Send me everything you have in stock and find more."

Harold Sparks listened to the warehouse manager's surprised response and didn't care how many swing-bar locks and window frame locking bolts he was ordering. It wouldn't be enough.

"Yes, everything. Send everything on the truck this afternoon. I can't keep the stuff on the shelves. People are scared."

Harold looked down the door and window hardware aisle of his store filled with frightened women.

"Hang on. Don't put the stuff on the truck. I'll be there in twenty minutes. Just have it ready to load."

A young woman in a State College hoodie stood in the aisle staring up at a wall of door locks while a single tear rolled down her cheek.

Her voice shook as she said into the phone at her ear, "No, Mom. They don't have any left, either."

"God, help us," Harold said, "God, help us all."

#

4:45 PM, Monday, January 19, 2015
Cookie Kutter Crime Beat Recording Studio
Durham, NC

"Good evening. I'm Cookie Kutter. CKCB. See a crime, come see me."

A formerly respected news reporter, gone the way of Nancy Grace sensationalism, Cookie Kutter began the recording of her nightly cable crime beat newscast, ready to explain to the masses why she was the only person watching their backs. She shook her judgmental bottle-blonde head from side to side and smirked for the camera before launching into tonight's rant.

"S. M. H. For those of you not text savvy, that means I'm shaking my head." She pointed at her head. "See? Shakin' it. Shakin' it."

Her smirk turned into an exaggerated frown.

"Another woman is dead at the hands of the Triangle Terror, and the multi-jurisdictional task force is no closer to catching this guy than they were when he started pulling panties off clotheslines two years ago."

More head shaking followed.

"A thirty-five-year-old woman was brutally attacked and murdered in her home on Glen Road in Chatham County. The name of the victim has not been released, nor has law enforcement divulged any details, but sources say it is the Triangle Terror's work. The attack occurred sometime Saturday night or early Sunday morning. This follows only twenty-two days after the shocking murder of twenty-six-year-old Tiegen Davis, less than four miles from the latest crime scene."

Cookie stared into the camera, as it moved in for a close-up.

"After fourteen fetish burglaries, three rapes, and now two ghastly murders, what are the police doing to catch this guy? All law enforcement can do is tell women living alone to watch out for a thirty-five to forty-five-year-old physically fit white guy, move a man onto our couches, lock the doors, and hope for the best. Is that acceptable, ladies and gentlemen?"

Cookie raised one eyebrow and sneered at the camera. "I think not."

She dropped her elbow to the desktop and pointed at the camera.

"You, multi-jurisdictional task force, can do better. Why do you depend on former FBI agent Rainey Bell as a consultant, considering her inability to identify her own rapist, letting him close enough to try again? And what about the fact she hired a killer and let her into her own home without realizing it? She's lucky all she lost were her signature long curly locks."

The pointing finger came down, but the character assassination of Rainey Bell continued.

"Last February, former agent Bell went to a funeral and ended up kidnapped by a psychopath. Really, is that the best we can do folks, a tragically flawed behavioral analyst? Why not contact the Behavioral Analysis Unit and bring in actual FBI agents? Don't the women of the Triangle area deserve an official state and federal investigation? This is obviously over the heads of local law enforcement and the apparently clueless has-been analyst with issues."

The camera pulled back as Cookie stacked and straightened papers on the desk in front of her while giving a sideways glance to her audience. Having given ample time for her disdain to sink in, she slapped the papers on the desk for emphasis and asked, "Are you kidding me?"

Another pause followed, a short one to rearrange her features in an alternative display of condescension and scorn.

"Speaking of Rainey Bell, she is in the crime news today on another matter. The three bodies pulled from the drainage pond near an airport long-term parking lot last month have been identified. DNA was determined to match two teenage boys reported to be runaways and missing since October of 2014. The names have not been released. The two were thought to have taken up homosexual prostitution as a way to survive on the street—which is another show altogether—and were last seen getting into a black sedan with darkly tinted windows. The deaths were determined to be homicides, and there are no suspects."

Cookie tilted her head to one side, gave the camera lens her best gloating sneer, and chided, "Imagine that."

She shifted positions, leaning in on her elbows to pull the audience in further.

"Now here's where the Rainey Bell connection comes in. The third body is that of Dr. John P. Taylor, a local veterinarian missing since July of 2010. He is thought to be the last victim of the Y-Man serial killer, who turned out to be former State Representative JW Wilson. If you'll remember, Wilson is also the man who kidnapped and raped the then Agent Bell, scarring her for life with a Y-incision on her torso. Wilson was killed by his wife, Katherine Anne Meyers, after he attacked Agent Bell and Ms. Meyers in their love nest on Lake Jordan. Oh yes, Rainey Bell is now raising triplets with and is married to the former Mrs. Wilson, whom we all remember from her drunken attack on moi."

The batting eyelashes were meant to draw sympathy from her supporters. After the short pause for effect, she moved on.

"The teenagers' and Dr. Taylor's deaths do not appear to be related, according to the medical examiner's reports. Sources tell us the bindings were still attached to the teenagers' remains, suggesting another type of killer is also on the loose in the triangle, one targeting teenage male prostitutes."

Cookie formed an impish grin for her fans.

"How long do you think it will be before Rainey Bell is somehow mixed up in these teenagers' murders? We'll see. Trouble seems to find Ms. Bell on a regular basis. Maybe she should try gardening and leave the crime fighting to those who don't end up in the middle of their own investigations?"

Her raised eyebrows were meant to give emphasis and credence to Cookie's assessment of Rainey Bell's investigative talents.

"We'll be back after the break to talk to Dr. Edward Teague, a forensic psychologist and research fellow at State College. He's going to tell us about sexual paraphilia and why the Triangle Terror is driven by these needs. We'll be right back with more on the Cookie Kutter Crime Beat Show."

"And cut," a voice said from the darkness in the studio. "Okay, Cookie. We'll have the doc set up with a microphone in two minutes."

Without an audience to charm, Cookie reverted to her off-camera persona.

"Why don't I have video of Rainey Bell at one of these crime scenes? Why don't I have an interview with one of the surviving victims? What the fuck am I paying you little weasels for? And, Dirk, yes you, Dirk, the one with the headset in the booth, the one that's supposed to edit this shit into something worthy of a number one local cable news show—make sure you run that clip in the background of precious little Katie Meyers punching me in the face."

She chuckled and shook her head from side to side, as she started editing the questions for her upcoming guest.

Under her breath, but easily heard by others, she chuckled and said, "I've gotten more mileage out of that fifteen seconds of video than should be legal. Love it, just love it."

#

Later that same evening...
Somewhere in the Raleigh-Durham Area

"Thank you, Doctor Teague. I don't know about you ladies," Cookie said into the camera lens, "but I think I'm headed to the dollar store for some big ol' granny panties."

Dr. Teague's voice could be heard off-camera, trying to explain, "Well, the style might not be a factor in this offend—"

Cookie's glare, focused on someone beyond the camera, had the desired effect. The doctor's microphone was cut, silencing him from stepping on her clever line.

"That's it for the show, ladies and gentlemen. Stay safe, and remember, CKCB. See a crime, come see me."

He clicked on "save as" in the file menu, labeled the file, "CKCB, January 19, 2015," and saved it to his special external hard drive. The files on that particular device represented his best work to date. He safely ejected and disconnected the slender, black drive, returning it to its hiding place inside the false panel of his home office desk.

The secrets it held were the reason he insisted on the heavy piece of furniture his wife disliked. She only agreed to his choice because he was so accommodating on the rest of the decisions made for the new house. He was like that, obliging to his wife's wishes most of the time. She thought him the perfect husband, as she should because he invested a lot of effort in fulfilling the image she had of him.

He actually loved her and wanted her to be happy. She was fun and outgoing. Their sex life wasn't half bad, probably better than most with their longevity. It would be twenty years in May since he walked her down the aisle. He thought her pretty damn perfect, too. Her job took her away for days at a time. She took a sleeping aid that knocked her out cold for hours when she was at home. Bouncing around through time zones wore on her, she said. He remained the perfect long-suffering, lonely husband, home alone while she flew around the world.

It would never cross her mind that he was anything but loyal, and he was—except for one thing. He was now a murderer, a full-on sadistic serial killer. He had spent years repressing his darker thoughts. An occasional dalliance, some panties here, a camisole there, was all he would allow himself. He focused on his work and creating the picture-perfect life with his wife. He ran mile after mile, worked out obsessively, fulfilled his wife's every sexual fantasy, trying anything to silence the demon in the night. He plunged into his work with vigor, becoming well respected in his field. No one would ever suspect he harbored sadistic sexual desires.

He could control it back then. He could turn it off, lock it back down, but that all changed with the move to Durham. His wife was overjoyed to be back near family. He was offered a coveted position and a chance to make a name for himself among his colleagues. His wife accepted the job offer she'd refused multiple times after he told her she should live the dream, follow her heart, see the world and take it by storm.

Once she was launched on her travels, the demon had no reason to stay hidden. Though he had fooled himself into thinking he had controlled his dark desires, he never did. On his own for days, sometimes weeks, the demon could no longer be silenced. He began to watch them, his girls, initiating the collection of victims and trophies. At first, it was just what he could pinch from clotheslines, gyms, and unattended washers at public laundries.

His fantasies grew violent. The desires overwhelmed him until he no longer tried to quell them. That first time, walking into that basement, finding a treasure trove of one of his girls' underwear in a pile of laundry, that was the first needle in the vein. Once he crossed that line, entered a home undetected, he was an addict with a growing habit. He was smart enough to know the demon's hunger for the drug it craved would only increase in frequency and dosage. He was also smart enough to know, if he did not stop, he would go the way of many an addict. Was the crash and burn worth the ride?

He picked up Shayna Carson's blood spattered thong from his desk. It was the last thing in which he posed her before he tightened the zip tie around her neck. He watched the petechial hemorrhaging appear on her cheeks and in the whites of her terror—stricken eyes.

His wife's flight wouldn't land for another hour. He unzipped his jeans and slipped the thong over his already hardening penis. Shayna's last breath had excited him like no other experience in his admittedly deviant hunt for the ultimate sexual high. He closed his eyes so he could see her again. He didn't need the pictures he took to relive the time he spent with her. She nearly fulfilled the fantasy to a tee. While he replayed her pleas for her life in his mind, he determined then that the next time he would cut the zip tie off and let the target catch her breath before slipping on a new one. He would repeat this reviving strategy until she did not recover. If he practiced on the next couple of targets, he was sure he could perfect the glorious ending to the fantasy.

He slid Shayna's thong along the length of his now rock hard penis. The mental movie of her last hours began to meld with his fantasies.

"Shayna," he whispered, "you were definitely worth the ride."

#

11:22 PM, Saturday, January 31, 2015
Falcon Ridge Subdivision, Durham, NC

"9-1-1. What is your emergency?"

"He's going to kill us this time."

"Who, ma'am? Is someone in your home trying to hurt you?"

The bedroom door splintered, but the dresser and chest of drawers she managed to topple in front of it held fast, for the moment.

"Oh, my god. He's going to get in here."

"Who, ma'am? I have your address and a patrol car just down the street coming your way. Tell me who is trying to hurt you."

"My husband, Aaron Engel. Tell them he's armed. He's ex-FBI. He runs a security company. He's drunk, and he will not go down without a fi— Oh, my god," she screamed as he moved the makeshift barrier a few inches with the superhuman strength of a raging drunk. "He's crazy. My kids are in here with me."

"Stay calm. They are almost there. Stay with me. What's your name?"

"Amy, Amy Engel."

He hit the door again, roaring her name, "Aaaammmmyyyyy!"

"He's going to kill me this time. Please don't let him hurt my kids."

"How many children, and are they with you?"

"Two, and they are here with me."

Amy turned to see her two young children wild-eyed and terrified. Too frightened to cry anymore, they made not a sound. The phone nearly slipped from her hand, as blood from the gash above her ear oozed out of her hair. She listened to a supervisor in the background, calling out to the responding patrol car.

"Unit 27, be advised, the suspect male is ex-federal law enforcement, armed, and intoxicated. Proceed with caution. Unit 42, Unit 53, assist Unit 27, domestic assault in progress. Wife and two children in the house. Suspect armed."

"Where are you in the house, Amy?"

"We're in the master suite, upstairs, in the bathroom. He's at the top of the stairs on the landing."

Crraack! The door splintered again, leaving a gap. He pressed his enraged face into the void. Amy closed the bathroom door and locked it.

"Oh dear God, hurry up," she whispered into the phone.

"Amy," he called, his voice flat with anger. "Hang up the goddamn phone and come out here. You think you can take my kids, bitch? You have no idea who you are dealing with."

"How old are the children, ma'am?"

The operator was back, asking questions of her. She didn't answer but instead said, "Please, God, don't make me shoot this man in front of his kids."

"Are you armed, ma'am?"

"You bet your sweet ass I'm armed," Amy Engel replied. It was not weapon-holding false bravado, but an accurate assessment of the danger she was in. "I know exactly who I'm dealing with."

The supervisor was obviously listening. She began calling to the patrol officers immediately. "Unit 27, be advised, the caller is also armed and located in the upstairs master suite bathroom with two children."

Aaron stopped slamming into the door. Terror permeated the silence with a threat worse than him entering the room. Amy could hear the children whimper, as the fear of the unknown replaced their father's pointed rage. All the moment lacked was a high-pitched violin note to heighten the tension before the climax of the scene.

"10-4, 27. Suspect in custody." Suddenly the supervisor's voice was louder and directed at Amy. "Ma'am, officers are at your front door with your husband. I need you to put the weapon in a safe place away from the children and come out of the bathroom. An officer is waiting in the hall."

"Oh, thank God. Thank you, thank you," Amy gushed into the phone.

"You're welcome, ma'am. Please assist the officer in securing your safety."

The children cried softly, holding tight to each other. Relief freeing them to express the emotions no child should have to feel. Amy knew this was the last time she'd see her kids cower in fear in their own home.

The operator prodded her once more. "Ma'am, can you let the officer in the room?"

"Oh—yes. Thank you for everything. Bye."

Amy hung up the phone and opened a cabinet door too high for her eight and seven-year-olds to reach, but she warned them anyway.

"This isn't staying here, but still, no touching."

"Ma'am, this is Officer King with the Durham Police Department," a female voice called out. "Would you mind moving some of that furniture so we can get you out of there? Your husband is in custody."

Amy pushed the dresser over and out of the way with the added strength of the adrenaline pumping through her veins. Two of its wooden legs broke off, and the contents of drawers cascaded onto the floor. She didn't care, because as of that moment Amy Engel didn't live there anymore.

#

He'd been inside the target's residence less than a minute, long enough to check the dryer by the back door for trophies, when he heard the sirens coming. He ran, leaving the back door open, too afraid he'd be seen if he stopped to close it. They were near. Screeching tires and the blue flashing lights reflected in the treetops drove him further into the darkness. He pushed through the darkness too fast and regrettably forgot about that little drainage ditch near the running trail.

His ankle gave way. He lay crumpled in a heap on the forest floor; sure men with flashlights and guns would be coming soon. He had quite a crime spree under his belt, but it would soon be over. He left enough DNA and behavioral evidence to be tied to multiple felonies, including capital murder. The Triangle Terror induced panic would come to an end, and women could sleep in peace once again. He was destined for the needle, or at best, dying an old man on death row while the public debated the humane way to put him down—an indulgence he found ironic since there was nothing humane about his murder victims' last moments.

He had noticed the added law enforcement presence in his hunting grounds, part of the prevention measures employed by the task force formed to take down the Triangle Terror. It was an attempt to quell the public's fears. It only made his game of cat and mouse with the cops more fun to play. Even with the additional patrol units, he had entered homes in search of trophies while the cops circled the neighborhood. His confidence grew with each outing—enough so, that tonight he brought his rape kit and planned to pay a visit to one of his girls. She must have heard him downstairs and called the cops.

He peered through the woods toward the sound of voices and the source of the blue flashing lights. That's when he started to laugh, not loud, but a low chuckle from his chest. The police were two doors down from his girl's house. They had not been coming for him. The chuckle ceased when the lost opportunity to take his victim with the cops right outside crossed his mind.

"That would have been mind-blowing," he whispered.

He pulled himself up slowly, using a tree for balance. He tentatively put weight on his ankle. The pain was almost unbearable, but bear it he must. Although the cops might not have initially been looking for him, it seemed his entrance to his girl's house had been discovered. Flashlights bobbed in the distance, coming toward the woods. He turned, took a deep breath, and disappeared into the night, hobbled but not defeated, at least not yet.

As he ran, he took the pain, burying it beneath the new fantasy he'd been working on. The planning and prep-work were half the fun. He was ready for the next step and only continued the burglaries to stay his boredom while he waited for the perfect opportunity to put his preparation to good use. Tonight's planned rape was just foreplay for his ultimate desire. He wanted to spend more time with his next girl. He had a couple of candidates already picked out. He knew the one he wanted, but he'd have to break the golden rule. His girls could never be someone he knew in his other life, the one where he was the loving husband and consummate professional. But when he closed his eyes, forming his ultimate fantasies, it was her face he saw.

She would be his end, he knew, but still he limped through the darkness while the fantasy of her bound at his feet pushed back the pain and kept him moving.

#

"What's your badge number? What's your name," the man growled.

"Officer Wendy King, sir. We met before, Mr. Engel, at your home, the night you broke a wine bottle over your wife's head."

"Oh, you're that bitch," Engel snarled.

Officer King's patrol car was parked at an angle, blocking the entrance to the women's center. She had volunteered to bring a witness to court in Durham, one seeking a protective order against none other than Mr. Aaron Engel. Several security officers stood on the other side of the gate, further preventing the infuriated man access to his wife and children, which was why he was in a screaming rage in the middle of the road.

Buying time for backup from the Chatham County Sheriff's Department because she was out of her jurisdiction, the young officer stood her ground and kept him talking.

"I guess you don't remember much from that night, do you, Mr. Engel? You were pretty drunk and worked up. I seem to have found you in that state again today, but I don't smell alcohol. I'm afraid that 'I was drunk, forgive me' defense is going to look kind of lame now. It appears you can be a raging ass without substance abuse."

"Do you have any idea who I am? I'll crush you. You won't be able to sleep at night. I can make you disappear without a trace."

"Threats to an officer. Wow, you really do want to go to prison. You were FBI. How can you not know that you are digging yourself into a deeper and deeper hole?"

"I want to talk to my wife. I want my kids out of this lesbo camp, you fucking dyke."

41

Officer King smiled. "No, that would be my sister. I'm the straight girl in the family photos, but they treat me just like everyone else. I think that's very nice of them, celebrating diversity like that."

"My kids are not going to be subject to this lifestyle."

"What lifestyle would that be? Are you referring to my sister and her beautiful wife and kids? They love each other, and their children are healthy and happy. I don't know if I'd call that a lifestyle though. I'd probably just say that's the way it should be. A home that focuses on love without fear and violence, where no one is worried about what will set Dad off in a rage."

Aaron Engel took two steps forward, ready to pummel Wendy King. Her hand slipped to her weapon.

It didn't deter his rage. "I'm going to take that pistol from you and teach you some goddam respect, you smart mouthed bitc—"

The derogatory term he was about to use caught in his cheeks when a large hand clamped down on his shoulder.

"I wouldn't do that, mister," a booming bass voice said.

Aaron took one look over his shoulder at the mountain of a man and deflated.

Officer King smiled. "Mr. Engel, I'd like to introduce you to my friend Mackie."

"Hands on the car," Mackie instructed.

Aaron Engel complied. He was still angry but evidently not in the mood for an ass whippin'.

"Looks like you're only aggressive toward women, Aaron. That's the second time I've seen your raging bull act come to an abrupt halt when a bigger man stepped in to take the upper-hand," Officer King taunted.

Miles McKinney, Rainey Bell's business partner and the guardian angel to those she loved—six feet six inches of solid muscle since his heart attack and newfound love of the gym—handcuffed his prisoner.

"Lil' sis, the man is in custody. No need to rub his face in it."

"He's a jackass and an abusive one at that," Wendy said, bolstered by youthful arrogance.

42

"I knew a girl like you once," Mackie replied while putting the handcuffed man in the backseat of Wendy's patrol car. "She paid an awful price to gain some humility. You might learn from that experience without it costing you, as well."

"I just want to talk to my wife," Aaron called out from inside the car. "If she hadn't brought her here," referring to Officer King, "she would have been home by now. She brainwashed her against me. I know they text all the time. I can see her phone activity. I know that bitch right there is unduly influencing Amy. I have to get her out of here."

"See? I told you he was a prick. Who spies on a spouse like that? Your wife is lucky she is rid of you."

Aaron made a show of coming out of the car before a large palm hit his forehead, sending him backward onto the car seat. Mackie, who had been dealing with men like Engel much longer than his badge-wearing young friend, leaned down and spoke softly to the fuming man.

"Mr. Engel, you're going to be arrested. Be good and you'll probably be out in twenty-four hours. Get a lawyer and listen to him. My best advice is throw yourself on the mercy of the court and get some help. But this behavior here, that's going to cost you if you keep it up. It's already cost you your career. Don't let it cost you everything else."

Mackie turned to Officer Wendy King with a sage piece of advice, "And you, don't let your mouth write a check your ass can't pay for."

\#

11:59 PM, Thursday, February 12, 2015
Colfax Park Drive, Chatham County, NC

He had to stay off his wrenched ankle for a week. He'd been bearing his full weight again for only a few days, but he could wait no longer. His wife was coming back Saturday morning for a Valentine's visit. She would be home for a week this time. He needed a fix, and he needed it now. With his injury, he couldn't chance an encounter with one of his girls, but Paige would be off to the school dance Friday night. Her parents would go to their usual date night dinner and a movie. Her room would be free, and he could spend a few hours working off some steam.

He was watching Paige's house, fantasizing from the bushes of the time he would come to take her away. Until then, he came and went in her world without notice. However, he planned to leave a message this visit. It was time to let Paige know he was coming. He reached under his waistband, about to pleasure himself while he thought of her when he saw the silhouette against the side of the house two doors down. He removed his hand from his penis and began slowly moving toward the intruder in his territory.

Another predator was in his hunting grounds. A tall, well-built, young man peeped into the window of two adolescent sisters. This was unacceptable. These were his streets, his girls. They were not to be used by some young developing pedophile with a hard-on. He thought about calling the police. Wouldn't that be ironic? But, he'd hate to be caught up in the arrest. His cell phone number would show up on the emergency operator's screen. How would he explain his presence? It would lead to his name on a report, and linkage was everything. Stay off the radar, he decided.

Instead, he followed the young man back to his home. He read the name on the return address labels neatly stickered to the mail the young man had already put out for morning pickup.

"Ummm, interesting. Good to know."

He would keep an eye on this peeper from a distance. He'd learn his habits and the houses he hit, and if need be, pin his crimes on this budding sicko. He could drop a few dozen pairs of stolen underwear in this guy's garage, slip a hard drive with incriminating images in the heater vent, and watch the cops eat him alive before they figured out his DNA didn't match the evidence. Even then, the prosecution could claim contamination at the lab, throw out the DNA, and convict on the possession of the stolen items and pictures. That would be fun. The future looked bright as he wandered back home through the woods. Yeah, that would be fun.

#

7:15 AM, Saturday, February 14, 2015
Colfax Park Drive, Chatham County, NC

"Holy shit, Sheila. My house is less than three-quarters of a mile from here." Rainey pointed over her shoulder.

"I know," Sheila said. "I'm sure it's disconcerting."

"Disconcerting? I've never been so glad to live in a fortress with redundant security systems in my life."

Sheila laughed. "I thought you pretty much lived in a state of euphoria over that virtually impenetrable wall you've built around your family."

"It's the virtually part that keeps me vigilant," Rainey said in all seriousness.

"So let's catch this creep."

"That's not going to be so easy."

Sheila looked around the latest victim's room. Paige Jeanerette was an eighteen-year-old high school senior. Her room reflected her bookish, introverted personality, and she seemed to have dedicated her life and much of her wall space to the Hunger Games.

"What's he doing, Rainey? Why is he back to fetish crimes? And what the hell is this all about?"

Sheila pointed at Paige's laptop on the desk in the corner. A word document left open on the screen contained a message to the young woman who occupied this room.

The note read, "I seen you at school in class. I think your pretty. I'm scared to talk to you. I hope you don't be mad I took the panties. Its cause I like you."

"He's just playing with us and terrorizing her. Bad grammar and spelling—he's trying to mimic a teenager, make her look over her shoulder."

Sheila slapped the laptop closed with her latex-gloved hand. "I hate this guy. I mean I really, really hate this guy. I want his balls on a plaque in my office."

"Sorry, but that isn't going to happen," Rainey said, looking out the window to the woods behind the house.

"You don't think we'll catch him?" Sheila questioned, incredulously.

"We'll catch him, but you won't get his balls. When he's cornered, he'll come peacefully. He's too smart to go out in a blaze of glory. No, the guys at the BAU will be talking to him for years to come, albeit from death row."

"Maybe he'll hit the wrong woman, someone like you who'll put a bullet in his ass, save the state some money."

"You do know I've never actually killed anyone. I've had opportunities, but nope, not a one. I'm not the 'out of control badass' Cookie Kutter would have people believe."

"You watch that show?"

Rainey laughed and fibbed a little. "No, but Katie does. She says she likes to know what the enemy is up to. I can always tell when Cookie uses that clip of Katie punching her. That pisses her off, but between you and me, I think Katie's glad she did it."

Sheila chuckled. "I can't help it. I love that clip. I saved it to my computer for days when I'd like to do something similar to Ms. Kutter."

Rainey smiled at her friend. "Me, too, but Katie doesn't know."

"Well, let's get you back home to your Valentine's weekend. I know last year's plans were a bust."

"I made no plans this year. I didn't want to jinx it. Katie is in charge, and I am blissfully ignorant of what lies in store."

"Just remember to take your weapon. You, of all people, can never be too prepared."

"Always," Rainey answered absently, refocused on the room. "Okay, back to business. This is a straight up fetish burglary with sadistic tones. The note is meant to extend his terror. But there is nothing new here, nothing to learn, other than he's treading water."

"What do you mean?"

"He's bored. The patrols slowed him down but haven't stopped him. I don't think this is regression, though. I think he's planning his next step up the sadistic ladder. This guy is a thinker. He has a fantasy—he fulfills it. He moves on to the next fantasy, seeking a higher high each time. It took him two years to build up to what he did to Shayna Carson. He spent more time with her than the others, extending her suffering as long as possible. He appears to be going through sexual sadist school, but if you look at the last four months, he leapt from middle school to college. Postgraduate work is next. Keep an eye out for missing women."

"He's not a kidnapper," Sheila countered.

"He wants more time. He needs more time, more privacy, a chance to focus only on his victim without fear of interruption. He has a private place. I bet it's near those Chatham County scenes down by the river. That's how you'll find him. Locate the lair. I'd deploy deputies in that area, account for all the residents. You're looking for a man who visits but doesn't live there. Locate the owners of vacated structures and seasonally occupied homes, hunting cabins, fish camps, anywhere a lone man would go unnoticed."

"Women go missing all the time. How will we know he took her?"

"Victimology should at least give you a clue. She'll be white, twenty-five to forty-five, live alone on a property near the woods, and if he is the planner I believe him to be, she will have no close relatives or friends that would notice her weekend absence."

Rainey pulled the latex gloves from her hands and locked eyes with Sheila.

"Realistically? You will know when you find the body."

#

8:15 PM, Saturday, February 21, 2015
A Place For Us Charity Ball
Feme Sole Nightclub, Durham, NC

47

Rainey leaned against the wall near the entrance as the woman she adored stepped into the center stage spotlight. The large women's bar inside a former tobacco warehouse was decorated to fit the refinement of the evening. Diamonds and jewels glinted at every table in the dimly lit hall. Hundreds of haute couture-wearing guests with exceedingly deep pockets sat at elegantly decorated tables. The bar owner, Phyllis, stood nearby, grinning at the stage. She, too, had been placed under the spell of the beautiful blonde at the microphone.

Katie had called out the country club set and the left-leaning movers and shakers in the Triangle area. They were there to raise money for homeless LGBTQ youth. Kids were on the street because parents threw them out or made life a living hell from which escape was the only means of survival. Molly Kincaid, Rainey's friend, lawyer, and sometime employer recruited Katie to head the fundraising campaign knowing Ms. Bell-Meyers could bring a crowd, and that she did.

Rainey's infatuation with Katie had never worn thin in the nearly five years they had been together. It seemed to grow stronger every day. The red dress Katie wore was stunning, but Rainey thought her wife more attractive with pancake batter on her cheek and triplets at her feet, just a few hours ago. The three-year-olds were fussy and wanted breakfast for supper. Katie, the triplet whisperer, went to dress for the ball after she fed and washed them, leaving Rainey to wrestle the hyper trio into pajamas and bed. The children noted Katie's transformation into the sexiest mom in the room when she came in to kiss them goodnight.

"Mommy is pretty," Mack said.

"Mommy is pretty," Timothy echoed.

Weather, the only girl and lover of all things shiny and expensive, pointed at the diamond necklace around Katie's neck.

"Mommy is sparkly."

Rainey's mother, Constance, the evening's overnight babysitter, took over the kid watch because they had to be supervised. They were into everything, constantly on the move. Katie was the only person they didn't try to outmaneuver. She never raised her voice and rarely lost patience with the children, yet they obeyed Katie without question. Rainey figured it was because they recognized Katie as their main food source. They pulled most of their worst stunts when Rainey was watching them. Their latest escapade involved stealing Katie's makeup bag from the master suite, decorating the nursery and each other while they were supposed to be napping.

Rainey dressed under Katie's watchful eye. She had refused to wear a man's tuxedo, and an evening gown was simply out of the question—not convenient for hiding her weapon—but the fundraiser was a black tie affair. Katie found a tailor who could recreate the look of the 1966 Yves Saint Laurent Le Smoking tuxedo for women and presented it to Rainey as a gift. The tailor had required a final fitting, which included Rainey wearing her sidearm. He wanted to make sure she didn't mess up the lines with a bulge in the wrong place. The Glock was a no-go with the tailor. They compromised on a smaller weapon and a holster close to her ribcage. Katie had not seen the finished product.

When Rainey stepped out of the walk-in closet dressing area still working on a cuff link, she said, "Thank you, honey. This is the most comfortable suit I've ever worn."

Katie smiled and winked, saying, "Oh, no. Thank you."

Now Rainey leaned on the wall and smiled at the pretty mommy on stage, listening as Katie wrapped up her short speech.

"Forty percent of the homeless youth in America are from the LGBTQ community. The Internet provides exposure to worldviews, opening minds and presenting opportunities. Along with this newfound awareness, the strides forward in social acceptance have given many young men and women the knowledge that they are not alone and the strength to be themselves. They are now revealing hidden truths to family and friends at earlier ages than ever before. These children are still dependent on the adults in their lives for food, shelter, and financial support. While many families are embracing and loving, others use archaic belief systems to justify throwing a child out into the street. These children need our help, and that is why we are here tonight.

Thank you all for coming and for the expression of care and concern you have shown our youth. I don't like to use words like 'straight ally,' which some would use to describe those of you in this room who are heterosexual. The only label necessary to comprehend that we are all equal is 'human.' We are all human beings deserving of respect and the right to be our unique selves, loving whom we choose. Thank you again for being compassionate souls caring for all of us. Have a wonderful evening."

Katie began making her way from the stage to the back of the room, stopping to speak to guests. Molly walked over to Rainey, accompanied by her girlfriend, Leslie. Leslie had become Katie's closest friend. The four of them spent many social evenings together.

"Is your babysitter spending the night?" Molly asked.

"Yes," Rainey answered. "Why?"

"Because if the way you're looking at your wife is an indication of your intentions, you two are going to need some alone time."

Katie arrived and stood on her tiptoes to give Rainey a quick kiss on the lips. "Hey, good lookin'. How'd I do?"

"You were perfect," Rainey said, beaming back at her.

Molly and Leslie gave Katie hugs and congratulations on the event's success. Wendy joined them. She was twenty-four years old and the mirror image of her older sister at that age. Wendy's evening gown was exquisite, matching the green of her eyes. The dress was the direct result of a shopping spree with Leslie and Katie, who were determined to dress Wendy properly because Rainey was a lost cause.

"Katie, that was a great speech, and you look fantastic," Wendy said, hugging her. She waved over Katie's shoulder at Rainey. "Hi, sis."

Rainey waved her fingers back at Wendy, realizing she was mimicking behavior she used with her kids. Life changed for her every day, even as some things remained the same. Rainey didn't want to think about nightmares and past mistakes tonight. Katie was dazzling, the night out with good friends was just beginning, and they had a babysitter. Life was good at the moment.

As Wendy introduced her date, Rainey noticed Molly glaring at him. The date was a casual one. Two young professionals attending an event, Wendy explained earlier. With no steady boyfriend, she was focused on her career, as Rainey had been once.

"Rainey, Katie, I'd like to introduce you to Nick Prentiss. Nick, this is my sister, Rainey Bell-Meyers, and her wife, Katie Bell-Meyers."

Rainey and Katie shook Nick's hand and exchanged greetings. He was starkly handsome. His dark hair and tanned skin contrasted with his hazel eyes and playfully pouty pink lips. His tuxedo was not a rental, but a tailored fit worthy of his model good looks. He was also charming.

"I can see the family resemblance," Nick said. "It's a compliment to both you and Wendy."

Rainey took note that Molly still glared at Nick. She wanted to know what was up, so she sped things along.

"Nick, these are our friends, Molly Kincaid and Leslie Walker."

Leslie stuck her hand out first and said, "It's nice to meet you, Nick."

Molly never lifted a finger. Instead, she said, "Sleeping with the enemy, Wendy? Hello, Nick. Aren't you just a little too Fox News for this crowd?"

Rainey grinned. She loved to watch Molly take somebody on, even if it was her sister's date. Molly was usually the last one to show her colors. She must have had an intense dislike for this young man. It was sure to be entertaining.

Nick came back with, "Ms. Kincaid, you'll find I'm a man of many passions. It's good to see you again."

"Your passions are for sale, I take it," Molly quipped.

"Of course," Nick answered honestly. "A good lobbyist can be passionate about anything if the price is right. I'm paid to sway people to my clients' position, much like you make a living swaying juries on your clients' behalf. It's not my fault the system is broken. I'm merely making money until they fix it. It isn't any more of a crime than representing a murderer in court."

"At least if one of my clients claims God made him do it, I can plead insanity," Molly countered.

Everyone in the social circle had been following the conversation like a tennis match. So far, the score was fairly even. However, Rainey counted on Molly to have the last word.

Undaunted, Nick said, "It's politics. It's not personal." He offered his hand to Molly again. "Truce."

"Oh, but it is personal, Nick. If I recall, and I do recall quite clearly, you were on the front lines protesting funding for the women's center named after my mother with that asinine Jedidiah Lilly horde. What was it they were shouting? 'God hates dykes,' and my personal favorite, 'Sarah Harris was a white-trash drug addict.' I understand you were responsible for that little ditty." Molly raised the Champaign glass in her hand in salute to Wendy. "You look ravishing, Miss King, but I'd work on the arm candy. This one won't taste as good as he looks. As my mother used to say, sugar coated crap is still crap. Well, actually, she would have said, 'shit', but as I've left my white-trash roots behind, I thought I'd clean it up a bit."

Most women would have delivered that line, followed by a quick turn of the heel and a sachet away, but not Molly. She sipped from her glass, handed it off to Rainey, and slipped her arm around Leslie's waist.

"Let's dance, honey," Molly said. "They're playing my song."

Rainey started laughing when she realized the band was playing "Devil With The Blue Dress On." It was indeed, Molly Kincaid's theme song.

To Wendy's credit, she turned to Nick. "Did you actually make that sign?"

Nick blushed red, losing some of his charming composure. "No, I didn't make it. I just did the research on Sarah Harris and forwarded the information."

"But you did work for Lilly?"

"Hey, Molly Kincaid's mother's history is public knowledge," Nick argued.

Rainey narrowed her eyes at Nick. "I'm quite sure you have no idea what the real history involves in Molly's mother's case. That part of the story is not public knowledge."

"If she doesn't want it to be a political football, she should not have put the name on the building and then asked for public funding. It's the reality of politics today."

Katie had been uncharacteristically quiet, but that was about to change. The Sarah Harris Battered Women's Shelter was her baby.

"No, Nick, the reality of politics today is that a few rich men have bought some elections, using lobbyists such as yourself for the dirty work. Playing political football with the lives of women and children is shameful. Claiming it's God's work is despicable. Come on, honey," Katie said, grabbing Rainey's free hand. "Let's dance."

Rainey tipped up Molly's glass and finished the contents. She was being pulled toward the dance floor when she handed the glass to her sister.

She winked and said, "Choose wisely, young one. If you need a ride home, I got you covered."

Wendy handed the glass to her date. "Catch you later, Nick. You look good in that tux, but my mother agrees with Molly's— you can't polish a turd." That said, and in typical little sister form, she called out, "Hey, Rainey, wait for me."

#

Later that night.
The Bell-Meyers Residence
Chatham County, NC

Rainey stood outside the nursery doorway hugging Katie close, watching their children sleep. They were both a bit tipsy. Rainey was glad Molly had arranged a car for them. They dropped off her slightly more inebriated sister at her little home

53

in a nearby neighborhood, at Wendy's insistence. Her house was smack in the middle of the Triangle Terror's hunting grounds, which made Rainey nervous. But Wendy was a grown woman, and she was determined to sleep in her bed. Rainey made the car wait while she checked all the doors and windows before leaving Wendy tucked in bed, a trashcan by her head and the alarm system on.

Now she watched her children sleeping while holding the woman she loved, truly at peace for the moment.

Rainey whispered, "They always look like angels when they sleep."

Katie tilted her head back to look up at Rainey. "Well, those little angels will be awake in a few hours, and if you want some of your slightly sloshed wife, we best get at it."

Rainey began leading Katie toward the master suite without further delay.

She chuckled while saying, "I love that our foreplay has become 'we best get at it.' "

Katie spun away from her. "You want foreplay?" she asked playfully.

She then reached for the bottom of her long red dress, shimmied it over her head, threw it on the floor, and started dancing down the hall with her back turned to Rainey. She peeled the remaining layers from her body and tossed them over her shoulder. Rainey stood frozen in place. Katie disappeared into the bedroom and crooked a finger out the door, beckoning Rainey to come hither. A few seconds had passed before Katie stuck her head out the door to see why her invitation was being ignored.

"Oh, hi, Constance," Katie said to Rainey's mother, who was standing next to her daughter. "Sorry about that."

"Oh, no, nothing to be sorry about. I heard noise on the baby monitor. I just came to make sure they were still asleep. Sorry to interrupt. Good night." Constance elbowed Rainey as she turned to leave, trying desperately not to burst out laughing. "If I looked like that, I'd dance naked in the hall for John, too."

Rainey didn't speak or move until she heard the door close on the guest bedroom her mother occupied. Katie leaned on the bedroom doorframe giggling.

Rainey sighed heavily. "That's going to take a while to forget. I may never have sex again."

#

10:35 AM, Monday, February 23, 2015
Durham County Sheriff's Office
Criminal Investigations Division
Interview Room

The soldier stood when she entered the room.

"Good afternoon. I'm Detective Robertson."

"Good afternoon, ma'am. Staff Sergeant Russell Whitaker," he said, shaking her extended hand.

Sizing up the young soldier, a living recruitment poster for the armed services, Sheila commented, "You're mighty young for a staff sergeant."

Russell Whitaker smiled. "I just received the promotion. The Army has an up or out policy. I like to keep the Army happy, ma'am."

"Please, have a seat." Sheila gestured to his chair. She took the one opposite and continued, "A career man, I take it—'Be all you can be.' "

"Hooah, ma'am."

"I understand you think something may have happened to your sister."

"Yes, ma'am. I've been to her house. Drove up from Bragg this morning. I got worried when Kaitlyn didn't check in this weekend."

"You and your sister, you stay in touch regularly?"

"Yes, ma'am. We have a standing appointment to check with each other on Friday nights. Our parents are abusive alcoholics. Me and sis, we fought our way out of that life. She's four years younger, so when I was eighteen and joined the Army, I came back to get her after I got out of basic. I got custody of her from the state. While I was deployed she stayed with my colonel's family. She went through high school pretty much on her own."

He became emotional but smiled through the welling tears.

"She made straight As. Got a four-year scholarship, graduated magna cum laude from State College last spring. She started graduate school and working at the research library on campus in the fall. She loves books and—" His voice cracked with emotion, saying, "Oh, God," before he broke into sobs.

Russell Whitaker was scared and helpless. A big tough soldier, straight and tall, who was realizing that even with all his warrior skills, he could not protect his baby sister.

Sheila gave him the time he needed to recompose before seeking more information.

"So, am I to understand your sister missed a standing check-in time on Friday?"

Russell's breathing calmed. He wiped the tears from his cheeks before visibly resuming a soldier's posture, eyes forward.

"Yes, ma'am, but that was prearranged. Kaitlyn had dinner plans with colleagues after work before attending a lecture she had been looking forward to Friday evening. We agreed to speak on Saturday morning. She did not respond to my calls, texts, or emails. That is very out of character, ma'am."

Sheila smiled, trying to ease the impact of the next few questions.

"Has Kaitlyn ever ignored your communications before? Maybe you sometimes disagreed. Is she a bit rebellious, a little resentful of having to check in with her big brother? Does she have a boyfriend?"

"I understand why you are asking these questions, ma'am, but if you will permit me to tell you what I discovered at her home, I think we might be able to speed the process up a bit."

Sheila sat back in her chair. A seasoned investigator, she could read people and knew when to be quiet and listen. This young man was bursting to have his story heard.

"Okay, Staff Sergeant, tell me why I should be looking for your sister."

"When Kaitlyn didn't respond to anything by Sunday morning, I went to my CO, explained the situation, and caught the next transport back to Carolina. I can't tell you where I was unless you get some clearance from someone above my pay grade."

"That probably will not be necessary, but why didn't you just call the police and ask for a welfare check."

"I did, ma'am. They went by the house. Her car is still there. They found a note taped to the inside of the front storm door. It's addressed to someone I don't know, but it says Kaitlyn was sorry she missed them and would see them soon. She wouldn't do that, ma'am—just leave without telling me. I knew something was off."

"Not to mention, who leaves notes on doors these days? You say Kaitlyn texts and emails, has a phone. Do you have this note?"

"Yes, ma'am." Russell reached into his chest pocket, but before he handed over the note enclosed in a plastic bag, he finished his story. "When I got to her house, I used my key to get in. The minute I walked in, I knew something was wrong. Her purse and keys were on the table by the door. I found her phone on the bedside table in her bedroom, resting on top of the program from the lecture Friday night. It looked like she came home, went to bed, and then just vanished into thin air. I came straight down here to report her missing."

He handed over the bag.

Sheila read the handwritten note through the bag. She hoped the gasp that left her throat had not been too noticeable, but when she looked up to see the expression on the staff sergeant's face, she knew he heard it.

The note read:
Rainey,
Sorry, I missed you. See you soon.
Kaitlyn

#

A few minutes later...
The Bell-Meyers Residence
Chatham County, NC

"No, I don't know her. I've never heard that name to my knowledge," Rainey said into the phone, one whimpering child on her hip and two all out bawlers wrapped around each knee.

"Then it's him, toying with you—us."

"Ya' think, Sheila?" The sarcasm indicated the mood she was in.

"Don't be a smartass. Why are those babies crying like that?"

"Because they picked up a stomach virus at the women's center day care and have been spewing from both ends since 2:30 this morning. I'm not sick, but I've spewed a few times myself from the smell. I may not survive this."

"Oh, my," Sheila said. "Where's Katie?"

"Katie and her mom are cleaning the nursery and I'm really glad I am not involved. This is— Oh, crap— Hey, I'm going to have to call you back. No, no, no, don't puke in the vent. Hey, hey, hey. Oh, god—"

CHAPTER THREE

2:00 PM, Wednesday, March 4, 2015
Durham Police Academy
Durham, NC

Just over one hundred law enforcement officers representing four North Carolina counties—Wake, Chatham, Orange, and Durham—squeezed into the large conference room. There to hear what the multi-jurisdictional task force had to say concerning a two-year escalating crime spree in the area, the air was thick with conjecture. As she made her way to the front of the room with Detective Robertson, Rainey heard snippets of the speculation.

"This guy is a psycho. No doubt about it."

"Breaking into houses to jack off in some woman's underwear. This guy is a freak."

"Some of the victims were just barely teenagers. He's all over the map."

"He did some sick shit, man. Look at those pictures. Jesus."

"I don't care how good this guy is at hiding his tracks; he'll be caught and all this time we spent on profiling mumbo-jumbo will have meant diddly-squat."

"Maybe these crimes aren't related at all. Maybe it's two guys, could be three."

Rainey paused at the front row and leaned against the wall as Sheila moved toward the podium.

A male voice to her right said, "What's her name? That profiler? Cloudy? Stormy? Something like that, anyway I heard she has a good looking wi— uh, girlfri, uh—the woman she lives with is smokin' hot."

A female voice chastised him. "You can say wife, Jack. Join us in the twenty-first century."

A hushed and deeper male voice commented, "She ain't so bad herself. She's standing right behind you."

Equipped with a body-mic for her coming presentation, Rainey fought the urge to comment. Pretending unawareness she kept her eyes focused on Sheila. Seated behind the podium, a semicircle of brass-ornamented chests waited. Giving a respectful nod to all the officers outranking her, Sheila stepped up to the microphone.

"Good afternoon, everyone."

The greeting silenced the murmuring room.

"Thank you for coming. I am Detective Sheila Robertson with the Durham County Sheriff's Office Criminal Investigation Division. I will be serving as the spokesperson for the task force today. Behind me are …"

Rainey stopped listening to the obligatory salutes to the brass. She didn't care which dignitaries were in the room. The man they were looking for was not among them, or she didn't think he was, but anything was possible with an offender like this. Her eyes trailed over the task force evidence boards. Crowded with pictures and maps, they represented the sum of the known facts concerning the UNSUB or "Triangle Terror."

The media came up with the nickname, as they usually did, much to Rainey's displeasure and she supposed to the unknown subject or UNSUB's delight. They initially tossed around names like "The Bodice Bandit," "The Bustier Booster," and the "Corset Creeper," when women's undergarments began disappearing in the fall of 2013. The more intimidating nature of the current media designation for the UNSUB accompanied his escalation from fetish burglaries to rape and finally to a burgeoning serial murder.

"… consulting behavioral analyst, Rainey Bell."

It took a second for the introduction to register, prompting Rainey to turn her attention from the evidence boards and back to the podium.

She apologized, "I'm sorry," before moving to take her place at the front of the room.

Sheila prevented Rainey's need of an explanation for her inattention, saying, "Forgive her. She has three-year-old triplets at home with a stomach virus—for how many days now?"

Rainey answered, "Ten. Ten long days. And nights. Don't forget the very long nights. They appear to be on the mend, thank goodness."

A ripple of chuckles from knowing parents circled the room.

"After we hear from Rainey, we have some proactive initiatives and responsibility designations to discuss. We have a woman missing for twelve days, two unsolved murders, three sexual assaults, and countless fetish burglaries. We need to get this guy off the street and locate Kaitlyn Whitaker. Please give your attention now to the UNSUB's profile."

"Thank you, Detective Robertson. Good afternoon, everyone," Rainey said to the room. "Once again, it is a privilege to work with the departments and investigators involved in this case. The attention to detail in both documenting the known crime scenes and the collection of evidence has been exemplary."

She indicated the evidence boards with a sweep of a hand.

"The task force requested I give you a brief behavioral analysis of the unknown subject who committed these crimes. My only goal is to add to your investigative toolbox. I will define the characteristics of this type of offender. Please feel free to stop me and ask questions at any time."

Rainey paused to sweep her eyes around the room. Her gaze fell on a late entrant. Officer Wendy King slipped into an empty chair near the back. She was out of uniform and looked like a college kid among the veterans. Rainey was sure young Wendy had to charm her way into the room filled with case-hardened investigators and experienced patrol officers. Wendy reminded Rainey of her own impervious spirit at the beginning of her FBI career. She smiled at her little sister and received a youthful grin and thumbs-up in return. She then continued with the presentation.

"First, I'd like to address some comments I heard on the way in."

The Chatham County deputy who commented on Katie's looks shifted uneasily in his chair. Rainey surmised a little levity in advance of the somber process that lay ahead couldn't hurt. She peered at his nametag.

"To answer your question, Officer Tweed, yes, the rumor is true. My wife is smokin' hot."

The embarrassed officer turned beet red while the room filled with laughter.

Rainey eased Officer Tweed's discomfort with a smile. "Thank you for noticing."

Taking the ribbing well, he answered, "No problem."

Rainey refocused on the room at large.

"Some of you believe this UNSUB to be psychotic, crazy, nuts, a freak. You are ascribing to this perpetrator a mental state marked by illogical thinking patterns and behavior. That would be a mistake. The foresight and planning exhibited in these crimes indicates a rational and functioning individual. Although he may suffer from various personality disorders, he knows what he's doing, knows it's wrong and frankly does not care. He is sane in the legal sense. The fact he has been extremely active for two years and escalating rapidly without drawing attention to himself is an indication of his lucidity. Do not underestimate the intelligence and cunning at work here. His ability to blend into the norm and live above suspicion indicates an apex predator at work. In this way, he *is* a freak of nature. He seems quite successful at living a double life most of us could not maintain."

She drove the point home with her next statement.

"More than likely, the UNSUB has already spoken to law enforcement about this case and never blinked. He gave no sign of anxiousness or guilt and showed the appropriate response of a concerned citizen."

The rustle of shifting bodies into defensive postures told Rainey she needed to let them know she wasn't accusing them of incompetence.

"I am a trained criminal behavioral analyst. I've let people who wanted to kill me get very close to doing just that. I never saw them coming. But when that flicker of truth became evident, my training helped me identify the situation as dangerous and kept me alive. Nothing can take the place of sound investigation tactics, which your departments have exhibited. Despite how some of you may feel about "profiling mumbo-jumbo," you do need the tools to recognize the offender when he peeks out of his veil of normalcy. UNSUBs like this are consummate human predators hiding in plain sight."

Clenched crossed arms relaxed. Bodies leaned forward, as the room collectively opened to her message. They were ready to hear what she had to say. Rainey moved away from the podium to a map with the crime scenes indicated with colorful pushpins.

"Let's begin with how we know these crimes are attributable to one UNSUB." She pointed at a yellow pushpin. "The first reported fetish burglary occurred on Labor Day weekend, 2013, here on Chancery Court in Durham County. The rest of these yellow pins represent the other incidents of stolen undergarments, the last of which took place just a few weeks ago on February twentieth in the Brookhaven Subdivision in Chatham County, here. I believe you were all given a detailed list and timeline for these crimes. Correct?"

Nods and verbal confirmations accompanied the waving of information packets in the air. Rainey moved on, pointing to residences not far from where she and Katie lived.

"Six of the reported burglaries occurred in Durham County, four in Chatham, and two each in Wake and Orange Counties. With the exception of the two down in the southeast corner of Chatham County, all took place within a four-mile radius of the first reported fetish theft. If fourteen of these break-ins were reported, some not until days later when garments were eventually discovered missing, then I'm willing to bet there are twice as many intrusions that went unnoticed or unreported."

"So he lives in the middle of that area. Right?" a suit and tie-wearing detective asked from the third row.

Rainey nodded in agreement. "Yes, he more than likely lives in one of these subdivisions."

Another question followed from several rows farther back. "How do you explain those three pins down south in Chatham? How do you know they are related?"

Rainey had the answer. "Along with the two fetish burglaries, one on Buckhorn Road and one on Corinth Road, the second sexual assault also occurred in this area. The first assault took place in October of 2014 in Durham County. Then one month later, he committed the second assault down south, where these orange and yellow pins are located at the same address on Buckhorn Road. The UNSUB returned to the scene of his ninth reported burglary committed back in July, escalating in just four months to his first penetrative rape. The third sexual assault came in December of 2014, just over the Durham County line, at Madras Lane in Orange County. We found evidence he had visited this victim prior to the assault, although she was unaware. I recommend a close surveillance of his earliest known victims. They hold significance, which may drive him back to them.

"We initially linked the three sexual assaults, marked with the orange pushpins, through victim statements and perpetrator behavior. We then focused on the Wilde case. It is highly unlikely two different suspects, one a fetish burglar, and the other a rapist who also has a lingerie fetish, targeted the same victim in such a sparsely populated area. DNA found at one of the murder scenes, this one here—the rest are marked with red pins, as well—the DNA from this scene matched evidence collected at the Buckhorn sexual assault. This crime scene," she pointed to the orange pin near the Cape Fear River, where Arianna Wilde no longer lived, "was the key to linking the fetish burglaries to the rapes and ultimately to the murders. We're looking for a suspect who has a connection to both of these areas."

Rainey moved over to a board with pictures of the victims.

"In each of the three sexual assaults and the two murders, the victims were bound in similar fashion and blindfolded. The bruising is almost identical on each of these women. There were also injuries consistent with ritual binding. Unnecessary to restrain the victim, these bonds are part of a signature fed by a sexual fantasy unique to this offender. The assault survivors reported he took pictures with a digital camera, forcing them to pose in different undergarments. This is another signature behavior. Murder victim number two, Shayna Carson's bathroom trash can contained an XQD format memory card. A thorough search of her home turned up no camera other than the one on her phone. None of her friends or family ever knew of her owning a camera. He also took panties and other lingerie items from each of these locations. It's the same guy."

A wizened old detective spoke up. "I've been doing this a long time. I don't believe I've ever seen an escalation in deviance of this magnitude, not this fast. How does that factor into your analysis?"

"Good question," Rainey replied. "We shouldn't analyze the three phases of the crimes together but look more at the progression. The fetish burglaries were a prelude to future sadistic behavior but are more than likely not his first show of deviance. The UNSUB is a voyeur and probably began peeking into windows as a teenager, acting on his still forming fantasies. He may have started stealing women's undergarments then, as well, clandestinely poaching them from family, friends, and neighbors.

Two years ago he tired of the voyeuristic activity and embarked on the second phase of his development, entering unoccupied homes. The thrill wore off the anonymous burglaries, so he began to leave clues to his intrusion, at times taunting the victims with notes on their electronic devices. He escalated to taking a picture with a fourteen-year-old's tablet of her panties draped over his erect penis and left it for her to find. He taunted law enforcement, too, growing more and more confident. If he had not shown these sadistic tendencies and evolved so quickly into a serial murderer, I would have thought him to be much younger than the thirty-five to forty-five year age range assigned to this profile."

"That's old for fetish crimes, isn't it?" Officer Tweed asked.

"Yes, it is," Rainey replied.

"So, why do you think he's older?"

"We classify UNSUBs by analyzing the behavior of their worst offenses. Here, we have to look at the sexual assaults and murders. He exhibits organized offender traits; brings a rape kit, binds his victims, takes trophies and pictures. This type of sexual murderer chooses victims close to his age. The rapes and murders were of women ranging in age from late twenties to early forties. There is evidence of stalking behavior, extensive preplanning and surveillance. The assault victims said he was calm and in control throughout the time he spent with them, which was sometimes hours. He learned from each escalating experience, growing more violent and sadistic with every assault. He's simply too successful and confident in his actions to be on the younger end of the organized offender scale."

She paused and walked back to the podium to look at her notes, before continuing.

"We also have the descriptions given by the albeit blindfolded victims. Six feet or a bit taller, super fit, extremely strong, and well spoken. The words he used were commanding and authoritative. His voice was described as deep, although one victim thought it wasn't his natural speaking tone. The victims all had the impression that this was an adult male, not a teenager. And finally, his chameleon-like ability to project normalcy in his daily life while simultaneously acting out his sadistic fantasies takes maturity not found in younger offenders."

Young enough to exude the enthusiasm for behavioral analysis lacking in a few of the veterans around him, a smartly dressed detective with a shiny new badge protruding from his jacket pocket interjected, "Are we absolutely sure this is one guy? I know the linkage analysis points to one in some of the cases, but this timeline is all wrong. How does a fetish burglar escalate to sadistic murder and then go back to stealing underwear? A psychopath like this doesn't de-escalate, does he?"

Rainey started to answer, but the young man wasn't finished.

"And what about his behavior during the sexual assaults? The victims said he kept asking if they were comfortable and adjusted bindings so it wouldn't hurt as bad. He bandaged a head wound on the third one, even helped her use her inhaler when she asked for it. Then suddenly he is an anger excitation rapist and sadistic murderer. That's a big leap. Maybe it's a team? And lastly, how do you link the Whitaker disappearance to all this? That's a different M.O. altogether."

Rainey gave him a verbal pat on the head for doing his homework, "Those are valid questions," but she needed to send him back to the books.

"I'll talk about the Whitaker abduction in a moment. As to the others, I'm confident this is one man. The linkage is readily identifiable, even in cases with no DNA evidence. The signature elements are unique and present at each crime."

Now came the schooling.

"The UNSUB is not a psychopath. His concern for his assault victims' well-being and his continuation of the fetish burglaries throughout the timeline—even after he began sexually assaulting and ultimately murdering his victims—points to this UNSUB as a malignant narcissist, a less extreme antisocial personality disorder than narcissistic psychopathy.

"That distinction could take us hours to discuss. Let's just agree that the malignant narcissist is capable of compassion, showing loyalty and concern for others, and can feel guilt, unlike a genuine psychopath, who lacks many of these behaviors. That's not to say this UNSUB has no psychopathic traits. We can't forget that the concern he showed for his victims came between the terrorizing moments of the assaults.

"The malignant narcissist will gain higher levels of satisfaction from his crimes over the course of time, driving him to commit more and worsening offenses while weakening his impulse control. We've seen that escalation in this series of crimes. Our UNSUB is a sadist, always has been, but that doesn't mean he feels no remorse. In part, the returns to his base paraphilia, the underwear fetishism, are an attempt to mollify his growing sadistic sexual needs. He may hope he can regain control of his desires. It's a sign he may have been frightened by the extremes he's reached. That's one possibility."

"What's the other?"

Rainey ventured into feel-it-in-her-gut territory, and despite her recent battles with self-doubt, she was sure she was correct about this UNSUB.

"There are some power issues at work here. While you patrolled the streets, he was able to enter homes seemingly at will, even with all the warnings to the public. That's powerful foreplay for a sadist. He also used the burglaries for surveillance and to stay sharp, keeping boredom at bay, until the perfect victim for his next phase of sadism could be found and followed. These types of killers are incredibly patient. He waited until the fantasy was most likely to come true before he took Kaitlyn Whitaker."

"That makes sense," the young detective replied, "but you didn't explain how you know he took the Whitaker girl."

"The task force has decided to keep that information confidential at this time, and I agree it is best for all concerned."

An anonymous voice called out, "Do you think she's still alive?"

Rainey knew the likelihood of Kaitlyn Whitaker living longer than twenty-four hours after the UNSUB took her were slim. Unless he completely switched gears, he couldn't wait much longer than that to kill her. She was a means to an end, his sexual gratification. When he was done with her, he tossed her body and started the hunt for his next victim.

Rainey said none of that and instead answered, "We can hope that she is still alive and investigate accordingly."

She realized her time was running short and quickly made her final points.

"I'm going to close with some suggestions as you continue with your investigation. The UNSUB is on foot. He's in great shape, according to the victims. Running trails and woodlands surround the crime scenes. This guy is a runner."

Rainey turned to Sheila, who resumed her place at the podium. The remainder of this presentation they would do together.

Sheila explained the next steps in the investigation. "The task force has recommended we pick up more checkpoints on the trails. We will continue to stop and question runners, only with more frequency. In your packet, you see the make and model of a shoe consistent with a print found at several of the crime scenes. This shoe is a favorite with off-trail runners. We will have people in the woods around the trails, too. Make note of anyone with this type of shoe or someone that fits other aspects of the profile. We'll also be asking for voluntary searches of any bags runners may be carrying."

Rainey joined in, "When you interview the UNSUB, he will have a runner's bag or vest that he will happily hand over for inspection. The items it contains can be harmlessly explained away. In addition to water and protein bars, he will have a camera. He'll show you some great nature shots if you ask. He'll have a survival bracelet, maybe more than one, made of paracord, which we know he uses for bindings due to trace evidence left at several scenes. He will have a multifunction tool, like a Leatherman, and a flashlight large enough to be used as a weapon. He'll have a beanie and a neck gaiter he uses to cover his head and face, leaving only his eyes visible to his victims. He'll have a roll of athletic tape and large cotton bandages he uses to blindfold the women. He'll have zip ties—and I'm sure a creative reason for their use. We know he also has lock picks, but he probably conceals them on his person rather than in his bag. He will be carrying a smartphone, and he may have something that looks like a garage opener."

"Garage opener?" The question came from somewhere in the middle of the room.

Shelia answered, "He is using an app on his phone or another device to disable wireless security systems and cameras before entering the property. Our UNSUB is also very computer savvy."

Rainey completed the profile, "He's better than average looking, intelligent, and socially adept. He'll have a college degree or two, based on his vocabulary and the literary discussion he had with Glena Sweet, who is an English professor and his third rape victim. He's at least upper middle class economically and has a good job where he is in a position of leadership. He has an exceptional relationship with his wife or girlfriend. His car, his house, his lawn will all be well maintained. He's not a joiner, though, so you won't find him in running clubs. His acquaintances will say he's sometimes quiet, a bit of a confident introvert, but he's a great guy. He will be delighted to help any way he can during the interview."

Sheila held up her copy of the packet given to everyone in the room. "Rainey's comprehensive profile is included in the information we gave you, along with the UNSUB's physical description. Please make sure the personnel assigned to the trails are aware of details contained in this literature." She turned to Rainey. "Is there anything else you would like to add?"

Rainey looked out at the faces in the room. "When you have a suspect, there is a list in the packet of items you'll want to name in the search warrants. He'll have security measures on his computer, so make sure the tech guys are the ones to handle that evidence. He'll probably have a removable hard drive or two. Any audio-visual recording devices should be seized. He'll have a private place where he can be alone with his trophies, and that is where he probably has Kaitlyn Whitaker. He'll have items to restock his rape kit. You'll also find documentation of each of his crimes and victims. There will probably be a journal detailing his fantasies, whether a physical document or a file you'll find on his computer. You'll find the pictures he takes of the victims and newspaper clippings about his crimes. And as with almost every single one of these guys I've studied, he will have an extensive sadomasochistic porn collection. Good hunting. You'll find him, I have no doubt."

"Thank you, Rainey," Sheila said, shaking her hand.

"You are welcome. Call me if you need anything."

The room began to fill with movement.

Sheila asked for attention. "Wait, we are not finished. We're going to let Rainey go, but we need to discuss the positioning and staffing of the checkpoints."

Rainey headed for the exit. Wendy stood and followed her out.

#

Once in the hallway, Wendy asked, "You don't think Kaitlyn Whitaker is still alive, do you?"

"Why would you say that?"

Wendy grinned. "Answers a question with a question—definite sign of deception."

"Analyzing my behavior after only one complete semester of grad school. You must be a very bright girl," Rainey teased, but she still didn't answer the question.

"You were quibbling when you said 'we can hope that she is still alive and investigate accordingly.' I can tell when you're lying or at least being evasive. Call it familial insight. Why didn't you tell them they are looking for a body?"

"The same reason they let rescue dogs find a live victim, even if they have to plant one, so they can feel good about finding the dead ones. Just like the dogs, those cops know to look for a body, but they can still hope for a live find. I can't take away the prospect that Kaitlyn Whitaker is still waiting to be found. This UNSUB is changing. Maybe his fantasy is now to keep a woman."

"But you don't believe that," Wendy said, not letting up.

Wendy's career goal was to follow in Rainey's footsteps to Quantico and the BAU. She should know the horror show to which she wished to buy a ticket. Pressed for an answer, Rainey pulled Wendy to the side of the wide hallway and spoke in hushed tones.

"The probability that Kaitlyn survived twenty-four hours is essentially zero. She was his first long-term guest. He had a fantasy planned out, but he rushed it in his excitement. He's done that with every escalating phase until he mastered each element of his crimes. It's also important to note Kaitlyn was introverted and inexperienced sexually. These guys watch hours of porn with victims portrayed by skilled porn actresses, filling deviant fantasies with unrealistic expectations. It probably didn't go as planned because she had no clue what was happening to her."

Wendy interjected, "So, she didn't follow his script."

"Right," Rainey said. "The terror would have been real enough, but the degraded 'bitch' he was looking for was probably a scared, checked out, childlike mess. He got what he could out of her and then killed her, which were probably his most satisfying moments and the most terror-filled for Kaitlyn. Her death, however, did not end the assault. He spent time posing and photographing her dead body. She became the ultimate objectified woman, dehumanized, and available to his whims. As horrible as all that sounds, it opens a window of opportunity in the investigation because he's added a new element—body disposal. He could make a mistake. He's transporting live victims and dead bodies for the first time."

"This is one sick-ass dude."

Rainey laughed. "Do me a favor. Don't ever put that as your analysis in any official documents or term papers, Officer King."

Wendy laughed with her, and Rainey couldn't help but notice the family resemblance in the sound. Rainey knew of Wendy's existence only after the two met face to face for the first time almost two years ago. Nearly a year went by before Rainey finally broached the subject of their kinship. She spent a few sleepless nights, wondering how to tell Wendy the truth and whether she should. She was already part of Rainey and Katie's family life by then. The anxiety had been unnecessary. When she finally sat her half-sister down to have the talk about Billy Bell's dalliance with Rex King's wife, it came as no surprise to the younger woman.

"Dad spilled his guts on the way home from the emergency room the night I met you. He said I was bound to find out. There were a few tears from Mom and some sort of explanation. I never knew Billy Bell, so no big deal. Rex is my dad, flaws and all, no genetics required. You and I share some DNA—quite a bit from the looks of things—so I guess we should give this sister thing a shot."

"Well, okay then," had been Rainey's response. There was nothing else to say.

Wendy was busy being a young woman with a social life, a new cop, and a graduate student in criminology. Somehow she found the time to be the cool aunt, hang out with the big girls on poker nights, and sometimes be the nuisance little sisters are supposed to be to older siblings.

Rainey had thought herself an only child for forty-three years, so the sibling thing was new to her. She watched Katie and her high-strung clan for sisterhood clues, ignored most of what she saw in that drama, and found it took no effort to spend time with Wendy. Despite growing up in separate homes, they were both Billy Bell's daughters and, as Katie often noted, seemed cut from the same cloth.

Katie would shake her head when Wendy and Rainey had identical simultaneous reactions to a basketball game or shared a facial expression.

"That Billy Bell had some dominant genes. You two could never deny the blood relation. Bookends. You're bookends," she'd say.

It was a new and enjoyable experience, this big sister thing, until the day a cop asked Rainey if she was Officer Wendy King's mother. She was old enough, of course, if she had the girl at twenty, but it wasn't a comfortable realization to live with. Besides, the cop was insinuating she had slept with Rex King, the only father Wendy ever knew, and someone Rainey loathed. She had to start telling people Wendy was her sister to stifle even the slightest supposition there might be another reason for their uncanny resemblance. Rainey also warned Wendy that being in her life was not the safest place to be.

With the mischievous smile of youth, Wendy had replied, "Yes, but it's certainly never dull."

Now, Rainey stood with her little sister as the task force briefing ended. The hallway filled with a swarm of law enforcement officers.

Wendy finally got around to why she was there. "Hey, do you have a couple of hours free this afternoon?"

"I was headed home to give Katie a break. With me leaving in the morning, she'll be on her own."

Wendy was prepared for that answer. "Katie isn't alone. Her mom is there, and Grandpa John should be there any minute."

Grandpa John was Dr. John Herndon, Rainey's stepfather and doting grandfather to the triplets. A heart surgeon by trade, he'd been keeping a close eye on his grandchildren during the stomach virus episode.

Whatever Wendy wanted Rainey to do, it must have been important because she added quickly, "I talked to Katie, and she said you could go with me. Supper is at six, so you're all clear until then."

"You have permission from my wife to take me where, may I ask?" Rainey said with a grin.

"I have some kids I want you to listen to. They have a story I'm not sure I believe, but I'd like a second opinion."

Rainey stopped smiling. "Is this an open investigation? You know I can't be involved without an invitation from the investigating jurisdiction."

"It's not official. I'm looking for a kid who ran away. I used to babysit him when I was in high school. He was just a baby then. He's sixteen now. His dad is a prick, and his mom is a traumatized useless fundamentalist who keeps praying to God for a miracle and standing by her man."

"You know that thing you said about knowing when I was evading the truth? It works both ways," Rainey said, prodding Wendy for a more honest answer.

Wendy's shoulders dropped, her plot foiled.

"Okay, look," she began, "there is an official missing person report on this kid, but nobody is looking. He's gay, so I started asking around in places homeless LGBT teens hang out. I heard these stories, almost identical experiences, from some of the boys. I don't want to say too much. I want you to hear it from them."

Rainey wasn't about to cross the blue line without an invitation.

"If it is relevant to the missing person investigation, you should give that department the information."

Wendy pled her case, undeterred by Rainey's reluctance.

"The thing is, I think there may be something real shady going on, but I'm not sure. It could be some urban myth, taking on a life of its own. I don't want to look like an idiot if that is true." She lowered her voice to a whisper. "I think it could be connected to the two bodies they pulled out of that drainage pond."

"Oh, now it's getting more out of bounds," Rainey said, shaking her head. "This is the same pond with a body related to my case. You know I can't go anywhere near that investigation."

Seemingly as determined as Rainey had been in her younger days, Wendy would not take no for an answer.

"Rainey, you and I both know that case is not related to those teenagers' bodies."

"Until that is a proven fact, I'm not on that case, nowhere near it. They hired another consultant to work with the investigators."

Rainey thought that would settle the discussion, but she was wrong. Wendy was not above pulling the sister card.

"I would think that if a little sister felt strongly enough about something, a good big sister would trust her and ask how could she help."

Rainey was not that easily swayed. She chuckled at Wendy's tactics.

"Straight for the guilt trip. That didn't take long."

"Please, Rainey. I'm staying at your house tomorrow night so you can go to Quantico. Peace of mind from knowing your three kids and stressed out wife are secure while you're away, in exchange for two hours of your time."

"Whoa, layering it on now. This is great training for when Weather gets older and tries manipulating her mother and me." Against her better judgment, Rainey gave in. "Okay, I'll talk to these kids, but we agree right now, if there is anything at all I feel should be in an official report, we call it in. Officer Wendy is not embarking on an unofficial investigation and dragging my businesses down with her. Understood?"

"Yes, ma'am," Wendy said with a mock salute and in perfect little sister style added, "Who are you kidding? When Weather is my age you'll be so old, you will be an easy mark for that child. She's already running the show."

"Oh, shut up," Rainey said, laughing because it was the truth.

A voice from the hallway cut short their conversation. "Wow, Wendy, you do look like your sister."

A handsome man approached with Sheila Robertson at his side, wearing fashionable glasses and a tweed suit to round out his professorial look. He was a little taller than Rainey, a few inches over six feet, and had the athletic build of a man younger than his slightly graying temples suggested. Rainey recognized him from the Cookie Kutter show but would never admit she'd watched his discussion on paraphilia. She looked him up, read his bio and the study he authored on fetishism. She also knew of him from her currently blushing little sister. Rainey could see the schoolgirl crush responsible for Wendy's gushing praise since she enrolled in one of his classes last fall. She was now on her second course with the dashing professor.

"Dr. Teague, what brings you to the Academy?" Wendy asked, her broad smile beaming up at him.

"I have an appointment with Detective Robertson and heard your sister would be discussing the Triangle Terror analysis." He turned his brilliant smile to Rainey. "I was most impressed, Agent, I mean Ms. Bell. I'm sorry, the agent label is hard for me to dismiss. I've studied your analysis of Dalton Chambers and his crimes. It's required reading for my advanced forensic psychology classes. He extended his hand. I'm happy to meet finally."

Rainey shook his hand. "Thank you, Dr. Teague. It's a pleasure to meet you. Please, call me Rainey. I've heard good things about you from Wendy."

Rainey knew the department heads had forced another analyst on the task force. Cookie Kutter wasn't the only person doubting

Rainey's skills. Rainey wasn't supposed to know about the request for a re-evaluation of her profile. Sheila clarified Teague's presence to keep the awkwardness at bay.

"Dr. Teague is reviewing the medical examiner's reports on those two teenagers Wake County found. One of them was from Durham County. While we try to determine the jurisdiction of the murders, we're cooperating with Wake. We're hoping Dr. Teague can give us some clues as to what we're dealing with," Sheila explained.

Rainey listened to Sheila, but her attention was drawn to her little sister. Wendy's blush had turned a darker shade, and red splotches were just becoming visible on her neck. The girl had it bad for teacher. At least fifteen years Wendy's senior, from Rainey's estimation, the handsome professor was charismatic, erudite, and from Wendy's description a "captivating" educator. Rainey saw exactly who was captivated. The age difference did not concern her, but Dr. Teague's wedding ring and his position of power did.

Wendy's crush was harmless, thus far, and Rainey hoped it flamed out before a discussion of ethics and power-imbalanced relationships became necessary. In the meantime, she had never seen Wendy so discombobulated and found it entertaining, but would save the teasing for a private moment. Rainey suppressed her amusement and turned her attention to the professor.

"I'm sure you'll be able to offer valuable insights, Dr. Teague. I'm glad you were available for the consult."

Teague offered a humble, "I wish we could work together on the case, but I understand there are complications with that scenario. Maybe soon. I would like to extend an invitation for you to speak with my graduate classes."

This excited Wendy. She enthusiastically urged her sister to accept the offer.

"Rainey, that would be awesome. You could present a case or something. I know my class would love it."

Commitments were hard on the fly for a woman with triplets and two jobs. Owning a bail bond business came with paperwork, lots of it, and the consulting and investigations business was

77

never ending. Requests for consultations piled up on her desk from law enforcement agencies around the country. The BAU was stretched thin. Departments sought help from a growing number of former FBI behavioral analysts when BAU involvement wasn't feasible or timely. Frustrated big city detectives and overwhelmed small town sheriffs sent Rainey the cold cases that haunted their dreams.

"I will check my schedule and get back to you. I'm sure we can work something out, Dr. Teague."

"It's Edward," he said, shaking her hand again and beaming. "I look forward to hearing from you. I would love the chance to discuss some of the cases you worked. I apologize if I appear to be a BAU groupie. I admit to it if it makes me less creepy." He laughed easily. "Maybe we could have coffee sometime."

Rainey noted his smile was genuine. He wasn't blowing smoke or playing politics. His presentation on paraphilia for Cookie had been thorough and straightforward. He wasn't seeking fame, like so many analysts for sale to the highest bidder. He seemed to have a genuine interest in the research.

"Coffee sounds great, Edward. I'll be in touch."

Rainey saw up close what was fanning her sister's flames. This guy was one fine looking man, he had a brain, and he was out of bounds. Billy Bell's daughters inherited their father's attraction to the inaccessible. Katie had been about as off limits as a temptation could be—married, straight, and Rainey's security assignment. That's pretty much the list of ethical violations it took to acquire the best thing that ever happened to Rainey. Wendy, it appeared from her blushed cheeks, might be willing to violate a few ethics of her own. Rainey's fears were somewhat assuaged, as Teague and Sheila took their leave.

"I will look forward to your call," he said to Rainey. With a small wave to Wendy, he told her, "See you in class."

"See you tomorrow, Edward," Wendy ventured hopefully, and to Rainey's delight was immediately shot down.

Teague pointed a playful finger at her and, though he was smiling, put his student in her place.

78

"That's doctor to you. It will be Edward when we're colleagues."

Wendy was flustered but responded, "No problem, Dr. Teague. I'll see you in class."

Rainey felt sorry for her deflated sister but elated the professor gently but firmly drew the professional line.

When the professor and Sheila disappeared around the corner, Wendy said, "I can't believe I called him Edward. It just came out. That was awkward," and headed for the elevator at the end of the hall.

Rainey followed behind, trying to ease Wendy's embarrassment. "You aren't the first to crush on a professor."

Wendy glared at Rainey and argued between clenched teeth, "I-I don't have a crush on him," apparently not wanting the others in the hallway to hear.

Rainey stifled a laugh as they stepped into the crowded elevator. When the doors closed, she leaned over and whispered in Wendy's ear, "Now who's lying?"

#

An hour later.
Observation Deck
Raleigh Durham International Airport
Morrisville, Wake County, NC

"Look, boys. It's the Wendy bird."

Rainey and Wendy approached from the parking lot. A slender young man with sandy blond Bieber bangs covering his forehead smiled down from the observation deck platform. Five other boys joined him at the railing. Rainey judged them all to be in their early teens, except for Bieber bangs, who appeared a bit older, larger, and the leader.

Wendy smiled up at them and waved, calling out, "Ah, the lost boys."

They responded in unison, "Bangarang!" The sound was lost in the jet wash as another thundered off the ground at the busy airport.

The smallest of the boys pointed at Rainey, yelling through the noise. "Is that your mom?"

Wendy called up to him, "No, she's my sister," between howls of laughter.

Rainey leaned close to the still giggling Wendy as they climbed the stairs to the platform. She spoke over a landing jet, "If I remember my Peter Pan stories correctly, the lost boys shoot the Wendy bird. Keep laughing and I might let them."

Besides the five lost boys, a half a dozen people enjoyed a warm March afternoon watching jets land and take off. Rainey was sure that was not what the boys were watching. They were standing along the rail with a good view of the parking lot. A search of the Internet for gay cruising sites in Raleigh produced lists with the observation deck always among the top sites. The boys were fishing for supper. Headlights would flash, and they would stroll down to see what was biting. Rainey knew this was survival sex for these kids, the lost souls of which Katie spoke at the ball, the thrown-away beautiful children.

"She's another cop," the leader said, brushing his bangs from his eyes and indicating Rainey with his chin.

"Used to be," Rainey shouted over more jet noise, making sure to meet his accusatory stare with a smile. She extended her hand. "Rainey Bell, and you are Peter, I presume."

The kid let a slight grin creep to his lips, though he maintained his tough guy attitude. He was older than he looked. Rainey could see the age and shrewdness that was either chronological or street earned. He was a few inches shorter than Rainey. With a wiry, athletic build like Wendy's, he stood eye to eye with her.

He shook Rainey's hand and corrected her during a lull in noise levels, "It's Connor, but welcome to Neverland, anyway."

"What gave me away on the cop thing?" Rainey asked. "I thought I'd shed all of that badge swagger."

80

Connor proved he'd been on the streets for some time as he explained, "You're carrying, right-hand draw-over, shoulder holster."

"Very good," Rainey said, but Connor wasn't finished.

Over the next jet landing, he pointed at her ankle and shouted, "You have a small pistol in a holster on your right ankle."

Rainey congratulated him on getting it right. "Your observation skills are impressive."

The noise again quieted. The sound of idling jet engines hung in the air, but they could hear each other without shouting.

"I know who you are," a slight boy with a thick coastal accent said. "Cookie Kutter has your picture on her show all the time. You're that FBI profiler."

Rainey chuckled. "And you have questionable viewing tastes, but, yes, I am a former behavioral analyst for the FBI, emphasis on former. I'm a private consultant now."

"So Wonder Wendy—gonna save us all from the man—has a Fed for a sister," another boy said with a smirk. He was a few inches shorter than Conner, a little thicker, with dark features and brooding lips. He was angry and suspicious. "Either way, we'll end up in state custody if we talk to you. We don't know that kid you're looking for. Come on, boys. Let's go."

A young businessman topped the stairs, dressed in shoes more expensive than all the boys' clothes put together. Focused on the young men, he broke into a big smile, which disappeared rapidly when he noticed Rainey and Wendy. Both women turned to scowl at him. He immediately reversed his track. The roar of another jet leaving the airport accompanied his exit down the stairs.

When the noise quieted, Connor turned to Wendy. "There went a big score. How are you going to make our time worth what we lose talking to you? This is prime time—fat wallets getting their cocks licked before they go home to the wife and kids."

Brooding Lips, as he was to be called in Rainey's memory box for this event, asked, "How do we know you didn't already call the cops?"

81

"Wendy is a cop. She's under more of an obligation to report information she gets from you. She hasn't yet." Rainey gave Wendy a warning look before continuing, "She asked me to come talk to you, so here I am. As far as any conversation we have, I'm a private citizen subject to the same privacy laws as you. Failure to report a felony is technically a federal crime," another glance at Wendy, "but only if a person actively conceals actual knowledge that a felony was committed. So, unless you tell me about your involvement in a crime that caused or will cause serious bodily harm or death, I am not compelled to talk to the police on my own. I can't lie to them, but I don't have to report every minor lawbreaker I encounter. Wendy, however, is skirting the law as we speak."

Wendy spoke up, "They haven't told me anything that indicates they are complicit in a felony. I'm out of my jurisdiction. By the time I call for a car to pick them up, they will have scattered to the wind. Right, guys?"

"Yeah, Wendy's chill," the coastal boy commented.

While Rainey waited for another jet to land, she swept her eyes across the boys. When she could speak without yelling, she said, "Wendy says some of you have a story she'd like me to hear."

"It's not a story. It's the truth."

The boy speaking had not made eye contact before, but when he did, fear reflected in his brown eyes. Fading finger shaped bruises circled his throat. He saw Rainey see the marks and pulled his black hoodie over his matching thick dark hair.

She answered, "Someone is targeting young men like you, committing violence without consequence because they believe you expendable, that no one will care if you disappear. I care, and I'm not alone. I'm hoping what you have to say will help get this person off the street and out of your lives."

"It's all circumstantial," Connor said.

Rainey smiled at him. "Were you a lawyer in a former life?"

Connor spit over the railing, which appeared to be a commentary on his answer. "My father is a lawyer and a prick. He took my computer when he found out I had a boyfriend. He gave me law books and law reviews to read while he held me prisoner that last summer. When he wanted to send me back to conversion camp for re-schooling, I bolted. That was four years ago."

"I'm sorry to hear that." Another jet landed before Rainey added, "I know you don't have any reason to trust me, and you've heard too many broken promises in your young lives. I assure you I am here to help any way I can."

Connor smirked. "Yeah, well how about twenty bucks. I could use some help with my late night snack budget."

Rainey dipped into the pocket of her slacks and pulled out all the cash she had, which was just over two hundred dollars. She also reached into her coat to retrieve a business card. She handed it all to Connor.

"Here, take this. I know you can get more than that off the next rich guy, but this is free of obligation. It's enough to feed you all a good meal, which you look like you could use. How old are you, Connor?"

Connor stared at the money, answering absent-mindedly, "I'm seventeen."

"Do you have an I.D.?"

"What, you need to verify my age? October 17, 1997. Do the math. You don't need to see my fucking I.D." Distrustful had not described the depths of Connor's contempt for authority.

"You just looked older than the rest of these guys. I know someone who runs a catering business. She hires only LGBTQ kids off the street. You'll have a bed, food, a job. It's a way out. Any of the rest of you over fifteen?"

All but the youngest two nodded that they were. Rainey reached in her pocket and gave them each a card.

Rainey continued, "The card I gave you has my wife, Katie's, information on it. She works with homeless LGBTQ youth and battered women. Call that number. Someone will help you, whatever you need. You just have to reach out. Get a taxi, go to the address on the card, and they will pay the fare. Just get out of this cold. And you little guys," she looked at the two who were thirteen, maybe fourteen, "there are homes that will love you, take care of you, and no one will hurt you. Please call that number. Katie or someone she works with will see that you're safe."

Rainey pulled another card from the inside breast pocket of her coat. "This is my card. I run a bail business, too. If you need me, call. I have a pretty good line on a lawyer," she grinned at Connor, "and she is not a prick."

Wendy encouraged the young men, "Trust her, guys. I do, or I wouldn't have brought her here." She poked one of the youngest boys playfully. "You know how to find me if you need me, right?"

He nodded that he did but remained quiet. Rainey thought he was trying desperately not to need help, to be one of the boys toughing it out. She hoped he would be out of this life soon.

The coastal boy had had enough of winter outside. "Can I get a ride to this shelter, Wendy? I'm tired of this cold shit."

"I'll take you," a protective Connor answered as he slid the cash into his pocket.

"You have a car?" Rainey asked, surprised.

"Yeah, my Grandma lets me use hers. She's in assisted living now, anyway. They take them everywhere on a bus."

The coastal boy said, "If my boy Con didn't let me sleep in that car sometimes, I would've been a fag-sicle."

Wendy hurried things along. "Henrique, tell Rainey what you told me."

"It's Cane," the boy with the bruises spoke from under his hoodie.

Coastal boy, who seemed unable to stand still or be quiet, said, "Yo, that's 'cause he's Puerto Ri-cane."

"Bullshit, man. It's short for Hurricane. He came out of the Ninth Ward during Katrina." Conner punched coastal boy in the arm. "You just make shit up all the time, Water Boy." He said to Rainey, "We call him Water Boy 'cause he's always talkin' about that boat his family owns."

Brooding Lips threw a verbal jab, "Yeah, but no fags in the fleet, right, Water Boy?"

Cane piled on more verbal abuse. "We call him Water Boy because of his backwoods ass. He loves his momma, too."

Water Boy retaliated with, "Yeah, well your momma loves to suck my dick."

Cane slapped the back of Water Boy's head, daring him to fight back. Their shared pain made them bullies, even as they had been bullied themselves.

"Hey, hey, knock it off," Rainey yelled over a landing jet, trying to refocus them. "All right, then, Cane, my sister believed it was important enough to drag me to the airport to hear what you have to say."

Cane leaned closer so he wouldn't have to shout. "I knew the two guys they pulled out of that pond. They told people what they knew, and now look where they are."

"Two questions," Rainey shouted over a departing jet. "Who did they tell and what?"

One of the two remaining boys—too young for whiskers and cherub cheeked—moved to the front of the pack. He motioned for Rainey to come closer.

When she bent her ear close to his mouth, he said, "The man that comes in the black car, he took them. Everybody knows that. Connor told us to stay away from him, but I was hungry, and he offered so much money, more money than I've ever had in my whole life."

Rainey put her hands on his shoulders when he stopped talking. She could see the tears welling in his eyes. The noise became a distant roar again.

Rainey said softly, "You don't have to explain why you went with the man. What's your name?"

"Barron."

"Barron, where did the man take you?"

Cane relieved his younger friend of retelling something so obviously painful.

"This guy, he used to be one of us, he says. He's probably twenty-five, and he's rich now. He makes his money finding tricks for even wealthier men. I went with him. He'll only ask you once. He has all these rules."

85

Water Boy, as he would be known in Rainey's lost boys memory box, interjected excitedly, "Yeah, like you have to put on a blindfold as soon as you're in the car and keep it on until you're inside the house. Then he feeds you, makes you take a shower, and then you have to put on clothes he picks out. He has a whole room full of clothes, all sizes."

"Yeah, but you can't keep them," Cane complained over the next arriving flight.

Water Boy waited out the rumble before continuing the narrative, "It's not so bad. You eat, you get clean, and he even washes your old clothes. He let me spend the night after the party was over—fed me breakfast the next day. It's not what he does or what those other fucks do. It's nothing new."

The smallest boy, the one who wanted to know if Rainey was Wendy's mother, appeared the youngest and most vulnerable. With big blue eyes and the freckles of boyhood still covering the bridge of his nose, he burst forth with the real news.

"Those guys died because they knew who one of the men in the masks was."

Rainey needed clarification. "Wait, what men in masks?"

Connor filled Rainey in on the details. "Look, here's what happens. Ford comes to get them—"

Rainey stopped him. "Ford?"

"Yeah, he lived in an old piece of shit Ford car for a couple of years, so people called him Ford. That's what he said, anyway. I don't know what his real name is. He wants the little guys for a 'party' with rich pervs."

Water Boy continued his description of his evening at the party. "They all wear masks. Some are custom made. Some are those S 'n M masks, black leather, where you can only see their eyes. One guy wears the Guy Fawkes mask—you know, like Anonymous."

Barron spoke up, chuckling as if it wasn't the traumatic experience that it was. "One of them wears a hockey goalie mask with a skull demon thing painted on it. How fucked up is that?"

Conner waited out the next departing jet before he said, "The dead dudes said they knew one of the guy's voices and when he showed his dick, they recognized that, too. They started running their mouths about it, and the next thing you know they just vanished."

Wendy inquired, "What does Ford look like?"

Barron answered, "He has dark hair. He wears a mask, like a Lone Ranger mask. He wears nice clothes, and he's always tan."

Conner said, almost as an aside, "It's a Princess Bride mask."

Wendy, who entered information faster than Rainey could dream of typing into a phone, asked, "How tall? Is he overweight? Skinny? Average?"

Water Boy said, "He's about six foot tall, and he works out—got abs like a boss. He has a gym in his house."

"You think he killed those kids?" Rainey asked.

Connor answered, "There are some rich guys that have a lot to lose, too. I'd look there before I went after Ford. He's just making a living. Those kids were trying to figure out how to blackmail the rich dudes without ending up in jail, and then they were gone."

"Tell her who they said it was," Wendy prodded.

Barron volunteered, "It was Reverend Lilly. I recognized his voice, too."

Rainey peered at the boy. "Are you sure?"

"He came to conversion camp once a week. I'll never forget that voice."

"But you didn't see his face," Wendy added.

Connor's smirk returned. "Lilly's idea of rehab is to abuse the gay out of you. Says it's"—Connor adopted an exaggerated Southern preacher delivery—"natural domination practiced by the victors in the Bible and we need to understand it isn't meant to be enjoyable." He dropped the accent for his conclusion. "We're all graduates of the Lilly brand of re-education. Now he's been elected state representative. He's untouchable."

He shouted the last part over another jet roaring out of Raleigh-Durham International. Rainey had to wait for more convincing until she could hear herself think again.

She raised a brow and questioned the boys. "We are talking about Reverend Jedidiah Lilly, the guy who said all gays should be caged and left to die off? Which, by the way, proves what an idiot he is."

"Yes," the boys answered in unison.

"Do you have anything other than verbal recognition?"

Cane pulled out his phone and said, "How about a picture of his dick?"

"How did you get a picture of his penis?" Rainey asked.

"Blake, one of the dead dudes. He sent it to me. Said if anything happened to him to give this to the cops."

"How did those guys get a phone into the party? This Ford person must check for things like that."

Connor explained. "The dead kid from Durham, he had this spy cam he stole from his dad's house. It was small. I was going to pawn it for him because he wasn't old enough to sign the ticket. He had it with him that night, and he said he palmed it and then hid it in his pocket after Ford gave him clothes to wear.

Rainey turned back to Cane, "Why didn't you give the photo to the police and tell them what you know after they disappeared?"

His dark eyes bore into her. "I did. They arrested me for having a stolen phone and took it. I spent the weekend in youth detention and was sent back to my fucked-up foster family."

"Was the phone stolen?"

"No, one of my tricks gave it to me so he could reach me, but he told the cops he lost it. They gave it back to him after they erased all the pictures."

"So, how do you still have a copy?"

Cane looked incredulous. "Haven't you heard of the cloud?"

Rainey pointed at the phone in his hand. "Is that a gift from a trick, as well?"

"Yeah, but it is my phone. This guy likes me. He wants me to come live with him, but I ain't down for being no house boy."

"My email address is on the card I gave you. Will you email me the picture? It needs to be saved in more than one place."

"Yeah, I can do that," Cane said, smiling for the first time.

Connor ended the conversation with a warning to his friend. "If anyone finds out you have that picture, you'll be in that pond, too. That was a warning. Shut up or die." He looked up at Wendy. "We've seen superheroes like you before. We are still on the street. Leave these kids alone before you get them killed. Run your mouth too much, and you'll be in the pond with them. These guys will come after you, too. Come on, lost boys. Let's go get some food on the do-good cop's sister."

Brooding Lips contributed his brand of realism as he turned to skulk away, "Shit, ain't nobody going to believe a bunch of little fags anyway, right?"

Rainey turned to Wendy. "I can see why you were not sure of what to do with this information."

Wendy smiled at her big sister. "Yeah, but you will."

Part II

THE NIGHTMARE WAKES

"Even if she be not harmed, her heart may fail
her in so much and so many horrors;
and hereafter she may suffer—both in waking,
from her nerves, and in sleep, from her dreams."
— Bram Stoker

CHAPTER FOUR

Rainey entered the house through the door from the garage to see the triplets seated at the table in the breakfast nook.

"Hey guys," she said, happy to see them feeling better and eating a full meal.

"Nee Nee," they said in unison and scampered out of their chairs to surround her, but they had learned to stand and wait while her weapons were put away in the safe by the door.

Weapons secured, Rainey hung up her coat and threw open her arms for hugs and kisses.

"Where's mommy?" Rainey asked at the end of the greeting rumpus.

"Mommy is puke," Weather said, using the new word she learned during the stomach virus episode.

Melanie, Katie's mother, came back from the refrigerator with more juice for the kids and filled in the blanks for Rainey. "She took down just after lunch. She's upstairs in bed."

"Oh, that's not good," Rainey said. "Maybe I should cancel this trip."

"Katie wants you to go. Don't worry about the kids. Wendy will be here, and Constance said she'd come help, too."

Rainey's tenuous relationship with her mother had improved with the birth of the grandbabies but was still not the kind of mother-daughter connection Katie had with Melanie. Rainey had avoided her since the hallway striptease incident.

"Nee Nee, Mommy sleeped on da floor in da bafroom," Mack said. He was still having trouble with his 'th' sounds.

"She did?" Rainey asked, and was immediately inundated with commentary.

Timothy said, "Her sick. She say go get Nana, an' an' I go get Nana."

Weather's account was more detailed. "Mommy said, 'Get out.' She goed bleck, bleccckkk, in the potty."

"Okay, okay. Why don't you guys finish eating and I'll go check on Mommy." Rainey said, feeling her stomach turn as Weather's puking sound effects brought back the recent horror show of the triplets' gastrointestinal distress.

Rainey couldn't understand her queasiness after all the crime scenes she'd walked. Katie couldn't either.

Last week, as Rainey cleaned up yet another spewing while repeatedly gagging, Katie said, "You can examine a dead body with no head, and this makes you sick. You are too complicated for words."

Rainey responded, "You can't puke at a crime scene."

Katie had warned, "You can't puke on the dining room rug, either."

Timothy climbed back into his booster seat, saying, "Mommy say, 'Dammit, dammit, dammit.'"

Melanie chuckled.

Rainey tried to stifle a laugh and said, "That's not a nice word, is it?"

"Noooooo," the three chimed together.

"I'll tell her, okay?" Rainey said, still struggling to maintain a straight face. "But since she's sick, I don't think she should be in trouble, do you?"

Weather, who had experienced "trouble," said, "She can be timeout when she feels better."

"That will work," Rainey said. "I'll tell her."

Melanie, who was hiding her smile behind the kitchen towel in her hand, suggested, "You go check on her. I'll finish up here and then bring them up for bath time. Unless you want to eat first."

Rainey's stomach turned at the thought of what she might encounter upstairs. She waved off that idea.

"No, I think I'll wait a bit," she answered. "Eat your supper, guys, and then we'll do baths and story time."

Rainey climbed the stairs to the third floor and found Katie shivering with chills in the bed.

"Oh, honey. I'm so sorry," she said, as she sat down on the edge of the mattress.

Katie responded, "Don't shake the bed," without opening her eyes.

Rainey stayed completely still, asking, "Is there anything I can get you? Do you need another blanket? Do you want something to drink?"

"Rainey, I love you, but stop talking. I just need to sleep."

Rainey stood as gingerly as she could, trying not to shake the bed. "Okay, sweetheart. I'll check on you in a bit."

"Fine," Katie said, seemingly unwilling to say more.

Rainey changed clothes in the walk-in closet and tiptoed out of the room.

#

Three hours after arriving at home, Rainey finally sat down on the chaise lounge in the master suite. She had bathed the triplets with Melanie's help, read "If You Give A Mouse A Cookie" twice, and tucked the kids into their toddler beds for the night. Mack wouldn't go down without seeing Mommy, the love of his life. Katie came to the nursery door, pale and weak, blew kisses to each child, and said, "I love you." She immediately ran to the bathroom in the master suite and had only settled back down a few minutes ago.

Rainey could have slept in one of the second-floor bedrooms but thought the chaise would be okay for one night. She watched

95

the comforter on the bed rise and fall with Katie's shallow sleeping breaths. Freddie, Rainey's ever-faithful cat, now an old man prone to bed sleeping instead of the night wanderings of his past, curled up at Katie's knees.

Between bouts of sickness, Katie told Rainey to go on the trip as planned.

"It's just one night," she had said. "We'll be fine. You need to do this."

Rainey brought upstairs the case file she was presenting to her former colleagues at Quantico. She made herself comfortable, as best she could, and began to review the case once more. She knew every detail and had already prepared the visual aids for her presentation. Still, Rainey searched for the things she had missed, the ones she nearly paid for with her life. She opened the file folder and began reading.

Rainey woke sometime later from a deep sleep. She sat up quickly, suddenly aware that something was amiss. Katie had not moved. The comforter rose and fell slowly with her breathing. Freddie had left the room and was probably on his night prowl to the food bowl in the kitchen. Rainey stood and walked out into the hallway. She waited a moment, listening. She glanced back at the security panel by the bed. Her heart startled into rapid beating at the realization the alarm was disarmed.

Quickly she moved to the nursery door. The room was dark. The nightlights had been extinguished. Rainey rushed into the room, feeling of each bed to find them empty. Panic set in.

She screamed, "Katie! Katie wake up! The kids are gone," and broke into a run back toward the master suite.

Rainey reached her side of the bed, where she kept a small gun safe.

"Katie, Katie, wake up!"

She looked down at the bed. Katie was completely covered in the comforter from head to toe and not responding to Rainey's pleas. Movement at the door caused her to spin while feeling blindly for the fingerprint lock on the safe. A dark figure stood still in the hall.

"Katie, for god's sake, wake up," she shouted again.

Her finger hit the bio lock on the safe. The box sprang open. She fumbled for the pistol, keeping her eyes on the dark figure. She heard Katie move and turned her head to speak to her. The figure breathing slowly in the bed had not been her wife.

"Hello, Rainey. Thought you were rid of me, did you?"

Katie began to scream her name from somewhere in the house. The pistol was in Rainey's hand now, but he was on her too fast. He smashed into her body, sending the weapon flying across the room. He sat on her chest and smiled down at her, while she swung wildly, hitting only the air between them before someone grabbed her arms and pinned them to the floor. She could only see a glint of the second attackers blond hair.

"Rainey! Mom! Help me," Katie cried.

Rainey was in a fight for her life and couldn't break free of the two men holding her down.

"I'm going to enjoy watching you bleed to death," the one holding her arms said.

Suddenly, a scalpel appeared in the hand of the man sitting on her chest. He brought it down to her throat.

He yanked off the black mask he had been wearing to reveal his face, saying, "The cut will be deeper this time."

"Rainey! " Katie's voice was close, but Rainey couldn't see her.

All she saw was JW Wilson's face inches from her own, as she tried to buck him off her chest. The triplets began to cry and scream.

"Oh, God," she thought, "Don't let them see this."

"Rainey! Please wake up."

She heard Katie's plea and in a flash her eyes opened.

"Rainey, it's me."

Katie was bending over her, trying to hold her arms down. Rainey was on the floor by the chaise lounge, the contents of the file she had been reading spread around her. The triplets were in the doorway, crying. Melanie was attempting to shield them from the scene in their parents' bedroom. Rainey blinked a few times and realized her nightmare was over. She sat up and leaned back against the chaise, trying to calm her breathing.

Katie left Rainey and moved to the door to comfort their frightened children.

"It's okay. It's okay. Nee Nee had a bad dream. Nana is going to take you downstairs for a cookie and some milk. Okay?"

"Wait," Rainey said and crawled to her feet.

She walked to the door and got down on her knees. She hugged her children close.

"I'm sorry I woke you. I had a bad dream. That's all. I'm okay now."

Timothy said between sniffles, as he touched her face, "You were scared, Nee Nee."

"Yes, I was, but it was just a dream. Everything is all right now. Go with Nana. I'll come down in a minute and have a cookie with you."

Melanie looked down at Rainey, saying softly, "I hope this trip helps you, honey."

Rainey hugged the triplets close to her and responded with a nearly inaudible, "I do, too."

Weather patted her on the back and whispered against Rainey's neck, "You had a bad dream. You okay now," just as her parents did when the little girl experienced a terror in the night.

Suddenly, Katie took off for the bathroom.

"Go with Nana, now," Rainey said and patted each one on the butt, before turning them loose. "I love you."

Rainey watched them toddle off with Melanie before returning to the chaise to pick up the pages of the reports and crime scene photos scattered on the floor. Once that was completed, she went to the bathroom door and knocked lightly.

"Katie? Are you okay?"

The door opened, revealing Katie wiping her face with a towel. Wet wisps of hair stuck to her forehead.

"I'm so sorry," Rainey said before Katie could say anything.

Katie stared up at her for a second and then said, "You could have hurt me or the kids."

"I would nev—"

Katie cut her off. "You have no idea what you might do, and neither do I. The night terrors are worse now than ever." She held out her arms for Rainey to see. There were red marks where Katie had obviously tried to wake her. "I'm just glad I got away from you before you did serious damage. I can't stop you when you're like that, and that scares the shit out of me."

Rainey stared at the marks on Katie's arms and then moved her eyes to Katie's. The fear reflected there tore at her heart.

She repeated the only thing she could think to say, "I'm so sorry."

"Rainey, you started having these dreams again when they found John Taylor's body. It's triggered some form of delayed PTSD. If this plan you and Danny have doesn't work, we'll need to talk about some other sleeping arrangements. I have to think about the kids' safety. I love you, but—"

Katie left her statement hanging. Both of them were aware something had to give.

Rainey stared at the floor, unable to look her wife in the eye. "Don't give up on me, Katie."

CHAPTER FIVE

9:00 AM, Thursday, March 5, 2015
FBI Academy, Quantico, VA

"Good morning," Rainey said into the microphone.

The large lecture hall at the FBI Academy was filled, every seat taken by agents and trainees, with still more standing along the back wall. They'd all come to listen to Rainey discuss the worst moments of her life. Tired from lack of sleep, the sunrise flight out of Raleigh hadn't helped. Rainey's former BAU teammate and the triplet's godfather, Supervisory Special Agent Danny McNally picked her up at the airport in Washington, D. C. The hour-long drive back to Quantico, Virginia, gave them a chance to talk. Danny took full advantage.

After catching up on news of his godchildren and some small talk, Danny said, "Katie called me this morning. She told me about last night's incident. She's scared, Rainey."

"I don't want her afraid of me, Danny."

"She's not afraid of you. She's afraid of your memories and what they do to you in your dreams. Katie said that you've become more violent during these latest episodes. She's worried, Rainey, for all of you."

Rainey sighed, tears welling in her eyes. "I don't want to lose my family, Danny."

"I know," he said.

Rainey stared out the passenger side window. The Virginia countryside flew by as they traveled south on Interstate 95. She left Carolina's sixty-degree weather for freezing temperatures and rain. Snow and ice were on the way. The clouds overhead mirrored how Rainey felt inside, dark and foreboding.

After a moment, Danny continued, "I've talked to the psychologist you saw after the attack. She believes what we are doing today will help."

There was no one on earth who knew Rainey Blue Bell like Danny. He was privy to details about her life that even her wife did not know. Rainey never discussed the specifics with Katie of the night JW Wilson raped and scarred her for life, but Danny had been there and seen the aftermath. She remembered only bits and pieces right after the assault. One of the clearest images she retained was of Danny cutting her bindings loose with tears in his eyes. He loved her and she him. It was never a romantic love, but they shared an unbreakable bond. If anyone could help Rainey, it was the redheaded Irishman in the seat next to her.

When she didn't respond, Danny asked, "Are you okay with this?"

She had turned to him, forcing a smile. "I trust you, Danny. If you say this will help, then I'm willing to try."

Now, she stood at the microphone, facing old colleagues and new faces, about to bare her soul, in an attempt to bury the demons that haunted her dreams.

"My name is Rainey Bell," she said as she picked up the remote on the podium.

She smiled at the audience and pushed a button. The screen behind her came to life, displaying the last identification photo she had taken while still with the Bureau. Her once long curls hung over one shoulder as she sat in front of the FBI seal and an American Flag.

"Some of you will remember me as SSA Bell, when I had a lot more hair," she chuckled. "Some of you had more hair the last time I saw you, too."

Laughter rippled through the room. She let it play out before advancing to the next picture. The smile left her lips, as she watched the collective grimace overtake the room.

"And some of you have only seen me as a victim in a case file."

The image on the screen was of Rainey's badly beaten body. Her eyes were swollen shut, her face nearly entirely black with bruising, her lips distended and bleeding, her chest and torso lined with stitches in a Y-incision pattern. Finger marks were prominent on her neck. Her wrists and ankles showed bruising from the bindings.

The earlier image of SSA Bell reappeared beside a close up of Rainey's battered face.

"I'm here today to explain how I went from agent to victim. It is my hope that what you learn from my mistakes will help prevent similar ones in the future."

Rainey changed the image to a photo of Representative JW Wilson seated in front of the flag and seal of the state of North Carolina.

"This is my attacker. Before he was a lawyer and state official, he was my neighborhood friend, a guy I grew up with, played hooky with, and got into some teenaged shenanigans with."

The image changed to one of JW and Rainey from their high school yearbook. Sports trophies surrounded them as they smiled for the camera, an arm draped around each other's shoulders.

"We lost touch after high school. I became a behavioral analyst with the BAU. JW, in addition to his political aspirations, married a beautiful woman, had a successful legal career, and became a serial rapist and murderer. I would not knowingly see him again until he walked into my business a little more than a year after he raped and almost killed me. He would nearly kill me again before I saw through his façade."

Danny took his place at a podium a few feet away from Rainey.

"Former Agent Bell is not the only one who made mistakes on this case. I made them as an agent and an analyst."

"We both did," Rainey added.

She exchanged a nod with Danny, an acceptance of their mutual complicities in the events leading up to her abduction. Rainey never blamed Danny for what happened. He was hard enough on himself. She knew they were both there to bury demons. She pushed the remote button, bringing up headlines from newspapers about the Y-Man murders.

Danny turned back to the audience. "For those of you unfamiliar with the case file, we were looking for an organized UNSUB—an intelligent, affluent male the media dubbed the Y-Man for the signature eviscerating wounds on his victims. The killer had the means to abduct high-end call girls from business establishments frequented by wealthy, powerful men. He planned carefully and used forensic countermeasures to prevent his identification through trace evidence. He did not want the bodies found. Three were recovered before he improved his concealment techniques. He was learning and escalating. He dumped the first bodies in Lake Johnston. We recommended a stakeout of the bridge he was traveling in the early morning hours."

The image on the screen switched to the parking lot of the boathouse, where Rainey's nightmares had begun.

"On May 28, 2009, SSA McNally and I were watching the north entrance of the Advent Ferry Bridge, where we believed the UNSUB was accessing the lake for body disposal. We also thought he might come back to relive some elements of his fantasy. Local law enforcement had added patrols in the area. Agent McNally and I were there to experience what the UNSUB saw, the traffic patterns, the patrols, the way the shadows fell, in an effort to more clearly understand his methods. We were grasping for ways to get out in front of this guy. This type of killer needed to be forced into deviating from his plan. We needed him to make a mistake." Rainey paused and then added, "But a mistake had already been made—by me."

Danny interjected, "This is where Rainey and I disagree. I do not believe the sole responsibility for this error is hers. It belongs to the Bureau and her teammates, as well. I bear a particular burden here."

"Wherever the responsibility lies," Rainey said, "there is a lesson to be learned. My father had been murdered eighteen days prior to the stakeout. His murderer was arrested just four days previous to the evening in question. My frustrations and anger had no outlet when it was discovered my father's death was the result of a random drive-by shooting involving a fourteen-year-old trying to earn his way into a gang. I was distracted and should not have been in the field. My emotions were all over the place, and I let them take me out of the car and away from my stakeout partner. My preoccupations gave the UNSUB the opportunity to abduct me."

"Rainey's colleagues, including me, assumed what she needed was work to relieve her grief over the murder of her father. If an agent's head is not in the game, we don't allow him or her in the field, but Rainey hid her mental distress quite well."

Rainey nodded in agreement, adding, "Honest self-reporting is more important than feeling as if you must return to work after a trauma or loss. Whether you believe it will distract you from the pain of grief or that you may be perceived as weak if more time is needed, neither is a sufficient reason. Supervisors and agents alike need to take a frank look at mental state before a mistake such as mine is made in the future. Distraction can be deadly."

She let a grin creep to her lips. "I also learned to monitor the food intake of the person I'm going to be sharing a car with for unknown hours. I think my friend here learned that there is such a thing as too many collards with hot pepper vinegar."

A few chuckles rippled through the tense room as Rainey changed the image on the screen to a photo of the old office. She read aloud from the sign over the door, "Billy Bell's Bail and Bait. This is where I went to recuperate, my father's business, which he left to me. The UNSUB went dormant. I had taken medical leave after the minimum Bureau-required therapy appointments and escaped to North Carolina. The safe place I ran to happened to be very near my abduction site. Instead of the mental health help I needed, I turned to alcohol to silence the nightmares—my second mistake."

Rainey took a breath. The next part was hard to admit. "My third mistake was spending the time I should have been healing in a constant state of hyper-vigilance. I knew he was watching me. I could feel him. Paranoia? We'll never know exactly when JW Wilson re-engaged with me, but we do know he stalked me for some time before making the initial contact. His plan was extensive and took months to execute. In retrospect, I went home because I wanted him to find me. I never processed my father's death. The anger merely rolled into the baggage from my own assault. My extended family saw the self-destructive behavior and warned of the brick wall I was running at full steam. I was accused of having a death wish. What I had was a vengeance wish, and if that brought death, so be it. I needed help, but again I refused it when offered."

Danny expounded, "I kept an eye on Rainey. I had a Bureau psychologist contact her and, against medical advice, she rejected further treatment. She abandoned the Bureau support system and also refused to investigate her recollections of the assault. Although heavily drugged and unconscious during much of the attack, as it would turn out, she retained more memories than she was able or willing to recall. By using alcohol to dull the nightmares, Rainey was also preventing her brain from processing the information it stored for her there."

"With all my training and experience working with assault victims, I ignored the advice I had always given, 'Talk to someone.' I work with victims now. I spend a great deal of time encouraging them to take advantage of the help available. Above all else, I've learned as a victim that silencing the self-blaming voices in my head was most important. What I'm doing here today is an important part of that process."

Rainey pressed the button on the remote again. The image changed to that of the handsome couple, Representative and Mrs. JW Wilson, at a Republican fundraiser. She glanced over her shoulder at the picture, before continuing.

"In July of 2010, a little over a year after the assault, Representative Wilson asked me to investigate what appeared to be the stalking of his wife."

Rainey couldn't prevent the smile from curling her lips.

"Katie Meyers Wilson, as some of the agents who responded can attest, turned out to be a handful."

The familiar faces on the front row, her former team members of the BAU, smiled and nodded.

"I'll explain more about that in a bit," she said, suppressing a grin and continuing, "My attacker re-engaged shortly after I began shadowing Katie Wilson. Once aware of his involvement in the stalking case, I contacted the BAU. I moved into the Wilsons' home for a few days. Because I had not done the work of evaluating my assault, I had repressed what little I did remember. I could no longer trust my instincts or intuition, which were clouded by lack of sleep, alcohol abuse, and the fear of reliving too much.

"My body began to tell me things I chose to ignore or did not comprehend on a conscious level. When I was in JW Wilson's presence, I was nervous and unsettled. His cologne made me ill. I grew more and more uncomfortable around him as time went on. I attributed my behavior to the fact that I was struggling with an attraction to his wife, the woman I was hired to protect. Not only was I processing a heretofore unexplored element of my sexuality, I found myself in an ethical dilemma while being hunted by a serial killer."

Danny interrupted. "To Rainey's credit, she did try to distance herself from Mrs. Wilson and turned her safety over to us after we arrived. We had a plan to draw out the killer, putting a target squarely on Rainey's back. She returned to her home and waited for his next move." He chuckled a bit. "But as hard as we tried, we couldn't keep Mrs. Wilson away from Rainey. The attraction, it seems, was mutual."

The next picture appeared on the screen, one of Katie wearing a bathing suit and asleep in a lawn chair. Some appreciative murmuring came from the room.

"This is a photo JW gave me. His wife's stalker supposedly took it. I don't want to call our mutual attraction a mistake, but in reality," Rainey explained, "it was a significant diversion of my attention. I think you can see why."

107

Understanding chuckles filled the room.

The laughter subsided before she changed to an image showing only JW Wilson's eyes and continued, "The situation allowed me to excuse the warning signs my psyche was sending. The attraction was evident to everyone around us, including JW Wilson. He used it against me. He abducted Katie and used her as a lure to pull me in. It worked."

"Again, against my advice, Rainey made her next mistake, and this one is all on her. She engaged with the UNSUB on her own. I will give her points for leaving us breadcrumbs that enabled us to find her, but she broke the protocol she had been trained to follow."

This time it was Rainey who interrupted. "We disagree here. I made a judgment call that I stand by. The UNSUB gave me little choice but to follow his instructions. It was my training that allowed me to get close to him. I was able to rescue Katie and avoid us both becoming his next murder victims. Katie was heavily drugged during her entire abduction. She has had no notable recall in the years following. The event remains a black hole for her. She could not help us identify her abductor, and I never saw more than his shadow. He abandoned his plan to kill us when he heard the sirens closing in on our location."

"Now, just to be clear," Danny said, "we, the BAU members on site, interviewed JW Wilson. His behavior was questionable from the start. He fit our profile, but we allowed his prior relationship with Rainey to influence our assessment. We assumed it was someone in his social circle. We suggested that to Mr. Wilson, and like the consummate organized killer, he had a plan to hand us a suspect and deflect attention from himself. He was one step ahead of us the entire time. I allowed him to drive away from his wife's abduction site, and we're quite sure now, Katie was in the trunk of his car."

The image on the screen changed to a photo of a man who looked a lot like JW, smiling for the photographer and dressed in blue scrubs.

Rainey explained the image. "Dr. John Taylor, a local veterinarian and another former high school classmate of mine, fit our assessment of the UNSUB to a tee. He became a suspect, was questioned, and released under surveillance. JW Wilson had tied Dr. Taylor to the crimes with circumstantial and physical evidence. Had he gone to trial, it's very likely Taylor would have been convicted. JW couldn't take that chance, though, so he orchestrated our suspect's apparent flight from justice. As I've said, JW's plan was longstanding and extensive. He'd given his exit strategy quite a bit of thought. What he did not plan on was leaving his wife nor me alive. I would realize only recently why my death was vital to his plan."

Danny took over for a moment. "We've had ample time to analyze JW Wilson's final attempt to murder his wife and his old friend. We concluded he was just that arrogant and confident he would not be caught. JW believed Dr. Taylor would be blamed and he could move forward without the worry of either of his victims recovering memories."

Rainey changed the image. A photo of the cottage she once called home appeared. The big bay window was shattered where Mackie had tossed JW through it and off the balcony. A large hole had been blasted in the wall beside the window, where she and Katie had made their escape.

Rainey informed the audience. "This is my former home, where JW found Katie and me together. His wife had planned to leave him before I met her. My appearance on the scene simply sped up the process. Mrs. Meyers had her own reasons for disliking her husband. JW drugged and killed two agents that day and nearly killed my oldest friend. Fortunately, my friend was large enough to survive the attempted overdose. And unfortunately for JW, I did recover a memory in time to spoil his plans. I was standing beside him when the veil he hid behind lifted. I knew in an instant who he really was. He saw me see him, and the gunfight that ensued concluded in his death. Katie ended his life with a shotgun blast to his chest. Had JW Wilson not come to my home that day, I believed I never would have identified him as the serial rapist and murderer that he was. But he knew something I did not, and the story doesn't end there."

The image of skeletal remains on an autopsy table replaced the one of the ravaged cottage.

"On November 31, 2014, the skeletal remains of Dr. John Taylor were recovered from a drainage pond near the Raleigh-Durham Airport, which answered the question of what had become of him. None of JW Wilson's other victims have surfaced, but we are confident there are at least four more bodies somewhere in the Triangle area of North Carolina."

Rainey's throat became dry and she stopped to sip from the water bottle on the podium. This was the hard part, admitting the consequences of her errors. Danny did not interrupt this time. He waited quietly at his podium. He knew what she had to say. That late night phone call to Danny was one she would never forget.

She cleared her throat and began. "I had spent years burying the past. The compartmentalization I learned as a member of the BAU, which made me damn good at my job, was also nearly my undoing. When John Taylor's body was discovered, the mental boxes where I stored the bits and pieces of memory from the night of my attack flew open. Nightmare images flooded my dreams, more vivid than ever before. Lost details surfaced, and then I saw what I had refused to remember."

Here it was, the moment of truth. Rainey looked out at the audience and admitted the proof of the costly error she had made.

"Had I undergone the recommended treatment plan; had I allowed my teammates to question me about my attack and aided in the investigation; had I not silenced my mind with alcohol, distracted it by any means possible in order to forget; I may have saved lives and prevented the suffering of others. Before JW Wilson escaped the night of my abduction, he turned back to look at me and took off the mask. I saw him. He knew I saw him. That is the real reason he came after me again and again. Choosing to compartmentalize the memories and lock them away forever nearly cost me everything. It did cost the lives of two agents and an innocent man. It is also the source of the guilt and self-doubt that plagues me now."

Danny spoke softly into his microphone. "Rainey came to me for help. I believe that was the first step in her recovery. We came to the conclusion that her journey needed to begin here, among her former colleagues, people who would understand and possibly benefit from her experience." He smiled over at Rainey. "I think it is a brave thing to stand here, admitting one's flaws."

Rainey changed the image on the screen to show two young agents seated proudly in front of the FBI seal and the American flag, just as she had been so many years ago.

"Three families paid for the mishandling of my trauma, and the Bureau lost two fine young agents, Reed Hancock and Lee Watson. For the pain my refusal to seek treatment may have caused, I am truly sorry. I can only hope that by coming here today, I will have raised awareness of the importance of relying on each other and the Bureau support system in times of mental stress. The ability to compartmentalize our lives into little mental boxes is a necessary skill when one is exposed to unconscionable human depravity. It can also be detrimental to mental health when those boxes explode open without warning. Talk to someone. Unpack your boxes."

She tapped the remote, filling the screen behind her with the FBI seal.

"My time in the Bureau was the culmination of a lifelong dream, one I'm sure many of you shared. I can't remember not wanting to be an FBI agent. I am extremely proud to have worn those three letters on my chest and to have worked with the men and women who exemplify the motto—Fidelity, Bravery, Integrity. Thank you for taking the time to help me on my journey to recovery. It has been an honor to speak with you today."

She paused. The room was silent. Rainey was sure she could hear the audience members breathing for what felt like minutes but was only seconds.

Finally a voice from the middle of the room asked, "What happened to Katie Wilson?"

Rainey hit the button on the remote.

"Well, despite my flaws Katie married me. This was the Bell-Meyers family Christmas card this year." Rainey pointed at the picture of her and Katie laughing while helping the triplets decorate the tree. "These are our three-year-old triplets, Mack, Timothy, and Weather. Sometimes even tragic stories have happy endings."

The audience began to clap and was soon on its feet. With every second the ovation continued, Rainey felt the guilt she'd carried dissipating. She knew it was only the beginning. It was a sweet release, nonetheless.

#

Rainey called home on the way to lunch with some of her old teammates. Wendy answered Katie's cell phone.

"Hey, Rainey. Katie said answer if you called and to tell you first thing not to freak out because she didn't."

Rainey chuckled. "I guess I deserve that."

Wendy laughed, saying, "Yes, you do."

"Where is the lovely Ms. Meyers?" Rainey inquired.

"She's upstairs with Grandpa John. He came over to check on her. She's been puking like a freshman after homecoming."

"Oooh, that doesn't sound good. How are the kids doing?"

"You would never know they had been sick. I played with them in the backyard for two hours until it started raining. Your mom and Nana are feeding them now."

"I really appreciate you spending your days off there. I will be home early in the morning if the weather doesn't get too bad. They are calling for a big ice storm up here later."

"No worries," Wendy said and then asked, "Hey, you wouldn't happen to have a file or two on fetish burglars that escalate to murder? Teague is having my class do a case study on the Triangle Terror."

"There are perks to being my sister. A copy of the case file is locked in my desk. The key is in the cup with the paperclips."

Wendy chuckled. "That's some high tech security system there."

"I just lock it so no one accidently sees something that will scar them for life."

Wendy laughed louder. "Oh, Katie makes you do it."

"Yes, and if you keep laughing, I'll tell her you have a crush on a married man. She'll ride that one to the ground."

Danny, who was driving, started chuckling.

Wendy immediately stopped laughing. "Is that Danny? "

"Yes," Rainey answered, suppressing her own laughter.

Wendy insisted, "You tell him that's not true."

"There is nothing wrong with a little hero worship," Rainey said instead.

"Whatever," Wendy responded dismissively and changed the subject. "Hey, did you run that story those kids told us by Danny?"

"I haven't had a chance, but I will. Until then, you need to stay out of that investigation. Powerful people have powerful friends. You don't want to be in the middle if things get dicey for them. You could lose your badge or worse."

"Oh, just so you know, Aaron Engel followed me to your neighborhood security gate this morning. I called it in, but he didn't do anything but stare." Wendy said, bouncing from subject to subject like she usually did. "I let the guards know what's up."

"Tell your supervisor, Wendy. Now that his wife has gone into hiding and he's facing jail time, Aaron Engel is a desperate man. Do not confront him."

"Okay, but I have to protect myself, lethally if provoked."

Rainey heard herself say something that Ernie, Mackie, and Billy Bell had repeated to her ad nauseam.

"Don't get cocky."

"Yeah, yeah," came the reply.

"We're here at the restaurant. Tell Katie I called and I'll check back later."

"Okay. I'll tell her, but I'll probably send a note with her mother. Let's just say it isn't pretty—not pretty at all."

"All right. Talk to you soon. Bye."

Rainey hung up before Wendy could go into detail about Katie's viral emissions. On the one hand, she felt a pang of guilt for not being there. On the other, she couldn't be happier to be hundreds of miles away.

113

#

Roger pulled out a chair for Rainey after giving her a hug.

"It's good to see you," he said in his soft baritone.

He was a little grayer around the temples and resembled Harry Belafonte even more as he had aged. She'd known him the longest of her former teammates.

"It's good to see you, too," Rainey said, returning his smile. "How's life treating you?"

"I'm retiring to Florida next month," he said, wearing a broad grin. "Monique is already down there. Got a house right on the beach."

"I can tell you're shaken up about that," Rainey said with a chuckle.

She didn't sit because Paula was making her way around the private dining room table, swooping in for a hug.

She whispered in Rainey's ear. "I'm proud of you. That took guts." She pulled back and looked into Rainey's eyes. "But don't let me hear you take sole responsibility for what happened to those agents ever again. There were other people involved, including myself, who should have put a few things together without your input. We all missed things."

Rainey hugged her again. "Thank you, Paula. How's Julian? He's almost four, isn't he?"

"Yes," Paula answered, whipping out her phone to show Rainey a picture. "He's growing like a weed. His daddy is convinced he's going to be the next LeBron. Look at him dunking that nerf ball."

"He's precious," Rainey commented before being bear-hugged from behind.

"Rainey Bell, I've missed you."

She turned around and hugged the man standing behind her. "Curtis, you are still cherub-cheeked and happy. How the hell do you do it?"

"I love my job. I love my wife. Life is good." The young man, who once was an intern assigned to shadow Rainey, beamed at her with his answer. He worked with the team now but had

114

never lost his youthful exuberance. The team needed happy people mixed among the more solemn personalities.

James, the technology specialist who traveled with the team, followed Curtis to the table. He slapped him on the shoulder, saying, "Mr. Happy is in the house, ladies and gentlemen," indicating how the rest of the team dealt with Curtis's incessant cheerfulness. He extended his hand to Rainey and gave her a backslapping bro-hug. "Good to see you, Rainey."

"You too, James."

Danny suggested, "Let's have a seat." And to the waiter standing by, he said, "We have one more. She should be here—"

They heard her coming before she appeared in the door.

"I am at lunch. I will get back to you when I get back to you. You're new. So let me give you some advice. Don't be bitchy. Bitchy will get you nowhere. Ask around. I'm the biggest bitch in town."

Melatiah Brooks, as round as she was tall, which wasn't tall at all, walked into the room like she owned it. Brooks, as she was known, told Rainey once that if she demanded respect, it was more forthcoming. "Short, fat, African American, and a female computer nerd—I'd have a lot of prejudices to overcome if I gave a shit what people thought," she had explained to Rainey. She got away with her sharp tongue and occasional hostile attitude because Brooks was one of the best technical analysts in the Communication and Information Technology Unit at Quantico.

"Rainey Bell, how are my babies?" Brooks wrapped Rainey in her arms and squeezed hard.

Rainey grunted at the sudden thrust of her diaphragm, answering only after she had been released. "They are recovered from the intestinal hell they put us through and on the loose again. Thank you for sending the stuffed animals last week. They loved them."

"You kiss those cheeks for me and tell them Auntie Brooks will be down to see them soon."

"Well, now that we're all here," Danny said. "Shall we have a seat?"

The waiter busied himself with water-pouring while reviewing the special of the day menu with his guests. He took everyone's order over the small talk at the table, during which Rainey found out Curtis and his wife were expecting a second child. Since Rainey had seen him last, they had a two-year-old girl they named Beatrice. Paula spoke of having another child. Rainey passed around phones, including her own, participating in the proud parent picture parade. James and Brooks talked shop about a new program algorithm. Roger wanted to buy a fishing boat and planned to take up underwater photography. Danny was the only one not involved in a conversation. He watched Rainey interact with her friends. She saw him smile a few times, and he commented once or twice, but she could feel him analyzing her behavior. She expected no less.

The food was served, and Danny asked the waiter to leave the tea and water. They would serve themselves.

"We'll open this if we need you," he said and closed the door as the confused young man exited. After returning to his seat, while the others, including Rainey, dug into their plates, he began to speak.

"I asked you here because I think Rainey could benefit from your unique perspectives."

Rainey swallowed the bite of salad in her mouth and started to speak, but Danny raised his hand to stop her.

"Hear me out," he said to her.

Rainey acquiesced and waited to hear what Danny had to say.

"Rainey seems to be suffering from self-doubt concerning her behavioral analysis skills. After all, in the last six years, she's been abducted and raped by a man she knew and did not recognize as a psychopath until he almost killed her again. She found herself staring down the barrel of a gun when she missed identifying the partner of another. Then she let a dangerous woman into her home to guard her precious family. Last spring, she willingly got into a vehicle with a woman who was intent on killing her and never saw it coming."

"Well, when you put it like that, it does appear I'm not a very good analyst," Rainey commented.

116

"In the interest of fairness," Paula said, "while that woman was in her home, Rainey was saving Bladen Asher's life. And we were all in the room with JW Wilson and not one of us suggested he was the UNSUB. We also missed the partner's ID in that other case...Jared...Jared...,"

Rainey remembered. "Howard. Jared Howard."

"Thank you, Rainey," Paula said, not missing a beat. "The Jared Howard case. We interviewed Chelsea Thomas, and she wasn't a suspect."

Curtis spoke up. His sweet demeanor hid an encyclopedic knowledge of human behavior. Rainey had learned early on that this young man was exceptionally bright, if charmingly naïve.

"We examine behaviors. If a person does not overtly display a behavior, we have no extraordinary capabilities to recognize abnormal psychology. We study crimes after the fact. We identify traits of an UNSUB based on behavior already exhibited. We—all of us—we interact with psychopaths on a daily basis and have no idea. They survive by appearing normal."

"We were dealing with an organized predator in the Wilson case. They aren't easy to catch," Roger said. "It would be easy for us to put the blame on Rainey because she did not allow a cognitive interview, but there is no guarantee her memories would have returned any sooner. It's much more telling that we interviewed Wilson, stayed in his home, and not one of us spoke up about his resemblance to the profile. We all talked about the gut feelings we ignored, but only after the fact. It was Rainey who saw Wilson for who he was. We may never have caught him and instead lost more people that day, had her instincts not kicked in when they did."

"Hold up a minute," Brooks interjected, turning to Rainey. "How many of the cases mentioned were solved with your firsthand input? I seem to remember it was you who put together the Jared Howard-Dalton Chambers connection." She looked around the table. "You all fell for Chelsea Thomas's act, the broken-hearted, misled girlfriend of a serial killer. And Danny, didn't you spend time with Naomi Pierce? I ran the background check before Rainey hired her. No red flags. And that woman last

117

spring, she was a special kind of crazy-bitch and had a whole town fooled."

Danny answered, "Those are valid points, Brooks. And what Curtis said about not seeing things in people we interact with every day, that's extremely relevant. People in close relationships with these individuals never saw it coming, either."

Rainey knew he was talking about Katie and JW. She defended Katie with, "Who wants to believe someone they care for is actually a murdering psychopath? I'm more concerned with why I continue to find myself a target."

James, who had remained silent to this point, said quietly, "They come for you because they know you see them. Predators recognize hypervigilance in others because they survive on it. Instead of lacking in skills, it is precisely your ability to read behavior that draws them to you. An apex predator will attack when it perceives danger. They don't wait around for the hunter to see them first."

Rainey smiled at James. "The team has been wasting your talents. You should be an analyst."

"Nope," he said, returning her smile. "I don't want to spend my days sitting at a desk looking at what humans are capable of doing to one another. I know your work, Rainey. I'd follow you into any battle. Besides that, you are damn hard to kill."

The table erupted in laughter. When it subsided, Danny spoke again.

"I think what everybody is saying is we respect your talents as an analyst. What happened to you could have happened to any of us. It's time to cut yourself some slack."

Roger reached across the table and touched Rainey's hand. "You know I'd follow you, too, through any door. I got your six."

Paula wagged a finger in Rainey's direction. "If anything, you should learn to trust your instincts more. We all know there is a fine line between arrogance and self-confidence, but you need to get your swagger back. You're still standing. That has to mean something. I trust you, too, Rainey. I'd follow you."

Curtis grinned, saying, "I believe in you. I have your back."

Brooks raised her eyebrows and surrendered her palms when all eyes fell to her. "I don't follow or cover sixes. I listen. I direct. I provide key information, but I don't follow." She smiled at Rainey, offering a fist to be bumped, adding, "But you know Brooks got your back twenty-four-seven, Rainey Bell."

Rainey bumped fists with Brooks, saying, "Always."

Danny followed with his endorsement. "Rainey, you're good at what you do. I agree with everyone here. You wouldn't be alive if you weren't." He paused to give his words more weight. "I'll be there, Rainey—wherever, whenever—but you know that."

Rainey made eye contact with each person at the table, responding to their show of faith, with, "Thank you. Your trust is sacred to me. I wouldn't be sitting here if I didn't trust each and every one of you with my life."

Brooks reached for and squeezed Rainey's hand. Rainey returned the gesture and continued on her journey. There were unanswered questions. Some of the best behavioral analysts in the world were there to help her. She intended to take advantage of that.

"When I called Danny in December, I told him I couldn't deal with the knowledge I could have stopped JW Wilson before he killed more people, before he killed Katie's child, and almost killed her. It was a selfish act of preservation on my part. I needed help processing that guilt. Danny told me I needed to come home to you, my friends who know me, who have seen me in my best swagger," she smiled at Paula before continuing, "and who have witnessed my most vulnerable moments."

Rainey paused for a breath and exhaled slowly. Her audience waited for her to begin again.

"This bout of post-trauma stress hit me out of nowhere. My mind exploded with images and thoughts it had been examining for years. We've worked with victims. We know how traumatic an experience sudden recall can be. Knowing how PTSD manifests and experiencing it are two separate understandings, a difference I now comprehend quite clearly. From inside the

119

trauma, it's easy to forget what you know about the victim recovery process."

In an earnest quest for more knowledge, Curtis asked, "What do you think the dreams are telling you now? Danny said they've worsened and grown more vivid, yet you've seen the story's ending and it's a happy one. What more does your mind require of you?"

"I don't know, Curtis. That's why I'm here."

"I think I know the answer," Danny said.

His statement struck Rainey with the fear that maybe he did comprehend what was at the root of her problems, even if she couldn't recognize what that was. The anxiety Rainey was sure her facial expression projected did not deter Danny. Her body language alone was enough for a seasoned behaviorist to know he was treading on prickly ground, but he continued.

"We've talked over your dreams, analyzed them, and sought the meaning of each component. There is one recurring element you gloss over time and again. It's a new perspective added during this last round of nightmares. Do you know what that is?"

"I don't blame her."

The words were out of Rainey's mouth before she actually thought them. The others remained quiet while Danny asked Rainey to face her demons.

"I know you don't blame Katie, but she's appeared in your dreams bound and gagged beside you on that bed. JW asks you why Katie hasn't had to pay for her sin of not knowing who he really was. Where is that coming from?"

All eyes shifted to Rainey. She stared at Danny but remained silent.

When Rainey worked with Curtis, she always had to remind him to let the suspect think and be patient in waiting for the response. He had not changed. He spoke up when the quiet was too much for him to bear.

"It's the same source of her own self-doubts and guilt. Her psyche needs someone to blame. On a conscious level, Rainey knows she did everything right. The unconscious, more lizard-brained reaction, is the one saying, 'I can't believe I missed that,' and is looking for the cause of this error or someone else to blame. The lizard doesn't like to be wrong, and rightly so. Recognizing danger is one of its prime directives."

Paula added, "We all think unfathomable thoughts for a fleeting second and then dismiss them just as quickly. At some point, it crossed your mind that some responsibility rests with Katie. Your training and experience immediately quashed that idea, but your subconscious has seized on every single doubt you ever had concerning your assault, from your own liability to what Katie should have known. It makes you relive those misgivings in your dreams."

Danny spoke again, "You've explained to me that during most of the nightmare retelling of your assault, you are disconnected, floating above what is happening to your body. During this phase of the dream, you're able to look around and recall new details. Your brain has let go of the physical assault. It has allowed you to see more because you can process it now. What you cannot process, and the moment your nightmare throws you back inside the body on the bed, is your inability to protect the unconscious Katie. He asks you to condemn her. He threatens her for your reaction but never hurts her. That pain is reserved only for you. Why, do you think that is?"

Rainey broke her silence. "Because he is a sadist," she answered.

Brooks corrected her. "He *was* a sadist."

Danny smiled at Brook's insightful comment.

Roger leaned forward, making eye contact with Rainey. "It's because Katie doesn't remember the sadist JW Wilson. Her abduction is a complete blank. She never suspected him and can bear no witness to his crimes. She's unconscious in your dreams because you alone have the burden of remembering. He's still alive in you because your mind thinks it has to keep the record. You are the only living witness. You haven't told anyone everything that you remember, not Danny, not even your wife. There is no one to help you carry the tale forward. Your mind doesn't want the event forgotten. You have to share that burden with someone so it can cease its vigilance."

121

Rainey sighed heavily, tucked her chin, and stared at her hands now folded in her lap. Her body language conceded the point and could be easily read by those in the room.

"I received an email this morning," Danny said, reaching for his phone, "in answer to one I sent asking Katie if she had any insights that might help you."

Rainey's head popped up at Katie's name.

Danny touched his finger to the phone's screen a few times and then read aloud.

"Rainey will not discuss the assault or her dreams with me. If I could say anything to her it would be this: Rainey, neither of us is to blame. If you must hold someone accountable, then I ask forgiveness for not wanting to see the evil in the man I married. You don't have to protect me from those doubts. I know they exist. You wouldn't be so damn good at your job if you didn't wonder what signs I ignored. Thank you for helping me forgive myself for those sins and for making possible this incredible life we built together. I'm not willing to share you with JW Wilson's ghost. Banish him from our home."

No one said a word when Danny stopped reading. Rainey knew they were all looking at her. She was staring at her feet. Her head had dipped slowly as Katie's words hit their mark. A single tear fell from her eye and landed on the toe of her shoe. Rainey knew what she had to do. She did not raise her head. She just began to speak.

"I had gone out on the footbridge to clear my head. I started back to the SUV, after about twenty minutes of being pissed and self-absorbed. I was just passing the boathouse when JW Wilson put a stun gun to my neck. That's the last thing I remember until …"

CHAPTER SIX

2:30 PM, Thursday, March 5, 2015
Behavioral Analysis Unit
Quantico, VA

Danny left Rainey in the conference room with Paula to discuss the team's analysis of the Triangle fetish case.

"We reviewed the case again," Paula began. "We looked at your assessment and that of Teague, the behaviorist Wake County asked to come on board. Our analysis agrees entirely with yours and for the most part Teague's. He thinks the UNSUB is younger, late teens-early twenties, and advanced because of exposure to Internet porn and information he can acquire online. He points out that size and strength are not necessarily signs of maturity. But we agree with you on the age range being higher. The victims' impressions, the UNSUB's quick escalation to sadistic murder, and the organization he displays outweigh Teague's arguments." There was a pause, followed by, "Are you listening to me?"

Rainey looked up from her phone. "I'm sorry. I was texting Katie again. She seems to have her phone turned off. I guess she's resting. She caught the virus the kids had." Rainey put her phone down on the table. "Yes, I'm listening."

Paula asked, "Did you hear what I said about Teague's age assessment?"

"Yes, he thinks the UNSUB is much younger. His point is valid. Sadists can mature at a faster rate with all the information available to them now, but his vocabulary and the in-depth literary discussion he had with his third assault victim, those indicate an older, well-educated UNSUB. He could be in college now, and we know he's smart, but Arianna Wilde, the second victim, said she was sure he was in his forties. She said a young man's skin feels different from an older man's."

Paula looked up from the file. "What's it like, Rainey? How do you sit across from victims, encouraging them to tell you what you were unwilling to divulge until an hour ago? It's hard enough for me to interview an assault victim, but you know what it feels like at that moment."

Paula only wanted to be better at her job and treat victims with respect.

Rainey answered without any defensiveness. "Every victim is different. Some need the time to process what happened. Some need to share. I let them know that I do understand exactly how they feel and if they want to talk, I'll listen. If they don't, I give them my card and tell them I'll be there when they are ready. I might have pushed harder before my assault, telling them that solving the case was their best hope of recovery. I don't believe that anymore."

"What do you believe?" Paula asked.

"There are a lot of unsolved and unreported assaults out there and many of those women recovered and moved on with their lives. Solving the case and locking up the assailant may be one victim's healing resolution. For others, that closure isn't possible or necessary. As evidenced by my own case, even the death of the assailant won't close the case for some. Every victim has her own path back to a healthy mental state."

"Have you closed the case now, Rainey?"

Rainey smiled. "I hope so. I suppose I'll have to forgive myself. I tell victims they should never second-guess their behavior during the attack. There is no right or wrong way to survive a sexual assault. The important thing is they did. I needed to be reminded of that myself. I really appreciate what the team did for me today. I do feel lighter after dumping that load."

Paula patted Rainey's hand. "Guilt gets heavy. My momma says, 'It's easier to clean someone else's house than your own.' It took me a long time to see the wisdom in that, but she's right. It's easy for us to sit across from you, analyzing your behavior through all of this, cleaning your house, so to speak. You did the hard part. You went after the dirt in the corners. I admire you. I always have."

"Thank you, Paula. The admiration is mutual."

Paula exchanged smiles with Rainey and then turned back to the case file. "Okay then, let's see if we can find more information you can take back to the Triangle and catch this jerk."

Rainey leaned forward, anxious to talk about anything but herself for a while. "I think the key to catching him is finding his lair. I'm pretty sure it's down here in Chatham County."

She pointed at a map on the table, marking the crime scenes. Her fingertip rested on the dot indicating Arianna Wilde's farmhouse.

"I suggested a comparison be done between the occupants of this area," she pointed at the cluster of crimes near her home, "and property owners near the crime scenes in this area down south. No matches thus far, but it could be listed in someone else's name, a wife or parent maybe. I doubt it's a rental, though."

Paula nodded her head. "I agree, he owns this place or has exclusive access to it. He couldn't chance a landlord stopping by. You should suggest they expand the search to include all household members. I know that's a lot of names, but I own property without my husband's name on it. It was left to me by my grandmother."

"Brooks would have a better shot at making the connections," Rainey said. "I can't ask her to do it. I'll have to get the task force to make a request."

Paula picked up her cell phone. "They already asked for a consultation. We'll just extend the evaluation a bit, shall we?"

She hit a few buttons and stuck the phone to her ear. "Brooks, I need you to do something for me." She paused and then said, "It's for Rainey. Would that move it up the list?" Another pause. "I thought it would."

Paula began giving Brooks the details of the search she needed. Rainey picked up her phone and tried Katie's number again, and still received no answer. She was thinking about calling Wendy's phone when Paula hung up with Brooks.

"Okay, she's on it," Paula said, just as Danny walked into the room.

"I just got off the phone with Detective Robertson. She had some somber news. Kaitlyn Whitaker's body was found this morning."

Rainey said, "Let me guess. In the Cape Fear River near here." She pointed again to the area around the Wilde farmhouse.

Danny said, "Don't ever doubt your skills, Rainey. They found her body here, tangled in a dead tree caught on the dam."

He pointed to a spot less than an inch from Rainey's fingertip.

Rainey asked, "How long has she been in the water?"

"You said she wouldn't have lasted twenty-four hours with this guy," Danny said, acknowledging with a nod that again she was right. "The medical examiner estimates the body has been in the water almost two weeks. She was dumped there soon after being taken."

Rainey shook her head. "Damn. This is one time I really didn't want to be right."

#

Rainey spent the next two hours buried in the Triangle UNSUB file with Danny, Paula, and Roger. Their conclusion was the same. Rainey's recommendations to the task force were excellent—interview people on the running trails, add patrols within his hunting grounds, and look for property connections in both areas where he committed crimes.

"He doesn't seem to have an end game," Danny said. "He's left so much DNA and linkage evidence my five-year-old nephew could convict him. He isn't worried about a DNA match, so I doubt he has a record. He's not expecting to be questioned or face a DNA request. He's confidently above suspicion."

"These guys are the hardest to catch," Roger said as he stood and stretched, "but his narcissism will be his undoing. He may feel invincible right now, but his ego will trip him up. Until it does, he'll keep killing. He's been washed in the blood now. He couldn't stop if he wanted to."

"He could be working up to someone he knows, his true fantasy," Paula suggested.

Rainey had been pacing around the room, listening and thinking. She stopped suddenly.

"He's married, or in a committed relationship. To blend in where we think he lives, he has to be. He shares a home with someone. Why would a woman, living in the area blanketed with warnings of a late-night prowler, not question where her significant other spends his nights?"

"He has a reason to be gone, a job that keeps him away at night," Danny offered.

"He travels for his job. These crimes are near the airport," Paula said.

"Neither of those options fit our UNSUB. He spends too much time stalking his targets to be traveling for work. He has to learn their patterns and be there days on end to know what he knows." Rainey paused and broke into a smile. "Either she's the one traveling or she's completely drugged up on sleeping pills for hours at a time. Both of those things are searchable. Restricting the field to residents in this area, we can cross-reference that with connections to property owners in southeastern Chatham County."

"Frequent flyers might be easy to track, but a lot of women take a sleeping aid. That's going to be a huge list," Danny said.

Rainey started reeling off parameters. "Narrow the search. She's thirty-five to forty-five, white, upper-middle class. She started taking the drug or traveling approximately September 2013. That's when we believe the UNSUB began his fetish burglaries. If it's the drug, go back a few months. He would have had to gauge its effect on her before feeling comfortable enough to leave for hours. It might be a combination of both drugs and travel. People that move through time zones often rely on sleeping aids."

Rainey realized they were all looking at her, smiling broadly.

Paula chuckled and said, "Nice to see your swagger."

#

"Rainey, I'm sorry," Wendy said. "I left Katie's phone in your office and just now recovered it because she asked for it."

"It's okay," Rainey said, trying to calm her sister.

"I saw all those texts and missed calls and expected the door to be broken down any minute," Wendy replied.

"I'm not that over-reactive. I would have called your phone before I called the SWAT team," Rainey said, chuckling.

"Yeah, well, Katie's reaction was the same as mine. She freaked and told me I had to tell you to call off the tactical assault immediately." Wendy followed with laughter. "She's in the bathroom. Hang on. Here she comes."

Rainey heard Wendy say to Katie, "Here, the SWAT team has been told to stand down."

"Did she really call—" Katie's voice grew louder as she put the phone to her ear. "Did you really call the SWAT team?"

"No, I thought you were probably sleeping. I really wasn't worried."

"Bullshit," Katie said.

"You're right. I was getting worried. I was about to call Wendy to inquire about you when the phone rang. How are you, by the way?"

"John gave me some anti-nausea meds, and I actually ate a cracker a minute ago."

"I'm sorry I'm not there to take care of you," Rainey offered.

"I have plenty of people taking care of me and the kids. I've slept most of the day, anyway. I'm very boring. How did the presentation go?"

"It went well, I think," Rainey answered.

She slid a bit farther down the hall, away from the BAU's main doors, where she waited for Danny.

"Danny read your text to me," Rainey continued. "I'm sorry, Katie. I should have talked to you. I didn't want you to know. I thought protecting you from my pain was the right thing to do. I was wrong to shut you out like that."

"Have you forgiven me?" Katie asked.

"I never blamed you," Rainey responded.

Katie persisted. "Have you forgiven me?"

Rainey sighed. "Yes."

"Okay, then," Katie said. "I forgive you too."

Though Rainey carried guilt for the mistakes she made, she never thought Katie blamed her. Her failures blinded her to the perceptions others may have held of those same disappointments. Rainey carried a small seed of doubt about what Katie could have prevented. It made sense Katie would have reservations about Rainey's handling of the situation.

Rainey replied with only, "Thank you."

There was a bit of a pause before Katie said, "I love you, Rainey Blue Bell."

"I love you, too, Katie. I'll be home tomorrow, and we can put this behind us now."

"That must have been one hell of a presentation," Katie replied.

"I'm going to keep a regular appointment with the Bureau psychologist for a while, but yeah, it was a good day. I banished a ghost."

"Forever my hero," Katie said and then abruptly added, "Oh, I don't feel so good. Gotta go, honey."

The call disconnected. Rainey was still staring at her phone when Danny arrived at her side.

"Everything okay?" He asked.

"Yes. She's puking as we speak, but it could be worse."

"How's that?" Danny asked, leading the way to the elevator.

Rainey chuckled, answering, "I could be there sympathy puking with her. I swear I've lost control of my gag reflex."

Danny joined her chuckles with his. "I'm not sure it's just you. I can look at decomposing bodies, but when my nephew lost his cookies at Thanksgiving, I turned green and nearly followed his example on Mom's rug."

"We are a sick and twisted duo, my friend," Rainey said, tucking her arm through his as they entered the elevator.

"That we are, Rainey Bell. That we are."

#

They stepped outside into an ice storm, already in full progress.

"Hey, I have some of Katie's cheese ravioli and sauce in the freezer. Let's just go to my house before the idiots clog up the roads," Danny suggested.

That's how Rainey found herself in Danny's kitchen, standing by the oven, surrounded by aromas that took her home. She'd slipped into sweatpants and a long-sleeved tee shirt with UVA emblazoned in orange across her chest. Danny put the pan in the oven and went upstairs to change. He had not returned, but she could hear him talking on the phone. When he appeared in a tee shirt and jeans, she was pleasantly surprised.

"I was sure they were calling you back in," she said, sipping from a glass of bourbon she poured herself. She held up her glass. "Want one?"

"Yes, please," he said, sounding tired.

"Are you okay, Danny?" Rainey asked while putting ice in a glass for him.

"Yes. I'm leaving in the morning for Kentucky. Flights are grounded because of the ice, or I'd be going now." She handed him a three-finger pour because he looked like he needed it. He took it and clinked his glass against hers. "So, cheers to an evening at home, compliments of Mother Nature."

Rainey leaned back on the kitchen counter. "When's your next mandatory vacation?"

"A couple of weeks from now," he said, leaning on the opposite counter.

130

"Why don't you come down? I'll take some time off, and we'll take the kids fishing. It should be warm enough by then to go out on the lake."

"I'm going down to the Keys. Do a little sport-fishing," Danny said, not making eye contact.

He could never lie to Rainey. She saw through his attempt to omit details.

"Alone?" Rainey asked, grinning over the rim of her glass.

"Well, no, but she likes fishing, too."

"Is this Connie, or was the last one named Martha? I can't keep up."

"Her name is Cathleen. She's with NSA," Danny answered. "I met her at a Christmas party. She's a friend of Paula's."

"I approve of her security clearance," Rainey said with a chuckle. "Wow, it's March and you're still dating her. That's a record."

"I like her, Rainey. She never blinks when plans have to change. She knows what that's like. We see each other when we can and that seems to be enough. She has a life and doesn't want to change mine. She's fun. She makes me laugh."

"What's wrong with her?" Rainey asked, not laughing this time.

"What do you mean? Why does something have to be wrong with her because she's nice to me?"

Rainey's grin turned into a teasing smirk. "Because you haven't mentioned her, not once, and I've been talking to you nearly every day since December."

Danny stared at the floor.

Rainey's laughter filled the kitchen. "You like this one. Daniel John Bartholomew McNally, you have fallen in love."

Danny flushed red. "She's a great girl, Rainey. You'll like her."

"Why haven't we met her? Are you afraid we'll scare her off?" Rainey teased.

"I didn't want to jinx it, not yet."

"I know you have a picture. Cough it up," Rainey demanded as she placed her glass on the counter.

Danny reached into his pocket for his phone, pulled up a picture, but was reluctant to hand it over. He stumbled through the explanation for his reticence. "I—uh—she is—well, she's a lot younger than me," he finally sputtered out.

"Give me that," Rainey said, taking the phone from his hand. "How much younger?"

"She's thirty-five."

Rainey looked down at the picture. Cathleen had dark hair and hazel eyes. She smiled broadly at the camera, a genuine smile that said she liked the person behind the lens.

Rainey asked, "Did you take this picture?"

"Yes, why?"

"She likes you, too. She's pretty, Danny. Twelve years age difference might be a little much. Does she want children?"

"No, we talked about that. It's not a medical issue or anything. I'd be sixty-five when the kid graduated from high school if I had one now, so I'm good with hanging out with yours. Cathleen says her sisters and brothers have plenty and she can visit them whenever she wants. She is very career driven. I'm sure that's why she doesn't mind my erratic job schedule."

"I'm happy for you, Danny. I hope things work out. She sounds like the right fit."

"This will be our first trip together. We'll see how it goes."

"Well, she has to pass the triplet test, you know, so don't do anything rash." Rainey picked up her glass and offered a toast. "To happy endings, all the way around."

Danny touched his glass to hers. "I hope mine is as storybook as yours."

#

"Hi, Mom," Rainey said to the phone screen.

She was on video-chat with Wendy when she was taken into the kids' bathroom to say goodnight. The triplets were all in the bathtub, splashing Grand-mère, the designation Constance had chosen for herself, refusing the standard grandmotherly terms. It

132

came out more like Grammar from the toddlers' mouths, which made Rainey laugh every time.

"Hi, Rainey. Grandpa John is checking on Katie, and I thought I'd give Nana Melanie a break and bathe these rascals."

Timothy reached for the phone.

Wendy's voice said from behind the camera lens, "No, not in the bathtub."

"Nee Nee, Mommy sick," Weather said, hands on her hips. Except for her piercing green eyes, she was a miniature Katie, mannerisms included.

Hoping to avoid any of Weather's authentic sound effects, Rainey said, "Grandpa John will make her feel better."

"When you come home, Nee Nee?" Timothy asked.

"I'll be home early enough to eat breakfast with you. Okay, buddy?"

"Okay." Satisfied, Timothy went back to giggling and splashing Grammar.

Rainey saw Mack stand up behind Constance with a full cup of water in his hand.

"No, Mack," she said sternly.

He looked at the screen and judged his chances of getting away with his ploy. He surmised correctly that Rainey could not reach him and Mommy was too sick to care. With a grin Rainey recognized as Katie's genetic influence, he dumped the cup on Constance's shoulder before she could move.

The triplets giggled with delight.

Weather pointed a stubby little finger at Constance. "Grammar taked a shower," she said and cackled with laughter.

Constance had softened in her advancing age. She laughed and picked up the cup Mack had dropped, filled it with water, and dumped it over his head, saying, "You little rascal."

More giggling ensued. Rainey laughed too, even though Mack had ignored a direct admonition. Sure the children already suspected her disciplinary shortcomings, she was saved from exposing more when Danny walked into the den with two steaming coffee mugs. Rainey turned the phone's camera toward him.

"Look, guys, it's Uncle Danny."

The phone emitted shouts of something that sounded like Uncle Danny.

"Hey there," Danny said, coming closer to the phone. He handed Rainey a coffee mug and then waved at the camera. "I'm glad you feel better."

Timothy was still giggling and Mack was eyeing the cup again when Rainey moved to stand beside Danny so they could both see the screen.

"Mommy puke all the time," Weather informed Danny. She seemed the most concerned about Katie's stomach issues.

"I heard about that," he replied. "Tell her I hope she feels better."

"Okay," Weather answered and started climbing out of the tub.

Wendy chuckled, telling Weather, "Not now, honey. In a minute, when you're dry."

"Okay," Weather said and looked back up at the camera. "Unc Danny, Endy say not now."

"Yeah, wait until you're dressed," Danny encouraged.

Timothy pointed at Constance, saying, "Unc Danny, Mack wet Grammar," before throwing his head back in laughter, which caused his butt to slide out from under him.

He splashed backward in the water, sending a spray directly into Grammar's face. She was drenched. The camera started shaking with Wendy's laughter, as her arm came into view holding a towel out to Constance.

The triplets fell into a belly-shaking fit of cackles. They were near bedtime, and it was one of those contagious laugh cycles to which they were prone when tired. No one was immune from the giggles when the triplets found something amusing.

"Good gracious. What is going on in here?" Rainey heard Katie say.

"Hey honey," she said, as the camera view swung around to focus on Katie in the doorway.

"Mack wet Grammar, an an Timoty splash her," Weather reported.

"Mack?" Katie said, calmly.

He stopped laughing and said, "I sorry, Grammar."

"Timothy?"

He, too, responded with, "I sorry, Grammar."

Constance, who would have grounded Rainey for life for such an infraction, wiped her face with the towel and said, "It's okay. That was funny, wasn't it?"

The triplets started the rolls of laughter again.

Katie threw up her hands and looked at the camera. "Hi, Danny."

He waved while Weather narrated. "Unc Danny say he hope you feel better."

"Thank you. I'm going to go back to bed. You guys be nice," she said to the giggling children in the tub. She looked back at the camera. "I'll call you later, Rainey," she said before darting from the room.

Weather continued her narrator's job with, "Mommy puke too many times. Bleck, bleccck."

"Okay, you guys be good for Nana and Grammar," Rainey slipped and used the kids' pronunciation and quickly covered it with, "Goodnight. I love you. See you in the morning."

"Night, night, Nee Nee," they said, almost in unison.

"Night, night, rug rats," she said before the screen filled with Wendy's face.

"Hang on a sec, Rainey. I need to ask you something."

Rainey waited as Wendy moved away from the bathroom and down the stairs before she began to speak again.

"Hey, did the kid in the hoodie send you that picture?"

"Cane? Yes, it was in my inbox this morning," Rainey said, hoping she wouldn't die with an image of Jedidiah Lilly's dick on her phone.

"I got a message from Connor. He said Cane disappeared last night. Nobody has seen him. When did he send the picture?"

"Hang on, let me look."

Rainey pressed her finger to the screen, pausing the video chat, and checked her inbox for the penis picture. She pressed her finger on the screen again, re-engaging the paused chat.

"Wendy, he sent that about fifteen minutes after we left yesterday. I think you should call Sheila Robertson and tell her what you know. That's what I would do. Let her take the heat from Lilly's people and the higher ups. You are not equipped to deal with this on your own."

Rainey heard a notification signal from Wendy's phone. Wendy frowned at the screen.

"Who is that?" Rainey asked. "Is that Connor?"

"No, it's Nick Prentiss. He's been calling and texting me for two days. He doesn't seem to get his unanswered calls and the lack of replies to his texts are signs he should move along."

Danny asked, "He does know that nearly everyone in your family, including you, is armed, right?"

"Hi, Danny," Wendy replied. "Yes, he is aware of that fact. He's harmless. He needs some arm candy for a fundraiser. His date probably dumped him when she realized he's a shallow prick."

A heavy sigh from Wendy immediately followed another ding warning of a new message.

Since he was the closest thing to a brother Rainey had, she guessed Danny's protectiveness of Wendy came with the territory.

He asked, "If that's him again, that's harassment. Give me his number."

Wendy laughed. "I got it, Danny, but thanks. It's another cop, the one that introduced me to Nick. He now has the bro-team in action. His bro either wants to date me or plead his case. Hard to tell."

Danny smiled at the screen. "Just keep playing hard to get. The right one will simply sweep you off your feet with no effort and no bro-team action."

Rainey was still mulling over Cane's disappearance. "How does Connor know that kid isn't staying at a trick's house?"

"They check in with each other. He said Cane just vanished. He thinks Barron might be with him. He's not answering his phone. I ran a check. He isn't in the system, at least not yet."

"Call Sheila, Wendy. It's all that you can do."

136

"I'll call her in the morning. I need to check out a few things first." Wendy probably didn't mean to add aloud, "If I break this, I'm golden."

Rainey wanted no further involvement in what was rapidly becoming a firestorm case and what she viewed as Wendy's mishandling of it. As her younger sister torpedoed her career with unbridled ambition, Rainey did not want to be along for the ride. She'd be there to pick up the pieces, but riding shotgun into a shit-storm wasn't in Rainey's book of familial responsibilities. Little sis was going to have to learn this lesson on her own.

"How's the paper going?" Rainey asked to change the subject.

"I haven't had much time to gather my thoughts," Wendy said, smiling at the screen. "These kids are a full-time job. I don't know how you guys do this when you're alone with them, one on three. Mack hid from me in your office for a good fifteen minutes. It's amazing how he managed to climb those shelves in the closet. He was lying on the top shelf when Katie came down. She used all of his names, and he came scampering down like the pied piper had called him."

"She is his muse," Rainey said and then cautioned, "Keep the closet shut while you're in there, and close the office door when you're not."

"It was closed, Rainey. I'm not inept. He was there one minute and then he wasn't."

"You can't take your eyes off of them," Rainey replied with a chuckle. "They're quick."

Wendy countered, "I don't know if those gymnastics lessons were a good decision. You're likely to find Mack on the roof."

"Not for a few more years, I hope."

Wendy arrived in Rainey's office. She could see her desk through the screen as Wendy moved behind it.

"I scanned through the file. I'm going to read your notes next, but I was thinking, what if the UNSUB's wife travels for a living? That would explain his freedom of movement. Can you trace that?"

Danny smiled at Rainey.

She returned it, before saying to Wendy, "Yes. We started a search this afternoon."

"I should have known you'd think of that."

Rainey reassured her. "We just thought of it today. That's good work, Wendy. Nice catch."

Wendy beamed into the phone screen. "Thanks, sis. Well, I'll let you go. I need to finish reading your file and start writing that paper, now that the kidlets are heading to bed."

"Oh, no, not yet," Rainey said, laughing loudly. "I promised them Endy would do story time tonight. It takes at least two books, sometimes the same one twice. Enjoy."

"I am never having kids," Wendy said and waved goodbye to the camera.

Rainey ended the call and placed the phone on the coffee table.

"She's pretty sharp," Danny observed.

"Yes, she is, but she's reckless. She's over her head in what is going to be a nasty scandal. That looks promising to someone trying to make detective with lightning speed, but she worries me."

"Reminds me of someone else I knew once," Danny said, as he took his seat on the couch.

Rainey sat on the opposite end, nodding her head. "I know exactly what she's thinking. That's what scares me, Danny. She's also got that hothead Engel following her around. Did you check on that for me?"

"Yes, I did. He's a piece of shit, between you and me. The Bureau line is Aaron Engel resigned after his wife filed domestic abuse charges. She dropped the charges, but the Bureau saw enough evidence in his file, alleged abuse of a prisoner, excessive force, things like that. He was forced to resign or be fired. He chose to leave. Sometimes a bad one gets through all the psych tests. This guy has issues."

Rainey nodded. "I would agree. From what Wendy and Mackie said, Engel is unable to control his rage. I'm worried he's targeting Wendy because his wife has gone underground until his

138

trial for assault and battery. There are more charges pending for threatening Wendy and violating his wife's VPO."

"Those victim's protection orders are not worth the paper they are written on," Danny said in disgust. "Perps walk right through those VPOs and kill people every day, it seems."

"Wendy challenged him. Mackie said she's lucky this guy didn't get to her. She's still young enough to believe she's invincible."

"Again, I say, I knew someone like her once." Danny tipped his coffee mug in Rainey's direction.

"You did not know me when I was her age," Rainey said.

Danny raised his brow in question. "Am I wrong?"

Rainey conceded, "Well, let's just hope the Bell family survival streak stays intact."

Danny asked the obvious question. "What about your dad? Didn't he break the streak?"

"That guy wasn't trying to kill my dad. We can't stop what we don't see coming, but head-up and straight into a fight, I'd put money on a Bell."

Danny laughed. "I would too, Rainey. I would too."

#

Rainey called Katie at nine o'clock. She and Danny had an early flight, and both were drained from the emotional day. Katie answered on the first ring.

"I'm so glad you called early. I haven't blecked in several hours, but I'm exhausted. I just want to sleep."

"I can tell Weather has been talking to you. 'Blecked' may be part of our household vocabulary from now on," Rainey replied.

"She's very concerned. I think she's going to be a doctor. She's fascinated by John's stethoscope."

Rainey yawned. "You thought she was going to be an astronaut last month because she learned the names of the constellations you taught her. She's a sponge."

"We should enroll them in foreign language enrichment now while they can absorb it quickly." Katie finished in a long yawn.

139

"You go to sleep. I should be there by 7:30 if the flight is on time and the traffic isn't bad. See you for coffee."

Katie made a blecking sound, followed by, "Don't talk about food or coffee or anything that has to go into my stomach. I'll see you in the morning. I love you."

"Get some rest. I love you, too. Sweet dreams."

PART III

SUCH STUFF AS DREAMS ARE MADE ON

"The world is full of obvious things which nobody by any chance ever observes."
— *Sir Arthur Conan Doyle*

CHAPTER SEVEN

7:15 AM, Friday, March 6, 2015
The Bell-Meyer's Residence
Chatham County, NC

Danny dropped Rainey off at the airport before five and headed back to Quantico to catch a helicopter ride to Kentucky. Another killer was on the loose, and Agent McNally had been asked to engage in the hunt. Rainey's flight landed a few minutes early. She grabbed her carry-on and exited with the first class passengers, ahead of the masses. She rushed to her car and sped away, hoping she hadn't missed breakfast with the kids. It was her favorite time of the day with them.

She entered the house from the garage to find Katie sitting with two of the triplets.

"Hello, family," Rainey said, as she came through the door.

She dropped her overnight bag on the floor and hung up her coat. Rainey had no weapons to put away this time because she had not carried them to the airport.

"Hey, honey," Katie said.

Weather mimicked her mother, "Hey, honey."

Timothy charged from his chair to wrap his arms around Rainey's legs, shouting, "Nee Nee is home!"

"Hey, buddy," Rainey said, reaching down to lift him into her arms.

Weather was not to be left out of the hugs and was soon standing in front of Rainey, arms raised.

"I don't know if I can still hold two of you. You're getting so big. Here, let me try."

Rainey faked trying to lift Weather into her arms while still holding Timothy. She crumbled to the floor in a pile of toddlers and laughter. She tickled them and kissed them and relished the moment. It always amazed her when the mere joy of loving her kids overwhelmed her.

"Okay, let me up, guys. I need to give Mommy a hug, too."

"Tickle Mommy," Weather suggested.

Katie put her hands up to stop the approaching Rainey. "Honey, you don't want to hug me. I need a shower."

Rainey brushed right through Katie's warning and gave her a peck on the cheek. "Good morning, beautiful. I'm glad you feel better. You look better than when I last saw you."

"I think I've turned the corner, but we'll see. I just ate two crackers, so the jury is still out. I'm a bit wary considering how many times the kids relapsed last week."

Rainey looked around. "Where is your mom? Is Mack with her? I didn't see Wendy's car, either. Did she leave?"

"Mom went home this morning. I told her to. She needs some time off. She's been here nearly every moment for almost two weeks. Wendy said she needed to get something from her house that she wanted you to read. She said it could break the case wide open. I don't think she slept at all last night. I found her this morning, still pouring over your files." Katie smiled. "She's so much like you. Anyway, Mack was being a bit of a brat before the sun made it over the horizon, so she took him with her. They should be back by now, though. That was over an hour ago."

"I'll give her a call, see what's up." Rainey chuckled to hide her apprehension. "Maybe he hid from her again."

Rainey had reason to be concerned. Katie knew about Aaron Engel's threats to Wendy. She didn't know about the other cases into which Wendy foolishly probed. Rainey pulled out her phone and dialed her sister's number. The call went immediately to Wendy's voicemail.

144

"Damn," Rainey said.

"Damn," Weather repeated.

"Not a nice word," Rainey admonished her. "I'm sorry I said it. I'll do timeout later."

Weather seemed pleased someone else was going to be in timeout today.

She responded, "Okay," and climbed back into her chair.

Rainey turned to Katie, expecting her to be smiling at Weather's correction, but instead saw a look of pure dread on her wife's face. Katie's brow was lined with worry, her skin going paler than it already was. She stared in disbelief at Rainey and then began shaking her head from side to side very slowly.

"Katie?"

"Go find Mack, Rainey. Something is wrong, bad wrong."

"Wendy probably let her battery die. She'll be here in a minute."

Katie stood quickly. Her hand was shaking when she pointed a finger at Rainey.

"Go get our son, Rainey Bell. Now!"

As much as Rainey believed in her own gut feelings, she believed in Katie's motherly instincts. She went straight to the gun safe and punched in the code, noticing immediately Wendy had left her service weapon behind. Rainey removed her Glock and holster, but did not stop to put it on. She carried it and her coat out the door, calling over her shoulder, "Don't worry, honey. It's probably nothing."

"Bring Mack home, Rainey."

#

7:30 AM, Friday, March 6, 2015
Wendy King's Residence
Chatham County, NC

Rainey pulled into Wendy's driveway. She felt the queasiness of Katie's dread in the pit of her stomach. She slipped into the shoulder holster, snapped the Glock into place, and exited the car—taking the time to put on her coat to conceal her weapon, but not soon enough. Rainey saw the look of bewilderment on the face of the gray-haired woman standing beside a running car in the driveway next door. The air was cold and growing colder, as an arctic front barreled south into the Carolinas. It appeared the weather had not deteriorated enough to dissuade the inquisitive neighbor's need to stop and stare.

Rainey approached the garage door and took a quick look-see through the window. Wendy's car sat under the glowing fluorescent light, indicating it was dark when Wendy and Mack arrived. Rainey moved to the front door, knocked a few times, and received no answer. She knocked harder.

"Wendy, it's Rainey. Open the door."

With still no response, Rainey began banging on the door and shouting for Wendy loud enough to prompt the neighbor to become involved.

The woman asked, "Is there something I can help you with?"

Rainey spoke in a commanding tone, "Yes, call 9-1-1."

She pulled out the Glock, stepped up to the window next to the door, and smashed the butt of the pistol into the glass. No alarm sounded. Either Wendy turned it off and did not re-arm it right away or it was disabled before she went in. That thought made Rainey angry. If Wendy took Mack into the house with a nonfunctioning alarm, there was going to be hell to pay. How many times did she have to remind her of the diligence necessary to survive being Rainey Bell's little sister?

"Never let your guard down, ever," she told Wendy repeatedly.

Rainey turned back to the stunned neighbor and yelled again, "Call 9-1-1. Now!"

She cleared the glass with the barrel of the pistol and called out to Wendy. Once she'd poked her head inside, she knew Katie had been right. Something was bad wrong. There was no time to fear what had happened as Rainey's adrenaline kicked into overdrive. She looked back at the neighbor, who was now speaking rapidly into her cell phone.

"I'm Wendy's sister. She has my three-year-old son with her. Something is very wrong. Let the police know I'm going in."

The house was silent. Rainey climbed through the window. She stopped calling out for Wendy because what she saw sped her breathing and heart rate to panic mode. The coffee table lay splintered into pieces. Furniture had been overturned or forcefully pushed aside. Bloody fingerprints smeared on the doorframe suggested the fight continued down the hallway toward the back of the house. Wendy had been in a struggle for her life.

Her heart pounded in her ears as Rainey cleared each room and prayed she wouldn't discover her son or her sister in a pool of blood. After making it through the rest of the house and finding nothing, she approached the back bedroom Wendy used as an office. The door was closed.

"Not my child. Please, God, not my child," she prayed in a whisper.

Rainey pushed the door open slowly. Unlike the rest of the house, the office appeared undisturbed. Rainey pointed her weapon in every corner and then approached the closet, the last place in the house she had not searched.

The sound of movement from inside drew Rainey's shout of, "Let me see your hands." Her law enforcement training and muscle memory took over. She commanded, "Open the door slowly and let me see your hands. Now!"

The first little whimper eliminated any training. Rainey rushed to the closet and threw open the door.

Mack stood there, tears streaming down his face, holding his hands out for her to see. Rainey dropped to her knees and placed the weapon on the floor.

"Oh, thank God. Come here, baby boy. Come here."

He took one slow step forward, then rushed into her waiting arms and sobbed.

"You're okay, little man. You're okay," Rainey said, hugging him close.

"I scared, Nee Nee. The man hurt Endy."

"Did you see the man?" Rainey asked.

"No," he said, still sobbing. "Endy say, 'Hide, Mack. Be quiet. Wait for Nee Nee. She come.' I hide, Nee Nee. I quiet."

"You did great, buddy." She looked him over. He wasn't injured. She hugged him tight, fighting back the tears of relief. "I love you, Mack. You're all right, now. You're safe. Nee Nee's got you."

Rainey put the Glock back in the holster and picked up Mack, who now cried softly against her neck. She walked out of the house, a hand shielding his eyes from the blood smears and chaos from the fight. The neighbor's mouth gaped open with surprise. She appeared to still be on the phone with the emergency operator. Rainey pulled out her own phone and hit Katie's number on speed dial.

Katie answered with a frantic, "Did you find him?"

"I have him, Katie. He's okay. A little shaken up, but he's okay."

"Why is he crying?"

Rainey took a deep breath, trying to calm the adrenaline rush still cycling through her body.

"Wendy's gone. She's not in the house and there was a horrendous fight in the front room."

Katie gasped. "Oh, my God. Is Mack hurt?"

"No," Rainey replied. She looked down at her son. "He was a brave boy. He hid when Wendy told him to. He's a smart little man."

"Bring him home," Katie demanded.

"I can't yet, honey. I need to wait for the police. They'll want to talk to him and me. I had to break into the house."

Rainey heard Katie sniffle. She was crying now, with the relief of knowing their son was safe.

"Call Mackie and Ernie. They'll know what to do. I'll be home as soon as I can. He's okay, Katie. We'll be there soon."

"Don't let them scare him," Katie warned.

"Don't worry. I won't let anybody scare him. They'd have a hard time removing him from my shoulder at the moment."

"Who took Wendy?" Katie asked.

"I don't know, but I have a few ideas."

148

"Not that fetish guy, Rainey. Not him."

"I hope so," Rainey said. "He's our best hope that she's still alive. Don't give up on her, Katie. She's a Bell. We don't go down easy."

#

Five minutes later, two patrol cars pulled in front of the house. The officers got out and proceeded to speak to the excited neighbor. They then drew their weapons and pointed them at Rainey.

"Show me your hands," they shouted in unison.

Rainey held Mack under her coat. She said as calmly as she could. "I need to put my son down. I'm a former FBI agent. I am armed, which I'm sure this lady told you. Do not shoot me. I'm a consultant for your department. My name is Rainey Bell. Call your supervisor, now."

"Get on the ground," the younger one yelled, his adrenaline pumping off-the-charts high.

Mack started to scream.

Rainey glared at the young officer. She shouted over Mack's shrieks. "This child has been traumatized. You are not helping."

An unmarked car jerked to a stop, blocking the driveway. Rex King jumped from the car. The man Wendy had called father all her life was not a fan of Rainey's, but she was happy to see him.

"Stand down! Stand down, I said," Rex shouted at the officers, flashing his badge and his command presence.

The officers lowered their weapons as Rex charged past them to where Rainey stood calming Mack as best she could.

"What happened? Where's Wendy?" Rex demanded, red-faced and breathing hard.

"Don't go in the house, Detective King." Rainey used his title in an attempt to speak to the officer and not the father. "Wendy isn't there. She's been abducted. I found Mack in the office closet. There's no one else in the house."

"What?" Rex's hand flew to the back of his head and rubbed his neck. His stress peaked, as a parent's worst nightmare came true for him.

Mack had reburied his face in Rainey's neck. He clutched her tighter at the sound of his name. The ordinarily inquisitive toddler wanted nothing to do with anyone at the moment. His body jerked with diaphragm spasms. She couldn't explain in detail what she had seen with her devastated child in her arms.

"Detective, I'll answer all of your questions, but first I need to attend to my son. I can tell you Wendy has been gone less than an hour. We have time to find her. Call it in. And Rex, alert the taskforce."

#

Rainey had been sitting in her car for fifteen minutes with the engine running, keeping Mack warm under her coat. Officers, crime scene technicians, and members of the task force swarmed Wendy's little house.

Did he come here because she's my sister? The thought rattled around in her mind. Had being part of Rainey Bell's life again put someone she cared about in danger?

Mack mostly clung to her and fought off the rib shaking spasms while his body attempted to regain its normal breathing pattern.

After a long period of quiet reflection, he said, "Nee Nee, are you gonna find Endy?"

"See all those people out there. They are looking for Wendy."

Mack raised his head to look. He spontaneously said, "Why are you in my house? Go home!"

"Did Wendy say that?"

Mack nodded and then became highly animated, relaying what he remembered in a burst, "Get da fuck out! Are you crazy?" Mack worked himself up to a loud, "Get da fuck out my house!"

"Okay, little man." She patted his back and spoke quietly, "It's okay now. You are safe."

"Nee Nee?"

"What, bud?"

"Is Endy safe?"

"Not yet, Mack. Not yet."

He placed his head down on Rainey's shoulder and returned to quiet meditation. She finally detached him from her neck when the neighbor knocked on the car window offering two chocolate chip cookies, a juice box, and an apology.

"I'm so sorry they scared him. I wasn't sure you were who you said you were, but I see the resemblance now."

"Thank you," Rainey said to her, and then to Mack, "Hey, buddy. Do you think you could eat a cookie? You haven't had your breakfast. Aren't you hungry?"

Mack nodded his head slowly.

"Okay, sit over here in the seat."

Mack climbed over the console and silently took the cookie from Rainey's hand. She slid the juice box into the cup holder.

"There you go. You'll feel better when that chocolate hits your stomach."

"Like on Harry Potter," the neighbor suggested. "Well, I guess he's too young for Harry Potter. I don't know what they watch these days or when. I don't have any grandkids yet. I hope he's all right."

Rainey smiled at the chatterbox neighbor. "Did you see or hear anything this morning, anything unusual."

"Like I told the other officer, I called about a prowler last night, but the police checked around our house and Wendy's. Everything was locked up tight."

"What time was that?"

"It was 3:35. I looked at the clock out of habit. I usually hear Gary Don when he leaves in the mornings. He sleeps in the room on this end of the house because of how early he has to go in. I got up to get a glass of water. My kitchen window looks right at Wendy's fence. I could have sworn I saw someone in her backyard. I knew she wasn't home, so I called the police."

"The police found nothing?" Rainey asked.

"Well, they found Gary Don. He was in the garage and hadn't left yet. He does that in the morning. He thinks I don't know he hides cigarettes in the garage. He mostly quit, but he sneaks a few. I don't say much—"

Rainey redirected the story, "Did your husband see anything while he was out having his morning smoke?"

"Oh, he's not my husband. He's my boyfriend. Can you believe I'm sixty-two and living in sin for five years? My momma would roll over in her grave. I got me a young one." The neighbor lady winked at Rainey. "He's only forty-one. He wants to marry me, but my son doesn't like that idea. Says he's after the money Barney left me. Gary Don doesn't need my money. He has a job. I just try to keep the peace between those—"

Rainey interrupted again, "Did the police look around or just take your boyfriend's word for nothing happening?"

"He said the cops looked around and didn't find anyone. All Wendy's doors were locked. Gary Don said I was seeing things, but I know I saw a shadow between the fence slats. The police left. Gary Don left. And I went back to bed. I got up at 6:30 like I always do. I turn my TV up real loud so I can hear the news while I take a shower and get dressed in the back of the house. I was leaving for work when you pulled up. I called my boss and told him I'd be late today. I'm just so frazzled with all this happening." She shook her head. "I told Wendy she'd love it here when she moved in last summer. It was a nice place until this crazy man started scaring the bejesus out of people."

"Endy say, 'Get da fuck out,' " Mack said, cookie crumbs flying from his lips. And then, in a whisper, he repeated the neighbor's words, "Crazy man."

The neighbor reacted with, "Oh, my."

Rainey covered for Mack. "I'm sorry, I didn't get your name."

"Juanita, Juanita Cashion."

"Juanita, you'll have to forgive Mack's language. He's had a bit of a shock."

"Bless his little heart," Juanita said. "How old is he?"

152

"He just turned three in December. Tell Ms. Cashion thank you for the cookies and juice, Mack."

He wouldn't look up. Rainey didn't press him.

She excused his shyness, saying to the neighbor, "He's a little overwhelmed right now."

"He's one of the triplets in the pictures Wendy showed me. So you're the sister with the triplets and the lovely niece and nephews. She talks about them all the time. Is your spouse coming to get him?"

Rainey was ready for the neighbor to go away. "His mother is with our other two children. I'll take him home in a few minutes."

She was hoping for the offended right-wing idiot so that rolling up the window wouldn't be rude, just self-preservation. But she got, "My nephew Jimmy and his partner are using a surrogate. Did you have them, or did your partner? Oh, I guess you said 'his mother,' didn't you? I just think it's wonderful that you people can marry now."

Rainey flinched at "you people" and was about to dismiss the neighbor for some peace and quiet when the woman suddenly changed the topic.

"Oh, my. I believe that is the biggest, blackest man I have ever seen."

Rainey glanced at the woman and realized she was looking back down the driveway. Rainey looked into the rearview mirror and chuckled.

"Yeah, he's big all right." She looked down at Mack. "Mackie's here, buddy."

Mack came to life. He loved the man for whom he was named. His head swiveled from side to side, trying to find him. Mackie approached the driver's side of the car, and the neighbor backed away.

Mackie's face filled up the open window. "Hey there, little man," his bass voice rumbled through the car.

Rainey unlocked the doors and prepared to get out when the passenger door jerked open. Katie was in the car, snatching Mack up from the seat in an instant. Rainey hadn't seen her, distracted by Mackie's approach.

"Mommy!" Mack was delighted. He loved Rainey, thought the world of Mackie, but Katie was his first love.

"Oh, my God. I'm so happy to see you. Are you okay? Are you hurt?" Katie rattled off questions too quickly for Mack to answer.

"Slow down, Katie," Rainey said, opening the car door to stand. "He needs some time to process, honey."

Mack said, "Crazy man hurt Endy. She say hide. I hided."

"You are such a smart boy, Mack," Katie said, hugging him tighter.

"You hug me too hard, Mommy."

"I'm sorry. I was worried." Katie eased her grip on him. "Is that better?"

"Nee Nee come, Mommy. Nee Nee say, 'Show me your hands.' I show her."

Mack held up his chocolate-stained hands.

"Did you aim a gun at him?" Katie glared at Rainey, who was now standing beside her.

Katie had more color in her face than she did earlier, but that could have been a blush of anger. Although Rainey knew that anger was the next stage after having the bejesus scared out of you, to use the neighbor's phrase, it didn't stop her defensive reply.

"No. He was hiding in the closet. I had no way to know it was Mack and not somebody else. I did not point my weapon at our child, Katie. Give me some credit."

Mack put his little chocolate-stained fingers on both his parents' lips. "Don't be mad."

"Oh, I'm not, Mack. I'm glad Nee Nee found you." Katie looked at Rainey and apologized. "I'm sorry. I was just so…"

Rainey cut her off. "It's okay, Katie. We are all a bit worked up." She tousled Mack's sandy blond hair. "We're all safe now. Right, Mack?"

"Endy not safe," he said, his little lip forming a pout.

Katie reassured him, "Nee Nee will find her. That's what Nee Nee does. She finds people."

"Nee Nee found Mack," he said with a beaming smile in Rainey's direction.

"I'm going to go look for her, buddy. You go home with Mommy. You're safe now."

"Safe with Mommy," he said and hugged Katie again.

Mackie wore a long black leather coat with matching fedora and stood on Katie's left. Rainey, on her right, wore her long black wool coat. Hence the comment Sheila Robertson made as she approached.

"Y'all look like the mafia surrounding this poor woman and child." She put an arm around Katie. "How is everybody doing?"

Sheila was keeping the conversation light because of Mack's presence, but she looked at Rainey with worried eyes.

"We're better now," Katie answered.

"Good, good. You can take Mack home, Katie. I'll need to keep Rainey, though. I'm going to depend on her statement, and you can call us if Mack remembers anything pertinent."

Rainey thanked Sheila, adding, "I'll be right with you."

"Take your time," Sheila said to Rainey. To Mack she said, "I hear you are a very brave boy. You did a great job hiding. You'll have to teach me how when I come to see you at your house. Okay?"

Mack smiled as his gregarious personality slowly returned. "Okay. I show you."

"Good. You're a smart boy, Mack. Very smart." Sheila patted Katie's arm and then moved away.

Katie said to Mack. "Will you go with Mackie to the truck? I'll be right there. I need to talk to Nee Nee."

Mackie held out his enormous hands. "Come on, little man. Let's go home."

Mack went willingly into Mackie's arms. Rainey stepped over and kissed his little cheek.

"I love you, Mack. You are safe now. No one's going to harm you. I promise."

"I love Nee Nee and Mommy."

"Good to know, buddy. See you in a little while."

Mackie walked away with little Mack waving over his large shoulder at his parents.

"He looks so small in Mackie's arms," Katie observed.

"I look small in Mackie's arms," Rainey commented.

"Is he going to be okay, Rainey? What did he see?"

"From what he's said, I don't think he saw anything. I have a feeling Mack's presence may have startled the UNSUB. Wendy realized what was happening right away and told Mack to hide."

"Should I talk to him about it?" Katie asked.

"No, don't ask him questions, but if he wants to talk, just listen. He's going to want to discuss it at some point. He'll probably talk to Timothy and Weather. You might have to rein in some little imaginations, maybe answer some questions. He's also mimicking some language we'll need to curb, but don't punish him for remembering. Redirect him. Don't get too complicated with answers to his questions. Keep your comments simple and truthful. 'We're looking for Wendy' is about all you can say right now. The most essential thing is a return to normal. Just keep an eye on him and remind him he is safe."

Rainey sighed, torn between her son's needs and those of her sister.

Katie patted her on the back. "Wendy needs you. You go find her. Mack will be okay."

Rainey's eyes began to water. She was compartmentalizing like crazy, shoving emotions into boxes so she could think. For a moment, those feelings slipped out as she said, "Wendy fought for him, Katie. There's blood everywhere. She fought for her life and Mack's. I have to find her."

"You'll find her. Remember, she's a Bell. You are a hard bunch to kill." Katie stood on her tiptoes and kissed Rainey lightly on the lips before adding, "You be careful."

"Always."

#

"Okay, Rainey, tell me what you think," Sheila said, standing in Wendy's living room.

"Is her underwear drawer empty?" Rainey asked.

"Yes. There is an empty drawer, and we found some clean ones dropped near the dresser. She may have surprised him in the act."

"Either the fetish UNSUB was here or someone wants us to think so," Rainey said before asking, "Did they find any evidence leading out to the woods?"

"Most of the prints around the house are marred by the earlier reported prowler response. Two sets of prints go out the back gate, up onto the paved trail, and then disappear. It looks like she was walking with him. That surprises me. I would have thought he'd have to carry Wendy or drag her out unconscious."

As if she knew exactly what her sister had been thinking, Rainey said, "When she realized she couldn't overpower him, she got him away from the house, away from Mack. It looks like they crashed through this table. If she was still walking, then all this blood might be non-life threatening, a possible head wound. You know how they bleed. It looks like her head hit over here on the wall and there is a big smear." Rainey turned to Sheila, stating matter-of-factly, "She went with him to save Mack."

They were alone in the room. Sheila stepped in front of Rainey and looked into her eyes, searching for something.

"Are you good? Should I call in Teague? Are you too close to this, Rainey?"

"Go ahead and call him. Your bosses will want someone else on this, but trust me when I say I'm better than I've been in a long time. Don't shut me out, but by all means, bring in whoever you need." She paused, returning Sheila's stare. "But you know I'm the best shot you have of finding my sister."

"I'll call Teague to please the bosses, but I'm sticking with you. You have never let me down."

"Okay," Rainey said, and that was the end of doubts. "I run by here some mornings and pick up Wendy. We run the trails behind her house. There's a parking lot not far from here with access to the trails. That's the only place he'd be sure a parked car wouldn't draw much attention. Everyone is on edge. They would have noticed a strange vehicle. The woman next door didn't see a car, and the cops didn't find one when they came out to look for the prowler."

"He stayed late this time," Sheila noted.

"If Wendy had been fifteen minutes later, he would have probably jogged off with the morning runners. He had to have left before 6:30, just before the sun came up. He probably took her through the woods straight to the parking lot. He couldn't risk anyone seeing them together."

"Okay, I'll have the woods searched from here to the parking lot."

Sheila spoke into a radio while Rainey began thinking aloud, "The fetish UNSUB would have known she wasn't here. Maybe she surprised him, which disrupts an organized killer's fantasy. He took Kaitlyn Whitaker without a fight. If he wanted Wendy, he would have planned better. At this stage of his game, getting caught unaware while on a surveillance mission would lead to mistakes. Mistakes are what we need at this point."

She stopped that line of thought and moved on to more possibilities, "Now, that's if the fetish killer has her."

Sheila, finished with the radio call, tried to keep up. "Who else could it be?"

"Were there any signs of a break-in, other than the window I broke this morning?"

"No. He must have picked the lock if he was already in here when Wendy arrived. He could have reset the alarm once inside, just like on the other houses. The alarms were always working when first responders reached the crime scenes."

"It wasn't working when I arrived. It was still disarmed. Either Wendy didn't think she would be in the house long enough to rearm it or it was off and she came in regardless of the danger." Rainey walked over to the wall, examining a blood smear near the baseboard. She spoke while squatting next to the wall. "Unless she let him in."

"Why would she do that?"

Rainey looked up at Sheila. "Because she knows him, or he could have used a ruse. Wendy would have opened the door to someone asking for help. She isn't jaded yet."

"Wouldn't it be one hell of a coincidence that a prowler and an abductor showed up at the same house, at nearly the same time?"

Rainey remained by the baseboard, still studying the smear. Bloody fingers had been drawn across the paint.

She asked Sheila, "Do you see anything here?"

Sheila moved closer. "No. Wait, kind of. It could be a '1' or an 'I,' maybe a '4.' I don't know. It's one of those things where your mind tries to fill in what isn't there."

Rainey pulled out her phone and took a picture of the smear before standing and asking Sheila, "Let's go back to Wendy's office. I don't want anyone to hear what I have to say." She led the way and closed the door before she spoke again. "Wendy came home to get something she wanted me to read. I didn't see anything out there, so it must be in here."

"Any clue what we're looking for and why?"

"Wendy told Katie she thought she'd broken the case. I'm not sure which one. My sister has been playing detective. She was going through my file on the fetish UNSUB. She is also involved in a domestic abuse case. The abuser has targeted her, is stalking and has threatened her. His wife and kids are in hiding, and he's deteriorating rapidly. He's ex-FBI and in the home security field. The third case is bothersome, too. It involves high-level government officials and underage male prostitutes. It's linked to the bodies found in the drainage pond. I told her to back off and call you. So, you see, there are three very viable reasons Wendy was abducted. We have to figure out to whom she tipped her hand. I hope it was the fetish guy. She'll have the best chance of staying alive with him, at least for the next few hours."

"I want Aaron Engel's ass in custody right now," Rex King's voice penetrated the door before he burst into the office. He was looking over his shoulder at someone. "I said now!"

Sheila responded to this outburst calmly but firmly, "Detective King, you cannot interfere with this investigation. You can't issue orders. A father's participation could cloud the prosecution."

"What about her?" Rex said, pointing at Rainey. "She's Wendy's half-sister."

Rainey looked up from her study of Wendy's desk. Rex bored her. She rarely if ever paid attention to his frequent rants and conclusion jumping. She was honestly surprised he spoke of her relationship with Wendy so openly.

"He's right, Sheila. Run everything I say past Teague or call the BAU and ask for Paula Breedlove. She's the most up to date on the fetish case. I talked with her yesterday at Quantico."

Rex insisted, "Engel threatened to kill Wendy. He's a better suspect than the fetish creep. Why would an organized killer, as Rainey has called him, attack a cop? It's just foolish. She said he's smart. Does that sound smart to you?"

Rainey agreed, "I think Detective King has the right idea about Aaron Engel. We need to know exactly where he was early this morning."

"Okay," Sheila agreed. "I'll have Engel picked up and call Teague in. Detective King, I really need you to leave the premises. Would you walk out with me?"

"Why does she get to stay?" Rex complained.

Sheila grew impatient. "Because, you and I both know she's the best shot you have at getting your daughter back. Don't be an ass, King. You know Rainey is good at her job. Leave her alone and let her do it, for Wendy's sake."

Rainey continued her inspection of the desk while the other two argued.

"Don't shut me out, Robertson. I want to know everything when you know it."

Sheila proved she had more patience than Rainey. She calmly held out her hand, indicating the door, and asked Rex to leave with her one more time.

"I will keep you abreast of the investigation as much as possible. Now, will you walk out with me?"

160

Rex stormed out the door with Sheila following.

Rainey stopped her, asking, "Sheila, has anyone found Wendy's phone?"

"Yes, we found it under the couch."

"May I see it, please? She kept notes on there."

"I'll bring it back in with me after I call Teague and send someone for Engel."

"Thanks. I'm going to keep looking in here if that's all right."

"I'll close the door. Stay as long as you need to."

As soon as she was alone, Rainey said aloud, "Okay, Wendy, what did you need me to know?"

She stared at Wendy's neat desk. Everything was organized and in place. Wendy had binders for each graduate class she was taking. There were binders for "Theory of Criminology and Criminal Justice," "Crime and Public Policy," and Teague's "Forensic Psychology." Rainey picked up the binder for Teague's class. The syllabus contained a class description and a list of topics to be studied, including "eyewitness testimony, false confessions, child custody, juvenile delinquency, expert witnesses, civil commitment, insanity and competency evaluations, risk assessment, and criminal profiling."

"Survey class. Hit the high spots and move along, eh Teague?"

Rainey thumbed through Wendy's notes, pausing on the section on paraphilia, Teague's area of expertise. There were several case studies, a couple Rainey recognized from her work with the BAU. The lust killer, foot-fetish murderer Jerry Brudos, was the most well known. There were papers written by Teague himself on inmates he interviewed for the study he authored. Rainey put the binder down on the desk and went through the other classes' documentation. Nothing stuck out, but she didn't put Teague's class binder back. She wanted to read more. It seemed the task force had the right expert for the fetish case, at least.

Rainey opened all the drawers in the desk and in the file cabinet in the corner, asking herself, "What could she have wanted me to read? Which case was she talking about?" She

161

examined Wendy's bookshelf, filled with textbooks for the most part. There was an entire shelf dedicated to texts written about and by the initial Behavioral Science Unit members, Douglas, Hazelwood, Ressler, and others not so well known. The shelf's contents included FBI publications, some with Rainey named as a contributor. Another shelf held every Thomas Harris title and some other novels about well-known fictional mindhunters. Wendy had wanted to be a profiler long before she knew Rex King was not her father and that her half-sister once had her dream career.

Rainey opened the closet door. The memory of Mack holding his palms up flooded her mind. That image would stay with her, she knew. How long had her little boy hidden there? How many minutes was he required to listen as his aunt fought the attacker? How long was Mack forced to endure the uncertainty of the quiet that followed? He had to have been terrified. She hoped he would process it and move on, with no nightmares.

"Please don't terrorize him in his sleep," Rainey said to the universe, in hopes that someone was listening.

She saw nothing to read in the closet and was about to give up when she noticed a backpack hanging from a hook on the back of the door. Rainey recognized it as the one Wendy had with her often. She pulled the bag off the hook, took it to the desk, and began pulling out the contents a piece at a time. When she found an essay, she read the first paragraph.

The title page was missing. Rainey had no way to know the author of the paper, but within seconds, she knew this was what she was looking for. It was written from the point of view of an offender, one with a thing for women's undergarments. Rainey was positive it was the UNSUB she had been tracking.

The farmhouse sat back from the road, nestled into the surrounding woods. I saw her right after she moved in. She ran her tractor into a ditch. She was middle-aged, but still a hottie, MILF material. I had to stop and help. I went back that night, relieving her of a black bra and panty set. I repeatedly returned for more. She sure likes the pretty lacy ones. So do I. She knew someone was coming. She stopped hanging things on the line or porch. That's when the game began to change. I watched from the woods when the new washer and dryer showed up early one morning. I had visited the night before. I took a whole basketful of her dirties, mmmm. She called the cops. Like that was going to stop me.

Rainey stood behind the desk reading. The bedroom door flew open, smacking into the doorstop. Sheila nearly met it nose first when it bounced back at her.

"Oh, sorry," Sheila apologized to the door.

Rainey said. "What's got you in a tither?"

Sheila explained her haste. "Chatham County picked up a guy this morning. His live-in girlfriend found some disturbing things in their garage and called the police. The girl produced a gym bag full of underwear, and they were not hers. The officers emphasized she was adamant about that. One used the term 'hysterical.' They backed off and called in a supervisor. We are in the process of obtaining search warrants. They took the suspect into custody at his workplace and are bringing him to Durham. The son of bitch showed up at work on time, 8:00 a.m. sharp, after what he did here this morning."

"There could be more than one fetish burglar working the area. What makes you so sure he's the guy? And what did he do with Wendy in such a short span of time if he was already at work?"

"Maybe he stashed her somewhere, which could be in her favor, if—" ·

Sheila hesitated to finish the sentence, so Rainey did it for her.

"If she's still alive. Right?"

Sheila nodded. "Yes, if she's still alive. It is my hope that she is."

"Mine too," Rainey said, with a twinge of sorrow she was trying to ignore. She pushed it back inside the little mental box labeled Wendy and asked, "What else do you know about him?"

Sheila pulled a pad from her coat pocket and read, "His name is Shaun George. He's a teaching assistant at State College and is working on his graduate degree."

Rainey interrupted with a question. "What's his major?"

Sheila looked at the pad. "Uh, creative writing. Is that significant?"

"Just wondering," Rainey answered. "What's the rest of the story?"

"The girlfriend works four days on four days off as an overnight nurse at Memorial Hospital and sometimes stays with her mother because it's closer to work. That clears the way for his clandestine activities. The guy is obsessed with running, so the girlfriend says."

"I don't think he had time to take Wendy to where we believe his den is, do you?"

"No, but maybe we were wrong about that. The girlfriend also said the suspect goes off to hike and camp in the woods alone for days. She said he claimed he was working on his masterpiece, a 'novel about a man who gives up his everyday life to follow his base desires'—her description, by the way. She says she hasn't read it. He hasn't shared the text with anyone that she knows of. We included any original writings and his computer drives on the affidavit for the search warrant."

"What else might I have been wrong about?" Rainey asked, sensing that Sheila was holding something back.

"Teague was right, Rainey. The suspect is twenty-seven years old."

"I suppose I'm not going to be interviewing him. Have I been officially booted from the case?"

"No, but Teague is coming in. I caught him out for his morning run. He said he was five miles from his house and would meet us downtown as fast as he could. I convinced the bosses that two profilers were better than one and that your experience far outweighs Teague's. I emphasized that one mistake in the

164

interview could have the whole case thrown out and that Teague is a professor and an expert, but he's not and never has been a cop. You may both observe, but task force detectives will question the suspect."

"Good enough. Thank you for the support. Did you pick up Aaron Engel?"

"They are looking for him. He's not at home or his office. Do you still think he's involved in Wendy's abduction?"

Rainey stuffed Wendy's things back in the backpack. She included the essay and added the binder for Teague's class. Zipping it up and sliding it over one shoulder, she answered Sheila's question.

"If Shaun George is the fetish killer, then he doesn't have Wendy. He never would have taken her and not stayed with her. He would have called in sick or had a prearranged day off. At the very least, he would have been late. No way he takes a victim like Wendy without planning. The UNSUB we've been tracking doesn't do things spur of the moment. What good is a fantasy if you're going to ruin it by improvising and poor planning? Wendy would be a crowning jewel in this guy's cap. Degrading and torturing a female perceived to have authority, a police officer for instance, is the ultimate power trip for this type. He couldn't control that rush enough to simply show up at work on time."

"Well, you have a point and speak of what you know, so I can see that possibility. Are you going to tell me about the other case, the one involving high-ranking government officials?"

"What would you say if I told you State Representative Reverend Jedidiah Lilly is using a pimp to supply him with underage male prostitutes and is involved in a group of men who wear masks and have sex with young boys for sport?"

"I'd say holy shit, literally. Do you have any evidence to back that up?"

"Did you bring Wendy's phone?"

"It went back to the lab with the techs. I can get it for you when we get downtown. Does Wendy have evidence on that phone?"

"No, at least I don't think so, but she does have a phone number I want. What we need is an excuse to bring Jedidiah down to the interview room. A ruse so he doesn't suspect he's a target of an investigation."

"You think Lilly took Wendy? That's a stretch. She'd beat that little bald man senseless and feed him that god-awful toupee."

"I don't want Lilly. He wouldn't get his hands that dirty, but his pimp would if it threatened his income, which I understand is quite substantial."

"Oh, I see. What makes you think Lilly will admit to anything and give up his connection to this guy?"

Rainey pulled out her phone and touched the screen a few times. She smiled before turning the screen toward Sheila, saying, "Because I have a picture of Jedidiah Lilly's penis, which I'm sure he'll recognize from the identifying mole on the left there."

"Oh, good Lord. Where did you get that? And put it away. I could have gone my whole life without knowing what that idiot's dick looks like." Sheila chuckled. "But I can see why he's so unhappy and his wife always has that lemon-sucking grimace on her face."

"A kid that is now missing sent it to me. Three different teenagers identified it as belonging to Jedidiah Lilly, including the two fished out of that pond. There's only one left and he's not dead yet, but he will be if we don't find him soon. I believed his story, Sheila. I'm afraid someone else did, too, and if that someone found out Wendy knew anything about it, she could have been targeted for that reason."

Sheila headed for the door. "I'll get Lilly downtown. Let me think about how, but I'll get him down there. Nothing would please me more than to take down that lunatic and his church of fundamentalist idiots. How in the hell he got elected, I will never know."

"He will wet his pants when I show him this picture. Be sure to have the cameras rolling in the interview room. It will play well for the jury at his trial. And Sheila," Rainey reached out to stop her from leaving the room, "if the fetish killer did not take Wendy, she's in a lot worse trouble."

"How so?"

Rainey was painfully honest with her answer.

"If Aaron Engel or the pimp took her, they would have no reason to keep her alive."

Sheila was a good detective and made a valid point. "Why take her at all? Why not kill her here?"

"Who knows?" Rainey answered, again honestly because she could only think of one reason. "Wendy may have negotiated with him to remove her from the house because of Mack. You said she left walking beside him. Aaron Engel has kids. If it were him, he could have been empathetic toward Mack's situation. The pimp may simply have realized the circus he would have created if Mack were harmed or left with a dead body. The media coverage is relentless when a child is involved."

"Oh, speaking of media," Sheila said as they exited the room together, "your favorite cable crime reporter is outside."

"Cookie Kutter is out there?"

"Yes, and she knows Wendy is your sister."

"Of course she does," Rainey said, annoyed and preparing for the worst.

Sheila smiled up at Rainey. "If you hit her, make it a good one. I'll testify you were under mental duress. You'd probably get community service."

Rainey smiled back at her. "Ooo, now that is tempting."

#

Cookie started yelling questions the second Rainey exited Wendy's house.

"Rainey, how do you feel about causing your sister's abduction?"

Rainey said under her breath, "It's amazing how much damage hair dye can do to a brain."

Sheila heard the comment and covered her mouth to keep from laughing aloud.

Cookie persisted. "Why would you allow your child to be placed in such danger, knowing the Triangle Terror left you a note on one of his murder victim's doors?"

Sheila stopped laughing. No one outside of a very few people knew that information. She looked back at Rainey. "I'll get to the bottom of that."

"Rainey Bell, were you at Quantico yesterday for a mental evaluation?"

"Keep walking, keep walking," Rainey said to herself.

Cookie went for broke with the next questions.

"Is it true, former Agent Bell, that you nearly shot your own three-year-old child and ordered him to get on the ground like a common criminal? Have you no shame, Rainey? Isn't it true that you've endangered the lives of everyone in your family with your failures as a profiler and now your sister is probably dead because of your ineptitude?"

Rainey's eyes had been trailing the ground in front of her, but the last words from her nemesis snapped her head up to glare in Cookie's direction. It was that moment Rex King chose to jerk the microphone away from the crime show crusader and fling it to the ground. Unable to punch her in the nose and with no other recourse available to vent his anger, Rex snatched a fried pie from the hand of a gawking neighbor and forced it into Cookie's gaping mouth. "Shut up, you crazy bitch. Just shut the fuck up," he shouted.

Cookie threw her arms out and feigned a faint, but sadly no one tried to stop her fall. She fell backward onto the ground, where she rolled around, spitting out fried pie and screaming like she'd been shot.

Officers were quickly on Rex. His career was toast. He turned to Rainey and yelled, "Find her, Rainey. Find my baby girl."

Rainey walked over to Rex, who now had his hands behind his back as the handcuffs were being applied.

"Rex, I will find her. You have to trust me. And when this is over, the three of us will sit down and have the beer I'm going to buy you for doing something I have wanted to do for a very long time."

She turned to Cookie. Although there was some cherry filling visible on her cheek, it did not warrant the display of suffering Cookie's cameraman recorded. Rainey picked up the microphone Rex had thrown to the ground.

She called out to the cameraman, "Is this live? Are you still rolling?"

He nodded yes and moved the camera to focus on Rainey.

Rainey raised the microphone to her mouth and said with a smile, "My name is Rainey Bell. I'm Cookie Kutter's obsession. She's been in love with me for years. And no matter how many times I tell her I'm married and not interested, she cries and begs. It's really quite dramatic and pitiable the way she twists things in an attempt to get my attention. My family, in particular, my wife, would be grateful if someone would distract Cookie from this incessant and mentally unstable stalking behavior. Surely one of you is into trashy dyed blondes with loud mouths and questionable ethics. I'll pay for your wedding cake."

"Cut! Cut! Kill that fucking microphone," Cookie screamed from her supine position after realizing what was happening.

Rainey paid no attention. She concluded her airtime with, "CKCB, see a crime, call the police. Cookie is busy being a martyr at the moment."

The cameraman, who was laughing, turned the camera on Cookie's wallowing attempts to gain her feet as Rainey dropped the microphone on the ground near the crazed woman and walked away.

CHAPTER EIGHT

Rainey stood in the hallway outside the interview room with her phone held to her ear.

"How's Mack doing?"

"He's a little clingier than usual, but that's understandable. He has enriched the other two's vocabulary, which I'm trying to deal with gracefully. Hearing 'Get the fuck out,' randomly shouted from three-year-olds is disconcerting," Katie answered.

"It sounds like he's processing in a healthy manner," Rainey said. "Sharing the experience is good."

"Ernie has threatened soap usage, but I've quelled the desire thus far. Mackie is playing with them outside. He's like a giant jungle gym."

"Exercise will help ease Mack's stress. We may have trouble with him sleeping alone for a bit. There will probably be a few nights with five of us in the same bed."

"I will not mind that at all. We could all use a secure sleeping environment."

"All of us in one bed sounds like a good plan," Rainey said, just as Aaron Engel entered the hallway, escorted by two uniformed officers. "I have to go. I'll call you when I know something. Love you."

"Love you, too. Be safe."

"Always."

Rainey slipped the phone back in her pocket while she watched Aaron Engel approach. He saw her and immediately went on the offensive.

"Oh, this is fucking fantastic. You are here to interview me? Am I supposed to be intimidated by a has-been profiler?"

"No, I'm not here to interview you. I came to watch my sister's fellow officers question you. They don't like criminals who threaten one of their own, especially when they think you're responsible for my sister's abduction."

"I didn't touch your dyke sister."

"No, you have us confused. I'm the one with the wife and kids. But let's get back to why we're here today. You stalked my sister, followed her to my house where security caught you on the surveillance cameras. What happened, Aaron? You had a career, a family, a lovely home, and you couldn't control your temper. I'm just curious. Do you know why women make you lose your mind?" Rainey let her eyes drop to his crotch. "Does it have anything to do with your dysfunction?"

Aaron Engel flew into a rage in milliseconds. He lunged at Rainey. She sidestepped his attack and watched the two officers take him to the floor and cuff his wrists behind his back. He blew spit and air through clenched teeth in a state of rage. He roared and fought the cuffs. One of the officers pinned him to the floor with a knee on his neck. The other was on his radio, calling for an extraction team from the detention center next door.

"Whoa, Aaron. That was exciting. They should put a video of that on YouTube and title it 'Fucked up and lost my mind in a police station.' Nice takedown, gentlemen. No excessive force, and the prisoner is under control." Rainey knelt by the fuming man's head and spoke softly, "Aaron, I don't believe you took my sister, but I do believe you are dangerous and should not be on the street. You need help, brother. The Bureau saw something in you once. I hope you find it again."

172

Aaron's answer was to spit at her, which went nowhere because his mouth was so dry from the fight. The spittle hung on his lip, flipping in and out of his mouth with each panting breath. He had just enough energy left to growl out, "Fuck the Bureau, and fuck you."

Sheila opened the door to the interview room and stepped into the hall, asking, "What happened?"

Rainey looked up and smiled. "Aaron has anger issues. He would never have been able to control his rage. The person that was in that house wasn't trying to kill Wendy. He was attempting to gain control over her. Mr. Engel would have killed her if he ever got his hands on her. Right, Aaron?"

"I'll kill you, bitch. I'll kill your whole family. You are dead!"

Rainey stood up. "See what I mean."

"I'll kill all you fuckers," Aaron threatened while the officers added more restraints.

Sheila crossed her arms. "You pissed him off on purpose."

Rainey grinned. "I had only heard about Mr. Engel's temper. Now I've seen it myself. He didn't take Wendy, but he should be sedated and put in a psych ward for observation. He's a danger to himself and others."

She looked back down at Aaron, who was now hog-tied and played out from his rant.

"I'll be at your bond hearing, Mr. Engel. You have spent your last day on the outside for a good long time." Rainey knelt again and looked him in the eye. "Be well, Aaron. Don't come back for more. The best thing you can do is forget you ever heard my name."

Four extraction team members charged into the hallway, suited up in special gear used to handle aggressive prisoners. They checked his restraints and judged them sufficient. The officers recommended a spit mask, which really pissed off the prisoner. Once secured, each member of the extraction team grabbed a bound limb and lifted Aaron Engel from the floor. They carried him out like a side of beef while he continued his muffled rant.

"I'm going to find you, Rainey Bell. You're dead. You're dead. You're de..."

His voice trailed off as the elevator doors around the corner closed on his freedom.

Dr. Edward Teague came into view, backing into the hallway, his attention focused on the elevators. His professorial look remained intact, black turtleneck, tweed jacket, khakis, and suede saddle oxford shoes. He saw Rainey and Sheila and moved toward them.

"Wow," he said, "That guy is in the throes of a violent mental break. Is everyone okay?"

"Yes," Sheila said, "but that was one of the suspects we were going to interview."

Teague responded, "He's too out of control to pull off an abduction. He would have killed Wendy King on the spot." He focused on Rainey. "I'm sorry. That was insensitive of me. I know you must be tremendously worried."

"Thank you, Edward. We're all worried."

"Well, from what I know of Wendy, whoever took her has their hands full. Do you have any other suspects?"

Sheila answered his question. "We have a suspect in custody in the fetish case. We'll have to wait for DNA unless we can get a confession. Let's step in here."

Teague turned to Rainey. "Do you think this is the UNSUB?"

Rainey hedged her bet. "I'm open to the idea."

Sheila opened the door next to the interview room labeled Observation. "They're bringing him up now," she said.

"May I ask," Teague inquired as he followed Rainey and Sheila into the room, "how old is the suspect?"

Rainey answered, "He's twenty-seven. You may have been right about the age."

Teague let a smile creep onto his lips before covering his self-satisfaction with, "Well, we know age is the most difficult component of a profile."

"Yes, it is," Rainey agreed.

The observation room contained three large windows of mirrored glass that looked into three interview rooms labeled A,

B, and C. Rainey recognized the four detectives from the task force waiting inside. They were laughing and bumping victorious fists, assuming they had found the Triangle Terror. It was a career-making case, but Rainey still had doubts. The detectives all shook Teague's hand, congratulating him on his "perfect profile." They had only reserved nods for Rainey. She didn't care enough to point out the rest of the profile remained on point. Her only concern was finding Wendy.

All the backslapping stopped when a shackled Shaun George and his lawyer were escorted into Interview Room A. Rainey watched him shuffle to a chair at the table, a broken young man, scared and anxious.

This is no apex predator, Rainey thought.

In addition to his apparent distress, which was out of character for the type of UNSUB they were seeking, he had requested a lawyer immediately. Most of these guys welcomed a chance to talk to law enforcement, believing themselves the smartest person in the room. They may lawyer-up once they were sure the evidence was there to convict them or they became bored with the interviewer, but malignant narcissists would play the game until it no longer pleased them to do so. It was their last shot at control, and controlling others was a narcissistic personality's drug of choice. If they decided to confess, it was after there was obviously no way out. Then the game became when and how much information would be forthcoming. They were gamers, the lot of them.

Sheila glanced at Rainey. Rainey shook her head slightly from side to side, indicating her beliefs. Sheila frowned and crossed her arms, her go-to body language when she wasn't pleased, but said nothing.

One of the Chatham County detectives headed out the door, saying, "Time to bury this asshole for good." He chuckled. "Look at him. He'll be spilling his guts in minutes. Even with his lawyer sitting there."

The detective closed the door behind him. Rainey thought his arrogance premature. He had just the type of aggressive attitude predators loved and presented a challenge they could not resist.

Rainey focused on the sad young man at the table. He was guilty of something, but not sadistic murder.

"I never went into anyone's house," Shaun said the moment the detective entered the room.

His lawyer reprimanded him. "Don't talk. Just listen."

"Shaun, I'm Detective Charles, and we have a problem. Your DNA is all over two murder scenes, and the evidence in your garage seals the deal."

First mistake, Rainey thought. Don't lie about DNA evidence. It had been only a few hours since the arrest. It wasn't possible to know if there was a DNA match.

Shaun's lawyer called the detective's bluff. "That's a good one, detective. We both know that isn't true about the DNA. Try again."

"Well," the flustered detective said, "we have the underwear from the fetish burglaries and those pictures on the flash drives we found. That's enough to get the needle for your client." He turned his attention to the suspect. "Talk to me now, Shaun, and I'll see if the DA will make it life without parole."

The young lawyer, fresh out of law school from the looks of him, believed his client was guilty and jumped at the plea deal. "Let me see that in writing and we'll talk. Until then, my client has nothing to say."

Detective Charles tried a different tactic. "Shaun, you abducted a Durham police officer. If I walk out that door, they are going to make sure you get the needle. Tell me where she is, and I can help you."

"I don't know what he's talking about," Shaun said, frantically searching his lawyer's face for help.

"Quiet, Shaun," the lawyer admonished.

"You be quiet. You're ready to make a deal, and I haven't done anything really wrong."

There it was, Rainey thought, the admission of his guilt, but his confession wasn't about murder. Maybe he peeped and took some underwear off a line or two, but he wasn't a killer.

Teague spoke up. "He's guilty. That was an admission. Charles needs to back down some, be his friend, play down the seriousness of his crimes, get him to confess to the fetish burglaries first and then work his way up to the murders. Would you agree, Rainey?"

Rainey had a one-word reply. "No."

Teague looked surprised.

One of the other detectives lashed out. "You're just pissed you were wrong."

"No," Rainey calmly replied. "I think we're wasting time with what looks like a voyeur, but he's no murderer. He doesn't have my sister. Wendy would have taken a weak man like that and cleaned his clock."

"Look at him. He's over six-foot-three, weighs one-eighty-five, and built. Your sister is what, five-eight, a hundred and forty-five pounds? He'd kick her ass," the detective retorted.

Rainey took in a breath and let it out slowly. "Detective, size and strength don't outweigh determination. The man that was involved in the fight at my sister's home was not a whimpering coward. Look at this guy. Look at his body language. Does that look like a predator to you?"

Teague chimed in. "That could be his intelligence showing instead of cowardice. He might be playing at being weak. You're too close to this case, Rainey. Maybe your emotions are clouding your judgment."

"Pardon me, Dr. Teague, but exactly how many sexually sadistic serial murderers have you interviewed in person? I'd guess you may have been in the room with one or two reasonably deviant killers, but you've not dealt with a sadist, not like this. I have, Dr. Teague, and I have the scar to prove it."

Sheila stepped closer to Rainey. "Let's not start taking each other apart. I'm going to state for the record that I trust Rainey's judgment. She's never let me down, not once, but I agree you're too close to this."

A Chatham detective had an opinion also, which he let be known. "She's just covering her ass. There's someone smarter in the room and Miss FBI profiler can't stand it."

Teague's jaw muscles tightened, but his voice remained evenly toned. "It's okay, detectives. I'm sure Rainey is under quite a bit of stress."

Nothing made Rainey angrier than being dismissed as too emotional when she was right, and she was right. The doubts that plagued her just a day ago had vanished. She knew this wasn't the killer, and she could prove it. She just needed the chance to convince the people in the room with her.

Rainey challenged the Chatham detective. "Give me five minutes with Shaun George. He will confess to whatever he's done because he is guilty of something, but it won't be the sexual assaults or murders."

Rainey pointed at the men in the other room.

"What Detective Charles is doing in there will only result in a false arrest. You'll inform the public the case is solved. When the killer strikes again, will you be the face of this debacle? The task force will need someone to be the fall guy. Will that be you? It sure as hell won't be me."

Teague suggested, "Let her go in there. If she's right, then we can move forward with finding the actual UNSUB. If she's wrong, then no harm will have been done. Either way, Rainey is the expert in the room when it comes to interviewing sexually deviant suspects. I bow to her experience."

"Are you okay with this?" Sheila asked the detective.

Rainey's remarks shook his confidence. He seemed to comprehend that if she were right, he would go down in a blaze of negative publicity.

"Sure, let her in there." He acquiesced, but not too much. "If she's wrong though, I want her off the investigation. Agreed?"

"Fine with me," Rainey said, taking off her coat. She unbuttoned another button on her black silk shirt, revealing part of the scar where J.W. Wilson left his mark. While kicking off her shoes, she asked the men in the room, "Would you mind turning around for a second?"

Teague and the detective seemed confused but complied.

178

Sheila's eyes popped wide open when Rainey dropped her slacks and slipped out of the black lace panties she wore, her mouth frozen in an unfinished question, "Wha—"

Rainey winked at her as she pulled the slacks back on. "What, you want to give me yours?" Re-buttoned and re-zipped, she slid her feet back into her shoes, twirled the panties in the air, and said, "We'll see who this guy is in about fifteen seconds."

Sheila regained her ability to speak. "I could have had some brought up from the evidence in the lab."

"No time," Rainey said. "We're wasting a lot with this guy. I need to prove that so we can look for Wendy without this distraction."

"Let me tell you, Bell, swinging your panties on your finger is distracting."

#

10:45AM, Friday, March 6, 2015
Durham County Sheriff's Department
Interview Room 212A
Durham County, NC

Sheila beckoned to the detective, "Detective Charles, could I see you in the hall for a moment?"

He challenged, "What's she doing in here?"

"She's going to sit with Mr. George and his attorney while we confer outside." Sheila wasn't asking when she said, "After you."

Command structure recognized, even as Sheila and Detective Charles were from different departments, he stood and left the room. Sheila followed and closed the door behind her.

Rainey sat down and tossed her panties on the table casually, watching for Shaun George's reaction. He glanced down at them but looked right back up at Rainey.

"I know you. You're Rainey Bell. I've read all your writings on the Chambers case. Man, that dude was sick."

179

Shaun's lawyer again reminded him to be quiet. "Don't talk to her. Wait for the deal. And nice try on the panties. If that's evidence, I'll claim contamination."

Rainey never took her eyes off the suspect, as she explained, "They aren't evidence. They are mine." She leaned forward, giving a good view down the front of her shirt. "I just took them off."

Shaun smiled. "She's trying to judge my reaction. I can't believe I'm sitting here with Rainey Bell." He couldn't help himself. He had to look down her shirt. "That scar is from a guy she finally caught," he informed his lawyer. Then hopeful, he said, "You know I'm not a killer. You're too good not to see I'm innocent."

"May I call you Shaun?" Rainey asked.

"Please do," he answered, unable to control his excitement.

Rainey held up her phone with a picture of Wendy on the screen. "Do you know this woman? She's a student at your school." She added at the last second, "Do you take any of Dr. Teague's classes?"

He looked at Wendy's picture. "No, I've never seen her, but she looks like a younger you. I would have remembered her if I saw her. And I've sat in on a few lectures but never taken a class from Teague. He's too clinical."

"Don't talk to her," the lawyer warned.

"Shut up. You're ready to sign a plea deal for something I didn't do. You're fired. Get out."

Rainey interrupted. "No, he needs to stay. You invoked your right to counsel. If he leaves, we can't talk because I'm acting as an agent for the police."

"Okay, you can stay, but just shut up, before you bury my ass," Shaun said.

Rainey spoke directly to the flustered attorney. "I'm not going to ask him about the crimes he's accused of. I want to ask him about the novel he's writing."

That was all it took. Shaun George was more than willing to share his writings and inspirations.

"You know about that, huh? Well, if you've searched my house and computer, you also know I'm obsessed with the BAU and serial killers. I've been doing a lot of research that I know looks kind of shady on my computer. I used to joke that if the FBI showed up, I'd be toast."

"You're in quite a bit of hot water, now. I can only imagine how deep this rabbit hole will go," Rainey said, prepared to hear this misguided but fairly innocent man's twisted explanation for poor judgment.

"Do you have any idea what's out there on the Internet?" He didn't wait for an answer. "Of course you do. Anyway, I'm writing a book about a guy who lives two separate lives. One, he's a normal dude, wife, kids, nice job, essentially boring existence. The other life, he's a sexual sadist. I was trying to find the right profile to use for my bad guy. BTK has been done over and over. I wanted something fresh, and when the Triangle Terror case hit the media, I started studying fetish burglars and stupidly thought it would be helpful to walk in his shoes, so to speak."

"He's not an original," Rainey said. "None of them are. They all follow the same patterns and behaviors. The signature makes them different. What's your character's signature, Shaun?"

Shaun sat up closer to the table, excited to tell his story. "He cuts off their feet and takes their shoes."

"Come on, Shaun, that's Jerry Brudos. Everyone knows that one. What makes your killer original? What does he eat with his Fava beans?"

"Hannibal was great, wasn't he?" When Rainey did not reply, Shaun went on to admit, "I don't have a signature yet, but when the Terror is caught, I'll have all the rest written and then I can just go in and stick the signature on a few scenes. My UNSUB is a terrorist too, pretending to be an upstanding American citizen. Instead, he collects feet and makes bombs. My hero is this FBI agent who is returning to work at NSA after a close call and has chased this serial killer all over the world but actually lives next door to him."

Rainey didn't want to hear the whole convoluted story. She cut off his creative flow, pointing to a snag in his storyline. "FBI

181

agents don't work for NSA. They may be retired, transferred, even on some joint task force, but no active FBI agent works *for* NSA. Do the research before you put more misinformation on the street."

A dejected Shaun looked across the table at Rainey. "So, that whole storyline has to be rewritten? That sucks, man. Are you sure an FBI agent can't be an NSA agent, too?"

"Pick one or the other agency. Simplify the story." Rainey refocused the disconsolate author. "Have you been out, trying to get into character, Shaun? Have you pulled a few pairs of underwear from dryers, that sort of thing?"

"My guy's into shoes. I only touched the shoes," Shaun answered, as if that exempted him from any suspicion.

"So you admit to being a voyeur?" Rainey asked while smiling at how easy Shaun George was to manipulate. He was definitely not the UNSUB.

The lawyer was losing his mind and turning beat red, "Don't talk to her. She's going to fry you."

Shaun put a hand up in his lawyer's face. "Shush!" He then continued to talk to Rainey, "Look, I prowled around, peeked into some windows, but I never went into anyone's house, and I never stole any underwear. Ask my girlfriend. I don't have a thing for fancy lingerie. You should hear her when I don't notice something she spent bucks on. I'm like, 'Babe, I like you better naked.' She gets mad, and I know I'm done for the evening."

"Words of enlightenment, Shaun. In the bedroom, it's really not all about you." Rainey smiled at him. "So, you prowl about at night—"

Shaun cut her off. "I just wanted to see things through this character's eyes, so my writing would be authentic. Stupid, wasn't it?"

"Yep," Rainey answered honestly. "How do you explain the evidence found in your garage?"

"You're going to think I'm making this up, but I think someone's been following me. I can hear him, but I've never seen him. I thought it might be my imagination, but now, after all this, I'm sure it was him, the real Terror guy. He's setting me up."

"That would be very convenient for you. The UNSUB just happened to be watching and followed you home." Rainey shook her head, emphasizing her disbelief in his story. "How can you convince me you're just a misguided author and not hiding your real personality under a cloak of feigned stupidity?"

"That's harsh. I'm not stupid. Well, I guess it was crazy to peek into windows, but I'm not an idiot."

"That's debatable," Rainey commented.

"Okay, I'm an idiot, but haven't all these crimes been linked to one UNSUB? You used linkage analysis, right? I live right in the middle of his territory. There's a good chance I could have run into this guy. I mean, I actually kind of hoped I would. You know, for—"

Rainey finished for him, "Authenticity. Yeah, we got that. Still, you look real good for this, Shaun."

Shaun puffed out his chest. "Wasn't the first murder committed the day after Christmas? I was on a cruise with my family. Check my phone records. Call my parents. Ask my soon-to-be ex-girlfriend. As soon as I get out of here, she's moving out. I can't believe she didn't ask me about that stuff before she called the cops."

"You don't have to worry about her moving out. I understand she packed a bag and went to her mother's, but I'm pretty sure she's the least of your concerns at the moment."

"One of the assault victims, Dr. Sweet, is like a mother to me. She's been my advisor through undergrad and grad school. I was so pissed when she was attacked," Shaun offered in his defense.

Glena Sweet would have recognized Shaun as her student, Rainey thought. The professor remembered so clearly the conversation the UNSUB had with her, the exact words he had used.

Rainey asked Shaun, "What about the second murder? January 17th. It was a Saturday. Where were you then?"

He smiled. "Ask my girlfriend—ex-girlfriend. It was her idea."

Rainey smiled back, picked up her panties and stuffed them into her pocket. "I think you better go ahead and tell us. We'll verify your story, of course, but it's probably best if you just say where you were."

"We went to Asheville. She wanted to go to the Biltmore Estate. She's all into Downton Abbey. We stayed at the Village Hotel on the grounds." He beamed at Rainey. "I have the credit card receipts. No linkage, no suspect. Right?"

Rainey stood up and looked down at the lawyer. "You might want to hear your client's story and do some fact checking before you start talking plea bargains. You were about to send an innocent man to prison, asshat."

To Shaun, she said, "You're going to be charged as a voyeur. You've admitted to it on video, so they have you. I'd get a new lawyer and go to trial. You might find some jurors who are as dedicated to authenticity in books as you are or who have done some really bonehead shit in their lives."

"Hey," Shaun called after her as Rainey headed for the door, "can I send you my manuscript? I could use you as an expert. It would give me more authenti—"

Rainey's "No" cut him off, and the door's closing silenced any further requests. When Rainey stepped into the observation room, she landed in the middle of Sheila's reprimand of the detectives cowering under her glare.

"No one bothered to check where this guy was on the dates of the murders? Well, this has been a monumental waste of time. You better hope we find Wendy King alive. Total incompetence."

Rainey redirected her, "Sheila, I really need Wendy's phone."

Sheila was disgusted with the detectives. "I'll call down to the lab. In the meantime, you two go in there and find out where this idiot has been playing at peeping Tom. Maybe we can use that to catch the real UNSUB."

Two detectives slinked off, shoulders drooping, their hope of being the conquering heroes dashed. The other two left the room with phones to their ears, already moving the investigation forward. Rainey, Teague, and Sheila were but a small cog in the justice machine searching for Wendy's abductor. Sheila took out her phone and stepped into the corner, leaving Rainey standing with Teague.

He smiled at her. "I suppose we'll have to just keep looking for the Triangle Terror. Fascinating interview technique. The panties were brilliant," he said, glancing at the pocket that contained them with a smile that made Rainey uncomfortable.

The facial muscles around Teague's eyes were not participating in his smile, an indication it was not genuine. Rainey was in no mood to swap professional accolades, nor was she happy with his use of "we." Rainey had worked plenty of investigations with academics contributing considerably to the process. It was not his education, his title, nor his smugness that bothered her, but something did, even if she couldn't name it. It may simply have been that Rainey noticed the tarnish on the professor's polish. His research and class materials gave her pause, as well. She needed to talk to him about the essay. She needed to know if Teague knew how it came to be in Wendy's possession.

She said, "Excuse me. I'm going to the restroom. Tell Sheila I'll be right back."

Rainey exited without further comment and found the restroom down the hall. She slipped into a stall and put her panties back on, all while mentally running scenarios of what could have happened to her sister. If Rainey's calculations were correct, Wendy had been missing for almost five hours. Five hours with a sadist was a long time.

While Rainey washed her hands, the phone chirped in her pocket, signaling a text message had been received. She dried her hands and entered the passcode. It seemed Danny had been made aware of Wendy's abduction.

His message read, "Whatever you need."

Rainey typed, "I need the cross-referenced list of property owners and women who take a sleeping aid. Absent partner scenario is too broad."

She paused. Having ignored the thought since finding the essay, it was difficult to give into it. Deciding it wasn't all that crazy to want to know with whom she was dealing, Rainey added, "Run Dr. Edward Teague for me. Tell Brooks to look beneath the surface."

Rainey hesitated, not yet ready to send the message. She looked into the mirror above the sink and saw the reflection of the uppermost track of the Y-incision scar. Rainey's mind recalled the cost of ignored disconcertion. She was suddenly subjected to the memory of JW at the kitchen counter reading with detached emotion the newspaper article describing her attack. She discovered later that JW fed the media the details himself. Physically reacting to the recollected nausea brought on by the remembrance of JW's cologne, Rainey placed the phone on the counter and splashed cold water on her face.

With her face buried in a couple of paper towels, she heard Sheila's voice ask, "Are you okay?"

Rainey finished drying her face and forced a smile. "Yeah, yeah, I'm okay." She picked up the phone, hit send, and slipped it back into her pocket. "It's been a long day already. Just freshening up and putting my underwear back where they belong."

Sheila put her hand over her mouth, trying to contain the volume of her laughter. "Oh my God. When you dropped your drawers in there I nearly had a heart attack. Do you have any idea how many sexual harassment rules you just violated? I don't think the boys will bring it up. That would mean admitting what a shitty job of investigating they did."

"Don't be too hard on them. Shaun George looked guilty. He just wasn't."

Her laughter subsiding, Sheila collected herself back into detective mode.

"I have to tell you, Rainey, I'm not comfortable cutting a guy loose with that much evidence in his home. We will hold him until he's arraigned on the voyeurism charge Monday. Luckily, he admitted to his peeper pattern, and we can charge him here in Durham before sending him back to Chatham. That gives us some time to be very sure he's not responsible for any of the assaults or burglaries before he's back on the street."

186

"He's guilty of peeking, but as unlikely as it seems, I think he is telling the truth about the UNSUB following him."

The chirping of another text message arriving sang from Rainey's pocket. She paused to take out the phone and read Danny's short but direct text, "Teague?"

Rainey's reply was just as succinct. She typed, "Stranger things…"

Assuming wrongly that it was Katie, Sheila asked, "Is everything okay at home?"

Rainey slipped the phone into her pocket and moved toward the exit with Sheila. "All is well. Now, let's go find my wayward sister."

Rainey ran into Teague as she stepped into the hallway. He winced and grabbed his ribcage where she bumped him.

"Sorry," he said, clearly trying to disguise his pain. "I was looking for the men's room."

Rainey apologized, "I'm sorry. I should have been more careful. Are you okay?"

Teague answered with a pained smile, "I slipped on a wet boulder on my run this morning—bruised my ribs pretty good."

Sheila pointed toward the end of the hall. "The men's room is on the other side of the elevators."

"Thank you," he nodded and started away. Three tiny red scratches peeked from the top of his turtleneck collar and were just viewable in the closely cropped hair at the nape of his neck.

Ding. Ding. Ding. The jackpot bells were chiming in Rainey's mind. She called after him, "When you come back, I have an essay I'd like to show you. I think it may be from your class."

Teague stopped. He turned to Rainey—and there it was. She saw the blink. He was the consummate predator, above reproach, and yet she saw that split-second view of his lizard brain stare. Teague was the fetish burglar, rapist, and murderer they were searching for. Now she had to prove it. All she had was an essay and a gut feeling. No one would believe her, not even Sheila.

Yet, he proved an even more viable suspect when he walked back to them, explaining, "Well, I didn't have to go. Just thought it was break time, you know." He chuckled. "So, let's see the essay."

I'll be damned, Rainey thought. She didn't dare speak her observations aloud as her brain asked, *What are the freakin' chances of that?* And rightly so, but as she hinted to Danny, stranger things had happened in Rainey's life. Now what? As long as he was with her, he wasn't with Wendy. If he took her, Rainey needed to make sure he did not leave without a full confession. If she accused him, he would walk out the door and kill Wendy the second he reached her. She wasn't wrong about Teague, but she could be wrong about him taking Wendy. She needed Wendy's phone to keep the investigation moving on all fronts while she dealt with Professor Terror one on one.

"Sheila, are they bringing Wendy's phone up to you?"

"Yes, they should be here any—and there she is." Sheila tipped her head in the direction of a young woman in a lab coat carrying a plastic evidence bag and a clipboard down the hall.

"Sergeant Robertson, we haven't processed the phone yet, so could you leave it in the bag?"

"Yes," Rainey said and took the phone while Sheila signed for it.

She made Teague stand and wait, uninformed. Rainey didn't know if evidence on the phone to tied him to Wendy's disappearance, but neither did he. She knew Wendy's passcode. She knew everyone's passcode in her immediate circle or had administrative access. She put trackers and emergency alert networks on her loved ones' phones because they were her loved ones and thus vulnerable to the trouble that seemed to find her. Rainey went to the recent calls menu, ran her finger down the list until she saw what she was looking for, *Peter Pan.* She tapped the screen revealing contact information. She tapped a few more times and heard the ding on the phone in her pocket as Connor's information was received.

"Is that it? The tech can take it back with her if that's all," Sheila said.

Rainey saw Teague's eyes following the phone and replied, "No, I need it to communicate with this kid. I'll hang on to it for a bit."

She led Teague back into the observation room and went straight to the corner, where she'd left her coat and Wendy's backpack.

Turning back to Sheila, Rainey said, "Could Dr. Teague and I use one of the other interview rooms? I think we can help each other process if we work together, without outside influences."

Not waiting for Sheila's answer, Rainey was already moving with Teague right behind her. She entered the interview room and walked over to the table. She dropped her coat and Wendy's backpack in one chair and set about moving the table and the other two chairs. When she was finished, one chair sat in the corner, one chair held her coat, and the other chair, the only one on wheels, faced the one in the corner.

"I hope I didn't mess up the camera angles." Glancing at Sheila, she continued speaking only to Teague, "Have you ever been in an actual interview room, Edward?"

"No, not like this. I've interviewed inmates at Butner, and I did my study at Walpole."

Rainey stood in front of the rolling chair, leaving only the one in the corner open for Teague. She talked while she pulled out her phone and placed it with Wendy's on the table.

"Walpole, I saw that in your study. Did you get a chance to meet some of the guys in the DDU?"

"I'm sorry, DDU?" Teague asked.

"The special discipline unit, strictly geared to punishment, not for rehabilitative purposes. It's where the impulse-control-challenged go to stay for years in some cases. It takes that long to punish a man who has nothing left to lose after he slits a guard's throat or shanks his roommate."

"No, I never had the pleasure. I worked in group therapy sessions and one-on-one interviews within the general population, but there are still some individuals walking around in there I would not care to meet on the street."

"Yeah, no kidding," Rainey said and then switched gears again. She pointed at the various video cameras. "I believe they automatically record in this particular room. Is that right, Sheila, or is that in the new ones over at the detention center?" She smiled at Teague. "You may want to request a copy of this conversation for future use."

"That would be an excellent teaching tool," he said, smiling.

"I was going to have Sheila turn it off, but since you're aware that we're being recorded, it's all good then?" Rainey nodded as she asked the question, watching as he began to nod, too.

"Yes, sure. Record away," replied Teague.

Intentionally ignoring Teague for a moment, Rainey spoke directly to Sheila, "Hey, did you make contact with Lilly?"

Sheila searched Rainey's face while wearing a befuddled expression. "I did," she answered, "I'm waiting for a response from his personal assistant."

Rainey picked up her phone. "What's his number?"

Sheila hesitated and then reached into her pocket for her phone. "Do not use my name. You hear me? Rainey?"

"Yeah, yeah. I hear you. Just give me the number."

Sheila held up her phone for Rainey to see the information and then waited by her side to see what she did with it.

Rainey typed a text message, "Two teens dead, one missing, two unaccounted for, Lilly conversion camp tied to case. Evidence and two witness statements at Durham Sheriff's department. Will only deal with Lilly personally, as long as possible. Call Det. Robertson in CID before media gets story. Don't tarry. See you soon."

She pulled up the penis photo, copied just the small section containing the unusually shaped mole, saved it to a new image, attached it to the text and hit the send button.

Rainey tossed her phone on the table with Wendy's and said, "I really wanted to see his face, but desperate times and all that."

"You used my name," Sheila said, taking a playful swat at Rainey's shoulder. "And where are these witnesses?"

"You have to promise not to arrest these kids. I'll find beds for them, but you have to promise me they will not be thrown back into the system for trying to survive."

"Rainey, I can't ignore the law. Even if they aren't charged with prostitution, I have to report underage homeless youth to social services."

"Fine, then you get one seventeen-year-old witness you can't touch."

"That's probably for the best right now," Sheila said. "Get the others in a program and off the street before you bring them here. I don't want them going back in the system just to run again."

"We have nothing by way of evidence. I have a picture and a story, but that does not prove murder. It also doesn't get us any closer to the man who has Wendy."

"No, it doesn't," Sheila said, "but it will stop Jedidiah Lilly from harming any more boys. Wouldn't it be great to shut down that conversion camp once and for all?"

Rainey pointed at that not being the case. "Don't discount the forgiving forces of the Lord and his minions, nor the moneymaking power of a repentant sinner."

Teague grew restless. Rainey had ignored him too long. "What about the essay? Are we working on both cases together now, the dead teens and the fetish case?"

Rainey walked a confused Sheila to the door, gently holding her elbow and prodding her to move. "We're going to talk about a lot of things, Edward. Clear the air and make some headway on these cases, both of which could lead to my sister's abductor. Sheila, you will let us know when Lilly or his representative arrives, won't you?"

When she was more or less pushed through the doorway and out into the hall, Sheila wheeled around and mouthed the words so that Teague couldn't see her, "What the hell?"

Rainey spoke so he could hear her words but not see her facial expression. "I think Dr. Teague can be a huge help in locating Wendy. Make sure the recorder is running. He'll want it for later."

CHAPTER NINE

11:10 AM, Friday, March 6, 2015
Durham County Sheriff's Department
Interview Room 212B
Durham County, NC

Rainey closed the door and indicated the empty chair in the corner to Teague. "Have a seat. Notice how I've put you in the corner, symbolically showing you have nowhere to go without going through me."

Teague laughed nervously but played along. "Oh, so I'm to be the interviewee. This is a new perspective."

Rainey moved the backpack, rolled the chair so it was closer to Teague and sat down, blocking more of his view of the door. "Truthfully, you should be questioned. You are a part of the victim's life, in this case, Wendy's life. Surely you have observed the crush she has on you, professor."

"I would think you would want to be out searching for her," Teague said, ignoring Rainey's comment on the crush and his relationship with the victim.

"There are professional investigators out there looking for Wendy. I'm helping my sister the best way I know how. I'm using years of training, study, and experience to explore possibilities. Some people call it throwing spaghetti at the walls to see what sticks. I'd like to think of it more as paying attention to the details, the frequently overlooked but immensely telling minutiae."

Rainey smiled, putting Teague at ease. She picked up her phone and sent Connor a message, requesting his presence at the Sheriff's Department and giving assurances he would not be detained. She then sent a return email to the address from which the picture originated, with instructions on how Cane and Barron could reach her safely. She promised to personally come get them if necessary. She followed that correspondence with one to Brooks, asking her to track the email and find Cane's phone. Rainey did all this while she continued to talk with Teague.

"Wendy is mixed up in the murder case you're working on, the one with the two dead boys. She stumbled into it—a family trait it seems, stumbling into trouble. I'm afraid some very powerful men may have wanted her silenced. Wendy believes the young men I'm trying to reach can identify the person who put those boys in the pond. She may very well have spoken to the wrong person. Did she discuss the case with you?"

Rainey put her phone down and picked up Wendy's. After sending Connor the identical message she sent from her own phone, she scrolled through Wendy's call and text message history. Teague watched the phone, not Rainey, while he answered her question.

"Wendy sent a text last night. She asked about the profile I was working on. I called her back and told her there wasn't a lot of evidence. Two boys, bound. That's it. Runaways, male prostitutes, but not much evidence at all on which to base a profile."

"Oh, but there is more to cull from the information you have." Noting Wendy's text and Teague's call in the history log on the phone, Rainey continued to scroll through information as she spoke. "Two teens bound together and believed killed at the same time. The question is how did a single UNSUB take down two streetwise teenage kids? They weren't small, both fifteen. Right? They went with the UNSUB willingly, together, thinking that was safer. They were bound similarly with flex cuffs on their wrists. The ropes around the knees were tied with different knots, suggesting one victim may have been forced to tie the other, or there were two assailants. The ankles were not tied, so the victims could shuffle but not run, suggesting one UNSUB who needed to move two teenage boys without resistance. Either way, the bindings were for control, not sexual gratification. This was an execution."

"To what end?" Teague asked.

Rainey shrugged. "Silence, maybe? I don't know. Snapping the necks of two bound kids, that takes some hellacious motivation. How terrifying it must have been to be the second to die, knowing it was coming."

Teague stretched his legs and leaned back against the chair. Expressing with body language that the topic had moved into a more comfortable realm, a place where he felt empowered. He also purposely occupied more space, increasing his physical boundaries, the psychological equivalent of manspreading.

Marking territory. *How testosterone driven of you, Doctor*, Rainey thought, but remained silent and smiling.

"For someone who was supposed to stay away from the case, you sure have an abundance of information from the M.E.'s report," Teague challenged.

"There are perks to having connections in a few places. I made a call or two." Changing direction, she asked, "Did you know Dr. Glena Sweet, from the Literature Department?"

"No, I never had the chance to meet her. I knew of her, but I did not associate a name with a face until she became a victim. It's a big faculty, different departments. It's understandable that we would not know one another."

Rainey saw guarding behavior as Teague pulled his lower legs in under the chair and folded his arms

"Did you recognize Shaun George as someone who may have attended one of your lectures?"

"No, I heard you ask him that, and I've been trying to recall his face, but there are so many students sitting in. I have an open door policy. I'm available to work with the fledgling crime authors on campus," he paused to chuckle, "even if Mr. George finds me too clinical."

Rainey nodded, agreeing with him, addressing him as her commiserate colleague. "The truth of what a behavioral analyst does appears clinical to most. I'm surprised more books aren't written from the criminal's point of view. The action lies with the UNSUB. The analyst's chase is not glamorous enough for entertainment purposes. I guess that's why authors have one of us lead the way through the door at the end of the story. In reality, we are rarely if ever there at the moment of arrest or victim recovery."

Teague smiled at his inclusion, relaxed the grip on his biceps, and welcomed the exchange between peers. He wanted to belong in the room with her. Rainey could see it in his expression and hear it in his voice.

"I totally agree with that assessment. I've read numerous manuscripts from budding authors seeking my approval." Teague leaned in to lend his observation. "Too often they have analysts doing things that are out of the realm of possibility. We are not clairvoyant. Why should it be less exciting that we use our brains as weapons?" Teague chuckled. "Not quite as sexy as a Glock and knock approach, though. Is it?"

Rainey laughed with him, "There were a few times the knock turned into something entirely unexpected. One minute you're ringing doorbells looking for information. The next, some name on a list turns out to be the UNSUB you're looking for. You know what the bad part is?" Rainey asked.

"They see you before you see them," Teague offered.

"Yes, most of the time, they know they're caught before we know we've found them. That can be a very dangerous time for an unaware investigator. It's in the scurrying to get away that we see them. It's like when I watch my cat hunt in the yard. If the prey he's focused on quietly goes about its business, he'll stare at it long enough to be distracted by the one that runs away in a panic."

Rainey continued to examine her sister's life through the cell phone. She saw the texts and unanswered calls from Nick Prentiss and his friend, apparently named Junior. An exchange of texts with Connor informed Wendy of the missing Cane and

196

Barron and asked for help. Wendy explained she couldn't meet him until the morning after her "babysitting" job was complete. She told him to stay quiet and watch his back. Wendy, Rainey thought, was too cocky to have taken her own advice.

"Are you finding anything pertinent on Wendy's phone?"

"Not yet," Rainey replied, without looking up from the screen. "I took a look at your study on fetish burglaries evolving to sexual murder. It reads like a how-to-manual for the current UNSUB. The escalation follows the pattern of the most troubling cases at each step. This study has been widely distributed, I assume?"

"Yes, and if it's true someone used it as a study guide, it will be hard to track it. It's available online."

"I see," Rainey said, still watching the screen of the phone as Wendy's life flew by one finger swipe at a time. She appeared to become absorbed in the contents of the phone, but she had an eye on Teague. Rainey wasn't sure what she was looking for until she found it, but she waited for him to speak before the reveal.

Teague couldn't stand the quiet. When she stopped talking, he had to break the silence. He was used to commanding attention. Rainey's indifference to his presence didn't sit well with his narcissistic root personality.

"I thought you wanted to show me an essay?"

Rainey leaned forward, ignoring his question, and showed him the picture she had located. "I remember Wendy telling me about this," she said. "Isn't this you with her running group? Eno River Park, wasn't it?"

"Yes, I believe it was. I don't run with groups often, but Wendy invited me, and it sounded like fun. I had not run in that park before." Teague grinned at Rainey while she looked at the photo again. "I can see that mind of yours at work, Agent Bell. I'm an off-trail runner like our UNSUB. So are many Triangle residents, including your sister. I understand from Wendy, you grew up running through the woods around Jordan Lake."

"It's just Rainey. I did and still do run those old trails. You should come check them out. My dad made them for me when I ran cross country in high school." Rainey sat back, still thumbing through the phone. "Are you on Facebook, Edward? I'm not, except for the account I use to track bail jumpers stupid enough to post their whereabouts online. It's always funny when they 'like' their wanted photo."

"The school encourages us to be available to social media, as long as we keep it professional," Teague said.

Wendy was on Facebook and Edward was right there at the top of her friends list. Rainey clicked on his name to see what he shared with others. Not much, but enough. In the photos he shared publicly, she found another clue.

"So, since you say you've never experienced being interviewed like this, let me explain how this would go if I were still an agent. I'd inform you of your rights and let you know you're under no obligation to talk to me. I would make sure you knew you could leave at any time or request an attorney. Those same rights apply if I'm acting as an agent for law enforcement, as I am here today. I explained earlier that everything we do and say in this room is being recorded."

"This suddenly feels rather formal," Teague said, not yet losing his cool.

"Like I said earlier, as a friend or acquaintance of Wendy's you will be questioned. The first element of a crime we investigate is the victim. We need to know how and why Wendy was abducted."

"What do you need to know to take me off the table as a suspect?" Teague asked.

"I'm sorry. Are you a suspect?" Rainey made sure to appear surprised.

Teague seemed prepared for the duel. "Well, it is about removing possible suspects when you examine the victim's life. How do you eliminate me?" He paused to make sure his sly smile was fully realized and then added, "And how do they eliminate you, Rainey? You were there at the house. Maybe you had a fight with your sister that escalated."

Rainey let slip a slight grin of her own. "Okay, I'll go first. I was on a domestic flight from Quantico that arrived too late to have done the damage at Wendy's house, hidden her body, left my son behind, gone back to my house, and then sped back to Wendy's, where I was spotted arriving, and witnessed entering the house by way of a broken front window. My alibi is relatively tight."

"It would seem so," Teague said but didn't offer his own accounting.

Rainey asked, "Have you ever had reason to be at Wendy's house?"

"No, I've not been in her house, but I have run the trails behind her house."

Rainey's phone sounded a ding. A text message had arrived. She led Teague, "So, you do know where Wendy lives."

"Yes, I do. She told me when she found out I live just a few miles away in Falcon Ridge."

"You live in the center of the geographic profile for this UNSUB. How many of the other burglary, sexual assault, and now murder locations do you pass on your runs?"

"I'm sorry. I thought we were talking about Wendy. Are you now officially questioning me about the Terror case?"

Rainey listened to his response while reading the message from Brooks on the screen. She worked very hard at keeping her breathing steady. Rainey was once accused of having ice water in her veins, able to control the very beat of her heart, so as to never give the killer across from her a hint of reaction to the violent acts he or she described. It took all she had to maintain that stoicism now.

Rainey smiled at Teague. "I'm not questioning you, Edward. I'm a consultant. I'm gathering information. You can answer what and if you choose. I will tell you that answering a question with a question hints at evasion."

Teague admitted, "Yes, I run by all of the crime scenes, some before and some after I acquired the knowledge of their existence from the police files. I'm one among thousands who use those trails, you and your sister included."

She left Teague hanging, awaiting her next move while she copied the text message from Brooks and sent it to Sheila, with a postscript added, "Get a warrant."

Rainey then turned her attention back to the man in the corner. "And now you add qualifying statements to explain why you were at a crime scene. See how easy it is for innocent circumstances to become concerns for investigators. Something as simple as you run the same trails as a killer and wear the same brand of running shoes. Bet you have a new pair you're breaking in as we speak."

Teague tried to maintain the calm air of intrigued, innocent professor, but his forehead tinted pink, his ears flushed, and the smile he adopted to hide his concern did not do the job. He couldn't fake a genuine smile. He could project authenticity to the untrained eye, but not to Rainey.

"How do you know I wear the same shoes as the killer?"

"Social media, photos, likes, comments, posts, all that stuff says a lot about a person. A psychopath's toy box—that's what I call social sites on the Internet. That line, 'I can be whoever you need me to be,' is deadlier than it is romantic."

"The Internet is a source of much enlightenment, for good and bad," Teague noted. "These guys can find whatever brand of fantasy they want out there. Rule number thirty-six of the Internet: If it exists, it is somebody's fetish. No exceptions."

"Okay, now as an interviewer, I could consider your last statement deflecting, an attempt to draw me off the topic of what I found through your social media interactions."

Teague shifted in the chair, crossed a leg over the other, and rested his hand on his ankle. He attempted a depiction of calm. It would have been normal to show signs of stress, yet Teague tried pretending indifference. He didn't know how an innocent man would react because he wasn't one. Neither was he practiced in front of a doubter. For everyone else in his life, Edward Teague was absolutely convincing in his portrayal of the model citizen scholar.

He grinned at Rainey. "By all means, tell me what I've divulged about myself on the Internet."

Rainey obliged him. "I can see that you do, in fact, wear the exact shoe we've been looking for, or did a few months ago, before you were asked to consult on the case. Much like our

UNSUB, you're an off-trail runner, loyal to a particular shoe brand and have a new pair. You are an avid photographer, again fitting the profile, and prone to selfies, some of which show you wearing the exact clothing the UNSUB is said to wear. You even have the black hat and neck gator."

"All circumstantial," Teague said.

"If you were guilty, I'd call that peacocking-foreplay or an attempt at re-experiencing, standard behavior for a sadistic sexual murderer. It amounts to taunting, all that 'look at me, look at me' cock-strutting. The obsession with mocking documentation usually makes excellent evidence, especially in the penalty phase." Rainey let that sit a second before adding, "But as you say, it's circumstantial. Still, if you'd like to stop, you can seek an attorney's advice."

"Broad generalizations are not evidence," Teague said, waving off her intimations.

Rainey pointed out, "Circumstantial evidence does lead to questions, such as why your DNA would be inside the homes of the victims."

"I don't know," he answered, and then remembered he should deny and did so. "Well, it shouldn't be."

Rainey let out a little chuckle. "This UNSUB rather foolishly left deposits of DNA, so it will be easy to link him to most of the sites. We left some information out of the files for signature element verification. It helps maintain a pristine chain of linkage. If I were an investigator, I'd ask you to volunteer for a DNA swab for elimination purposes. Of course, I could just run the water bottle you left in the other room."

The blood left Teague's head and ran to his heart. He lost his color for a millisecond. It returned with a rush, bringing the blush of a guilty man.

Rainey continued closing in on him. "It's part of the signature, leaving behind sheets or a pair of underwear, a towel, something this UNSUB stained almost unnoticeably. Part of his fantasy is the hope the victim will wear or use it before noticing his prolonged violation. You write about this behavior in your study. In fact, you mention some of our UNSUB's behaviors precisely, attributing them to the fantasies and crimes of anonymous study participants. What do you think the chances are of two perpetrators' behaviors matching in such minute detail? One would have to assume they have compared notes or inspirations. The other option is a copycat."

Teague tried very hard to look entirely unconcerned. He was unaware his ears were now scarlet and his forehead was damp with nervous perspiration. Hell yeah, this guy was guilty. Rainey wanted to beat him with a chair until he told her what she needed to know, but remained in control. She'd heard worse, been closer to men who ate victims, took home heads to sleep with and other unimaginable things. Teague's only distinguishing note was one of his victims might be her sister. Rainey had forced him inside his head hunting for a way out, a way to explain the circumstances that brought him to each victim's home. His brain was occupied with calculating the chances of escaping the needle.

Rainey smiled at him as she pulled the essay and Wendy's binder for his class from the backpack. Teague's eyes followed her every move.

"My sister is much more organized than I am. She has an individual binder for her classes and appears to keep every scrap of paper associated with each one neatly tucked inside. I had time to read the notes and handouts in this binder when we first arrived this morning. The class description doesn't really fit the materials. It appears to be a survey class, and you do spend a moment or two on all the topics, but the focus is on your research area, paraphilia leading to sexual violence."

Teague had the academic answer ready. Rainey guessed he had probably justified his methods of teaching to some administrator along the way. He gave her the spiel, "Behavioral analysis, or profiling as some call it, is the sexy in the class. It's why people take it. My roster is always full and has a waiting list. I cover everything in the syllabus using my area of expertise as the basis for discussion."

"What brought you to this particular study topic, Edward?"

"An undergraduate assignment becomes a life study. Nothing more suspect than that, I assure you."

Rainey slid the essay to the end of the table, just off Teague's right. "Have you seen this, Edward? Is it from your class?"

He had to turn in his chair to see the paper. He winced with the movement and answered, "Yes, that's from my class." He picked it up and smiled, almost laughing, as he said, "You don't believe the Triangle Terror wrote this, do you?"

Rainey sat forward, closing the space between them. "As a matter of fact, I do."

"I wrote this," Teague said. "I used the file and wrote this for a class exercise in profiling. If it's too accurate, it's because it is based on actual evidence and Arianna Wilde's victim statement."

"What does your wife do for a living, Edward?"

"She's a fabric designer. What does that have to do with this essay?" He put the paper back down on the table.

Rainey didn't let up. "Does she travel a lot?"

Teague knew he was caught, but his ego wouldn't let him give up. He thought himself too smart. He thought he could still talk his way out of the trap he had walked into.

"My wife travels, yes. More circumstantial evidence."

"How did you get those scratches on the back of your neck?"

He reflexively reached for his neck, before stopping himself. "When I tripped on the boulder, I guess a branch got me."

Rainey pressed him, "Where exactly were you when you fell? You do know we can track cell phone locations. When you answered Detective Robertson's call, where were you?" Rainey wore the smirk now. "Be careful, this is where the lies start to become difficult to remember. Stories become convoluted the more they are told, especially the fabrications. Did you say, 'I slipped on a boulder,' or 'I tripped on a boulder?' Little nagging details like that are the threads investigators pull and then watch the whole thing unravel."

"Slipped, tripped, what's the difference? I fell in the woods and scratched my neck, bruised my ribs."

"How difficult do you think it would be for someone like me, who has seen countless violent injuries, to distinguish between bruises made falling and bruises made by a victim fighting a predator? Would you care to lift your shirt and let me show you?"

Teague sat back away from Rainey. She countered, moving nearer, closing off more of his escape route, reclaiming the space. She changed subjects quickly, not allowing his brain to process information thoroughly, before adding complications.

"Is your wife home now?"

"No. She's in India. No one saw me come home from my run injured if that's what you're asking."

Rainey rolled the chair closer, taking more control and freedom from her prey. "Edward, I took Arianna Wilde's statement. I know what was in it. I signed it. I know what was not included in any file. Can you guess your mistake?"

Teague's eyes darted to the paper. He started reading it silently. Rainey watched him try desperately to see his error. The fact that he was reading it at all and not screaming about his innocence spoke volumes about his guilt.

"I thought it interesting that you chose to make the UNSUB sound younger than you are, less educated, in order to match your profile. Serving that ego right up to the bitter end. You can stop reading. You read it in the first ten seconds."

His eyes jumped back to the beginning.

Rainey read the line from the page to him, "She ran her tractor into a ditch."

Teague pushed the paper back toward Rainey. "That's in the report somewhere. Just because she didn't say it to you, doesn't mean she didn't say it to someone. Whose ego is showing now?"

Rainey held up a hand. "Sheila, knock once if Arianna spoke with anyone other than me, twice if she did not."

One knock and his smile started to come. With the second knock, he deflated.

"You've done two things here, Edward. You used information only the UNSUB knew, and you've made it clear Arianna has seen you. She'll be able to pick you out of a lineup. We'll put you at the scene, and we both know the DNA evidence is going to bury you."

Teague fell into a blank staring silence. Rainey could see his brain trying to think of a way to explain it all away.

"Where is Wendy?" Rainey asked. "Is she at your wife's old family estate?"

He looked up from his now bent posture.

Rainey answered his silent inquiry, "Yes, we know about that too. What are you willing to put your wife through? Search warrants are about to be served for your residence here and the place in lower Chatham. I'm sure the college has been notified that a search warrant is about to be served for your office and work products. How is this going to play out, Edward?"

His knee began a nervous jitter. Rainey watched him, careful not to disturb the silence. An intelligent criminal needed time to process, to look at the circumstances from all angles. He had to know he was cornered before he would give over to damage control. Rainey let a full minute go by before she prodded him.

"If Wendy is still alive, you helping us find her will look good to the prosecution. Is she still alive, Edward?"

He looked up from his contemplation, making eye contact with Rainey. The supreme sadist to the end, still thrilled with the suffering of others, Teague calmly said, "I don't know."

He was now watching Rainey, waiting for her reaction. It was probably not what he expected.

"Dr. Edward Teague, well-respected research fellow, an up and comer. People are going to want to know what happened. How does a man who has a happy marriage, a noble job, and a bright future go so far off the deep end? What will that tale be, Doctor? The only thing you'll ever control from this moment forward is your side of the story."

He turned his eyes to the floor, mute again. Rainey fought internal battles of her own. She repeated the silent mantra, *Keep it together*, to the voice in her head screaming for vengeance. *Don't lose it now*, she told herself. *He's so close. Keep it together.*

After another minute and a half of listening to Teague sigh and snort, while he attended to the discussion in his mind, Rainey prodded again.

"What are you having trouble with, Edward? Maybe I can help you process what needs to happen now. What are your concerns?"

The first real truthful thing spouted from Teague's mouth. "I can't believe this is happening."

"What can't you believe?" Rainey knew the answer but wanted to see if he would say it.

"I can't believe I'm sitting here—that this is all happening."

Rainey tried to sound compassionate. "You did so much of it right, you can't believe you made a small mistake with such significant consequences. An act of hubris, Edward, was all that was necessary to bring you down. That flirt with danger, the moment you slipped that essay into Wendy's hand, you knew it was a risk, a gloriously exciting risk. You lost the gamble, and the game is over. Pride has no place here in this room. You have limited choices. The police will tear your life to shreds and get what they need. Your participation is not necessary to reserve your spot on death row in Central Prison. Help yourself out, Edward. Where can we find Wendy?"

Rainey waited again, listening to Teague's breathing. He switched positions, trying to find comfort that was not coming, not mentally or physically, for a very long time.

"What is your biggest concern, Edward?"

He lost his façade for a brief second, and Rainey saw the little boy beneath the polished man.

"Call me Eddie," he said, as casually as an exchange over a cocktail might have been.

"Eddie," Rainey complied immediately with his wishes, "what are we going to do? How can I help you get through this?"

Teague said, "Don't tear up my wife's place. Julia has spent a lot of time painstakingly refurbishing each piece. She remanufactured the 1810 wallpaper. It's her dream to see it entirely restored."

"Eddie, I don't want them to tear up your wife's things, either. You obviously care a great deal about your wife. There is no reason to drag Julia down with you. Tell us what we need to know. Where is Wendy?"

Teague dropped the professor charade. Eddie Teague, the flawed man, planted both feet squarely on the floor, sat up straight in the chair, rubbed his hands on his thighs, sighed loudly, and gave up.

"There is a storm cellar."

#

12:15 PM, Friday, March 6, 2015
The Hammond Family Estate
Cape Fear River
Buckhorn Road, Chatham County, NC

Within seconds of learning of Teague's confession, Chatham County Sheriff's Department personnel sped toward the old Hammond place. Deputy Rosie Rivera passed the tree-lined carriage drive moments ago. An eight-year veteran of the department, Rivera was canvassing homes for the task force when the call came over the radio. Familiar with Julia Hammond Teague and her husband, the handsome professor, she had spoken to them after the Wilde sexual assault near the estate. Rosie remembered thinking what a lovely couple they were.

"You just never know about folks," Rosie said inside her patrol car as she hit the siren and lights.

After a swiftly maneuvered three-point turn on the narrow country road, she powered the patrol car back toward the well-worn drive. At one time, the estate had been large, spanning both sides of the river for several miles and dating back to the late 1700s. Time and finances took a toll on the family holdings. All that remained was the old home and the ten acres surrounding it. Rosie knew all that because she'd been pouring over land deeds along the river, investigating every hunting cabin, fishing camp, and lean-to in that part of Chatham County. The task force believed the Triangle Terror was connected to the area somehow. Rosie took it personally that someone hunted women in her county—damn personally.

"Right behind you, Rivera," Haywood called over the radio.

She could see the lights of his patrol car in her rearview mirror as she slowed to turn into the drive. Rosie killed the siren and followed the path into the pine woods. The radio filled with chatter. An ambulance was on the way. Detectives, supervisors, crime scene techs, they were all on the move, but at the moment, Deputy Rosie Rivera was the only one on site. Dispatch said the victim would be found in a storm cellar. No mention was made of a perpetrator's presence, but Rosie's heart still pumped with the speed of the adrenaline rush.

"Let her be alive," she whispered.

After having been on scene when the young girl was pulled from the river yesterday, Rosie prayed the outcome would be different for this victim. She heard it was a fellow cop, a young Durham police officer.

"Hang on, girl, we're coming," Rosie said as she slid the patrol car's transmission into park.

She rolled down the window and listened. She heard Haywood's siren die on the breeze. The leaves rustled, birds chirped; all seemed peaceful if she discounted the sound of distant sirens closing in on the old river home on the banks of the Cape Fear. The restoration was going well. In the two years since she had taken possession of the property, the worn, rotting exterior had been "restored to its original Regency splendor," so Julia Teague had proudly proclaimed. Rosie felt a little sorry for the woman. If this house became linked to all the murders and rapes, Julia Hammond Teague might as well rename it the Triangle Terror Bed and Breakfast and charge people to stay there. Fans of the macabre would come with or without permission.

Haywood's patrol unit pulled to a stop beside Rosie's. She heard him check in with dispatch over the radio before they both exited the cars.

He turned to her. "No one is supposed to be here, but you know, be ready. Any ideas on the location of the storm cellar?"

Rosie pulled her weapon and led the way. "I think it's on the other side of the house."

208

Haywood came up beside her, weapon raised and spoke into the radio microphone on his shoulder, "Dispatch, be advised. Officers on foot, east side of the property."

"Isn't that a cellar over there?" Rosie asked, pointing at a rock structure, the majority of which was buried underground.

Wooden doors on the slanted entryway were chained and padlocked shut.

Haywood had aimed his weapon at the lock, before Rosie yelled, "Hey, wait a minute. You don't know where that bullet is going to go."

Rosie holstered her weapon and walked over to the doors. "Hello. This is the Sheriff's department. Is anybody down there?"

The doors started bouncing. Someone was directly under them, pushing frantically. The sound of muffled screams from a gagged mouth reached Rosie's ears.

"Hang on! Hang on! We'll get you out. Move away from the doors." Rosie took off running, yelling back over her shoulder at Haywood. "I have bolt cutters in my unit."

Haywood grabbed his shoulder radio. "Dispatch, we have someone in the storm cellar. She's alive. Expedite rescue."

#

12:30 PM, Friday, March 6, 2015
Durham County Sheriff's Department
Interview Room 212B
Durham County, NC

Rainey heard the words, "She's alive," from Sheila's lips and exhaled loudly.

She hadn't realized the tension in her body until she relaxed.

She heard the rest of Sheila's statement, "They don't have her out yet, but contact has been made with someone alive in the cellar."

Rainey turned back to Teague. He was smiling, a genuine, joyful smile. She stared at him, wondering what he had to be so pleased about. He certainly shouldn't be glad he left a living witness to his crimes, especially not one who was sure to have recognized him.

Without turning around to face her, Rainey told Sheila, "Tell them to be careful. Someone should read this guy his rights and get him in cuffs before he says another word."

Teague's smile turned to a smirk. The pleasant lilt left his voice. He shook his head from side to side. "Wendy, Wendy, Wendy. Too eager to please, that one."

"Well, well. Welcome to the room, Eddie. No need for a charade now, I suppose?"

Two deputies entered and moved over to Teague. They stood him up against the wall and searched him. When his shirt was lifted, Rainey saw the bruises he claimed were from falling.

"It looks like someone fought a bit harder than you were prepared for, Eddie. Oh, now that must really hurt. She damn near kicked your ass. What'd you have to do, knock her out with a flashlight, like the others?"

"Don't answer that until I read you your rights," one of the deputies said.

Teague remained quiet while the deputies cuffed his hands in front of him, connected the cuffs to a waist chain, and then attached that to another chain bolted to the wall. When they were finished, Teague was returned to the chair in the corner. The taller deputy read the Miranda rights to the new prisoner. The shorter one put a rights waiver on the table in front of Teague.

Rainey taunted him, "Feel the walls closing in, Eddie?"

Sheila stepped back into the room, holding her cell phone to her ear. "They are going in now, Rainey."

Teague smiled so broadly, Rainey knew she wasn't going to like what they found.

#

12:35 PM, Friday, March 6, 2015
The Hammond Family Estate
Cape Fear River
Buckhorn Road, Chatham County, NC

Rosie leaned into the bolt cutters with all her strength until the steel hasp popped from the stress. Haywood stood by, weapon still pointed at the cellar doors. The word came down to be cautious, and he was taking no chances.

"Rivera, maybe we should wait for the dogs. It could be a trap."

Rosie yanked away the board that held the door shut. "The way she was beating on that door from inside, if it were rigged, she'd have been blown to bits before we got here."

Rosie knew what blown to bits looked like. Army life still haunted her dreams.

"Back away from the doors. We're coming in," she yelled down into the cellar.

Haywood took a step back as Rosie threw open the door. The sunlight flooded the small cellar. A severely beaten and gagged woman shuffled into view.

Haywood started yelling immediately, "Let me see your hands."

Rosie pushed past him and said, "Put that away. Can't you see she's tied up?" She climbed down the steps to the young woman, who had now begun to sob. "It's okay, honey. You're safe now. We got you. We got you."

Rosie carefully pulled the gag from the woman's mouth and asked, "What's your name, honey?"

#

12:43 PM, Friday, March 6, 2015
Durham County Sheriff's Department
Interview Room 212B
Durham County, NC

Rainey listened to Sheila responding to someone on the phone, "I see. That's interesting. Please lock down the site. We need evidence techs in there ASAP. Search warrants are on the way."

Teague watched Rainey. He was intent on her every expression. She knew what he was doing and called him on it.

"You won't get the reaction you're looking for, the anger you so desperately want me to show. You want me to lose control, to somehow bolster your opinion that we are all capable of murderous rage. It won't happen. Not that I'm incapable. Touch my children and see. But you never had my sister in that storm cellar."

Sheila stepped closer. "It was Hannah Barker, the first fetish burglary victim. You were right, Rainey. His first was the most important." She asked a question about Teague as if he were no longer in the room. "So, what's this been all about? Why make us think he had Wendy?"

Rainey made sure he saw her sneer. "This was Eddie's last chance to cause and witness human suffering. The time we wasted with him could have cost Wendy her life. That would make his arrest somehow satisfying. Yes, he's caught, but he may have killed someone else in the process. A sadist to the end. Right, professor?"

"I'm sure the BAU will have plenty of time to examine my motives," Teague answered as the killer's swagger revealed itself. "I'll be a star interviewee like Big Ed Kemper, a brilliant criminal, the perfect study candidate."

"Kemper offered unique insight, Dr. Teague. You, they'll probably just send you a survey or two. You've already told us all we need to know in your class notes. The video and photographic evidence they will find, your computer history, and the files you kept on each target will be more revealing than anything you would tell us. You've left us nothing to wonder about, Teague. You never have to say another word."

Not having agents clamoring for his story and hearing he was not unique nor worthy of study did not sit well with the good doctor. He lashed out at Rainey.

"You still haven't found your precious sister. You didn't break my case. I made a mistake. You would never have known if I hadn't given Wendy that essay."

"You're probably right, Eddie. But that's what we do. The BAU doesn't break cases. We link behavior based on case studies. We tell investigators what to look for and then we wait for the ego of a guy like you to shout, 'Look at me. Look at me,' like the narcissistic brat you are. You are hardly unique."

He tried again to cause Rainey pain. "If they find your sister alive, tell her to come see me in prison. But then, what are the chances of that? She's been gone more than six hours. If she's still alive, she probably wishes she was dead by now."

"I really only have one question before I leave you," Rainey said as she stood to go.

"Why did I come down here today?" Teague laughed at his private joke.

"I want to know if someone could have taken Wendy through those woods at that hour of the morning without being seen?"

"Ah, ask the predator about what moves in his territory," Teague replied. "No, whoever has her took her in a car from her driveway or left her in the woods, probably dead, right out behind her house, while you've been here with me. It's cold out there today. Freezing rain coming down by now, I'll bet. Sure hope Wendy hasn't suffered too terribly and that this doesn't haunt you as your other mistakes have—"

Rainey left the room, letting the door close on Teague's words. She had made it all the way to the bathroom before her knees began to shake. She locked herself inside a stall and leaned her back against the door. The emotional energy she held at bay for the past hour had to go somewhere. Deep breaths and focused thoughts would calm the shakes and set her right.

"Come on, Rainey. You've ridden this horse before," she said aloud.

Sheila's voice followed. "You okay, Rainey?"

"Yeah, just give me a minute."

"I came to tell you Jedidiah Lilly is in Interview C. He isn't alone."

Rainey took a deep, slow breath, counting in her head, *one, two, three, four.* She held the breath, counting again, *one, two, three, four.* She blew it out, *one, two, three, four.* She counted to four again and then restarted the cycle. *Shut it out, all of it,* she thought.

In her mind, Rainey's father's presence remained as a voice of reason. She heard him say, "Focus on the numbers and the cycle. Calm the storm, Rainey. Calm the storm."

After a full minute of rhythmic breathing, she was ready to exit the stall. Sheila waited while Rainey washed her hands and face.

"I don't know how you can look so calm on the surface," Sheila said after Rainey finally gave her eye contact. "Teague had sweat popping out on his forehead, and you sat there cool and unruffled."

"That's what this situation called for. Had I let him see a speck of concern or fear, even a second when I wasn't in control of the room, he would have pounced on that. You're going to see something different in this next interview. Are you ready?"

Sheila smiled at her. "Yes, I'm ready. I have three suspects in custody for three different crimes in less than an hour. No need to stop you now."

Rainey walked toward the door to the hall. "I didn't get a message back from those kids and Brooks hasn't located the phone yet. I hope they just ran. I hope we aren't too late."

Sheila asked, "Is there anything I can do?"

Rainey stopped with her hand on the door handle. What was she missing? What clue had she not seen?

"One of those kids, Henrique—they call him Hurricane or Cane. He came from New Orleans, displaced by Katrina. He was arrested and put back in the system a few weeks ago. Can you find that cop? Maybe he knows where these kids go when they run."

"I'll see what I can find out," Sheila said. "If this isn't the answer, what else can we do to find Wendy? Can we be doing it now?"

"Teague's right. If he didn't take her, she was taken in a car or left somewhere nearby. Find the neighbors at work, the ones no one spoke to this morning, the ones that left before I got there, before sun up. Maybe they saw something." Rainey pulled the door open. "Get the dogs out there. Search the woods."

#

1:10 PM, Friday, March 6, 2015
Durham County Sheriff's Department
Interview Room 212C
Durham County, NC

They stood when she entered. Jedidiah Lilly and Nick Prentiss wore identical fake smiles—until Nick saw Rainey.

"Good afternoon," Jedidiah began. "Are you the one that summoned me with that grotesque photo? I assure you, there are better ways to ask for an audience."

"It would only be grotesque if one knew exactly where that particular mole is located," Rainey said with a smile. "Thank you for confirming the boys' story."

"I've confirmed nothing," the flustered Lilly exclaimed.

Rainey ignored him and directed, "Have a seat." When the two men hesitated to follow her order, she applied more authority to the command, "Sit down."

The men looked at each other and then slowly lowered themselves down into the chairs on the other side of the table.

"May I ask who you are, what agency you represent?" Jedidiah wasn't used to taking orders.

Rainey pulled her phone from her pocket, touched the screen a few times, and then put the phone down on the table in front of the men.

"I am the person who has the picture of your penis, Mr. Lilly. Or should I say, I have a copy of the picture of your penis taken by a teenage male prostitute. That young man and another were found murdered. Two other boys, who can verify the existence of this picture and that they previously encountered this identifying mole while confined to your conversion camp, are now missing. I want your pimp unless you brought him and that's you, Nick."

"Now wait just a minute. I have no such mole," Jedidiah complained.

"You're here, Mr. Lilly. You have or had a mole just like that or you wouldn't be. Did you have it taken off after the boys took the picture and word got around?" Rainey asked and dashed his hopes with, "You'd be better off if you hadn't. You could have argued pixelation made it hard to identify. Now, the jury will only know you tried to cover something up."

Nick sat quietly by, saying nothing, but Rainey could see he was thinking very hard. It was as if he wasn't listening, but was running scenarios of his own making through his mind.

Rainey watched him but continued to hammer at Jedidiah. "I don't think you are capable physically or mentally of snapping those two boys' necks. Who would do something like that for you, Reverend Lilly? Who has as much to lose as you? You know who killed these boys. You know who is cleaning up the mess. I need a name. Now!" Rainey slammed her hand down on the table.

Nick spoke. "Can you keep the Reverend out of this?"

Rainey laughed. "Are you kidding? All he has left is a Jim Bakker swan dive into the 'Forgive me, I'm a sinner' pond of mercy and hope the good people of his congregation see fit not to let him drown. And why are you so concerned about him? You're going down for pandering. You lived on the street and now you turn around and sell those children to these sick fucks. What the hell is wrong with you?"

"It's safer for them if I set them up. I know the men involved. I'm trying to help them," Nick said, defending his actions.

"It was so safe that two are dead and three are unaccounted for," Rainey countered.

The sound of loud voices and a scuffle had erupted from the hall mere seconds before a heavily muscled, uniformed Durham officer stormed into the room, with several deputies trying to restrain him.

"Don't say anything, Dad," he shouted.

Jedidiah Lilly stood up. "Son, what have you done?"

Just that fast the case of the murdered boys was well on the way to being solved. Sheila walked into the room after the deputies gained control of Officer Jedidiah Lilly, Jr.

"Where was this guy this morning?" Rainey asked.

"It wasn't him, Rainey. He was at the gym at five this morning and on duty by seven. He did not take Wendy."

CHAPTER TEN

1:40 PM, Friday, March 6, 2015
Wendy King's Residence
Chatham County, NC

"They ought to just tear that house down," the woman said.

Rainey parked on the street in front of Wendy's house and had just exited the car when the woman in the winter running suit stepped off the curb. Fit and proudly wearing her Senior Olympics sun visor, even as the sleet began to fall, she appeared in her late seventies and was moving at a pretty good clip toward Rainey.

She extended her gloved hand and introduced herself. "Hello. I'm Rita James. You have to be the older sister Wendy talked about. You look so much alike."

Rainey shook Rita's extended hand. "Yes, ma'am. I'm Rainey Bell. Why do you say that about the house?"

"That makes two young women snatched out of there in the last ten years. It's cursed, or the guy that took them lives close by," Rita said.

Rainey was immediately intrigued. She had not thought to ask about crimes committed ten years ago at Wendy's house, not that anyone would have. However, Rainey had forgotten the first rule of crime analysis and zeroed-in on the prominent suspects. Suspects clouded evidence interpretation. The men she questioned were all guilty of something, but not her sister's abduction. Back at the house to start over, this new bit of knowledge was as good a place as any to begin.

Rainey asked the neighbor, "Do you have a basis for the assumption that he's close by?"

"My husband, Earl, and I were one of the first to buy a house in this subdivision." Rita pointed at the house directly across the street from Wendy's home. "We lived right over there for the last twenty-six years. At least, I have. Earl passed six months after Joanne Bonner went missing in 2005."

"I'm sorry for your loss," Rainey said.

Her words left smoke trails as temperatures plummeted with the arrival of the cold front's arctic blast. Rainey watched sleet pellets bounce from Rita's visor bill while she explained the activities in the neighborhood ten years ago.

"I think he worried himself sick over who took her. She vanished without a trace. The two years prior, cats and dogs went missing, people's trash cans were set on fire, and everyone kept their doors locked. After Joanne went missing, it all came to a stop. I've read enough true crime novels to see the correlation. Earl retired from the Marines. He looked on the folks in this neighborhood as part of his family. He started the neighborhood watch. I think losing Joanne broke him."

"Did they ever find her?"

"No, they never did. I talked to Wendy about it when the Triangle Terror started up. I thought he'd come back, the one that worried us those two summers. I just heard on the news that it was that professor expert they had working on the case. Can you believe that?"

"You just never know, do you?" Rainey commented but did not explain she was the one who ended the professor's life of crime. She was focused on one aspect of Teague's confession. "He doesn't have Wendy, and that's my primary concern at the moment."

"I'm sure you're worried sick."

Rainey answered, "Yes, we all are," and then asked Mrs. James, "Did you speak with the police this morning? Did you remind them of the unsolved case?"

"No, I was at my daughter's house last night. I came home about an hour ago."

"Did the police have any suspects in the Bonner case?"

"I don't know if they did or not, but Earl thought he'd narrowed it down. He had a stroke before he had any proof. He went into the hospital and never came home."

"But he thought he knew who took the Bonner woman? Did he tell you?"

Rita turned her back to Wendy's house as if she didn't want the lingering police on the lawn to read her lips.

"Buddy Cashion, Juanita's boy. Earl wasn't sure, but he was watching Buddy like a hawk. The Cashions moved in right after we did. Buddy was just a baby. We watched that boy grow up. He was always shy and quiet. He was thirteen when he found his daddy hanging in the workshop out back. After that, Buddy turned dark, very dark."

Rainey grew more interested in Rita's story. Like the rest of the homes in the neighborhood, Wendy's shared fences with the houses on either side. The dwellings also shared identical floor plans with slight variations in exterior presentation. Both Wendy's house and the Cashions' had a small workshop or storage building at the back of the lot. Each fenced backyard had a gate allowing access to the Eagles Spur Rail running trail, which wound through the pine barren to the tip of Jordan Lake. Composed of sandy swamp, shrubs, and small pines, the outwash wetlands were the ideal place to hide a body. Sheila had told Rainey before she left the Sheriff's Department that the search team dogs were deployed. Dead or alive, the dogs were the best chance of finding Wendy in the woods.

"Mrs. James, did the police question Buddy about the missing woman?"

"That's the weird part. They did question him, and he confessed, but his story did not match the details of the crime. He was not in his right mind. He would have admitted to killing

221

Kennedy at that point. Juanita had to send him to Dix Hill to get help. I think he lives in a halfway house now. He's okay as long as he stays on his medications. Juanita said Buddy has schizophrenia just like his daddy."

While Rainey reached for her phone, she continued probing for information.

"Juanita mentioned that her son didn't like her boyfriend. Have you seen Buddy around?"

Rita glanced over her shoulder at Juanita's home. "Gary Don Miller is a convicted sex offender. He is a reformed heroin addict who claims the girl was fifteen and came on to him. All I need to know is he went to prison for it and now lives across the street from me. Juanita sure can pick 'em."

"And Buddy doesn't like him?" Rainey said, reminding Rita of her question.

"I haven't seen Buddy in years. It's Travis that doesn't like Gary Don. Travis is from Juanita's first marriage to Barney Odom. Barney was killed in an accident on a barge when a frayed cable broke, cut him nearly in half. Juanita got a lot of money from the settlement. She married Johnny Cashion afterward, had Buddy, and bought that house. Travis was five when they moved in."

Rainey held her phone, having already typed the beginning of the email to Brooks while listening to Buddy Cashion's history. She sought clarification from Rita, "What is Buddy's name? I'd like to check with a friend on his whereabouts."

"He's John Cashion, Jr. I'm pretty sure that's it," Rita said.

Rainey typed in Buddy's name and sent her request for information concerning all members of the Cashion household to Brooks, with an accompanying text to her private cell number to get her attention.

Rita continued her narrative. "Juanita is a good woman, but the men in her life are troubled." She paused before adding, "Travis seems okay, I guess. He works in the banking business. I think that's what Juanita said. His wife, Reece, is attractive, but she doesn't come here often because of Gary Don."

The sound of young boys mouthing off at cops reached Rainey's ear, just as the gate to Wendy's backyard flew open. Two heavy-breathing uniformed officers appeared unamused by the two handcuffed and complaining teenagers. Steam rose from all four of their bodies, signaling recent physical activity.

"I want a lawyer," the smaller boy said.

The other asked, "What did I do wrong, officer? I was fuckin' walkin' on a walkin' trail."

Rainey recognized the voice and the teenager that went with it.

"Excuse me. I need to deal with this. Thank you for the information," she said to Mrs. James and left to intercept the duo.

"Rainey Bell. Hey, I'mma need that bail money," Cane said.

Barron smiled in relief. "Hey, she knows we ain't stealin' nothin'. She knows us. Hey, Rainey, tell these guys Wendy told me to come here."

Rainey gave the officers the respectful dip of her head they deserved and spoke to them as if the boys were not there, "Officers, I'm Rainey Bell. I am consulting on a case with the Sheriff's Department involving these two material witnesses. If you'd like to call Sergeant Detective Sheila Robertson to verify that, I'll wait here."

One of the officers smiled and began removing the handcuffs from Cane. "I know who you are. If you want the paperwork that goes with these clowns, be my guest."

The other officer followed suit. Rainey wanted to hug him when he bent to look Barron in the eye. "You're too young to be out here. Get off the street, kid." He stood and playfully rubbed the top of Barron's head. "And don't run from the police. That's how you get hurt."

"Thanks," Barron said to Rainey after the policemen walked away.

"Where have you guys been?" Rainey asked. "I tried to reach you all morning. Conner sent Wendy a message saying you were missing."

Cane answered, "We had to run from that cop that keeps harassing us. His name is Lilly, too. Any connection to the old man?"

"As a matter of fact, yes," Rainey answered.

"Anyway, my phone battery is dead and I lost the charger cord," Cane said.

Rainey motioned to them. "Come with me, and we'll fix that problem."

When Rainey opened her car door, Cane said, "Damn, girl, this ride is bitchin'."

"I'm not a girl. I'm a woman. I have a name. I'm not your homie, so don't talk to me like one. I'm the person that just got you out of handcuffs. Show some respect for yourself and me. Give me your phone."

Cane handed Rainey his phone, but he couldn't keep his mouth shut, "Who pissed on your donut? You're all cop when Wendy ain't around. And what are all these cops doing here?"

Barron chimed in with his softly spoken question, "Where's Wendy?"

Rainey placed Cane's phone in the rapid charger she pulled from the console of her car and handed it to Cane. "Hold this." She pushed the button on the key fob to open the trunk. The boys followed her to the rear of the car. "Wendy is missing. She was taken from her house this morning," Rainey said while digging through a leather bag in the trunk.

Cane commented further on the car, "This ride is legit. Is this the 2013 SRT8?"

Barron, though smaller and younger, showed no fear when he elbowed the much larger Cane in the ribs. "Didn't you hear what she said? Wendy's in trouble."

Rainey smiled at Barron and answered Cane. "It's a special order pursuit model. I'll be happy to explore your fascination later." She pulled some cables from the bag and closed the trunk lid. Moving back to the driver's seat, Rainey shook the accumulated ice pellets from her hair and sat down. She held out her hand, "Give me your phone."

Cane handed the phone to her, watching as she removed it from the rapid charger and plugged cables into the car and the phone. Rainey fired up the laptop attached to the console and talked while she worked.

"Wendy needs me right now, but I need you guys not to disappear. I can't take you myself, but if you let me, I'll have someone come drive you to a safe place. You'll be fed, given clean clothes, and a place to sleep until we can figure out a permanent solution to your problems. Your other choice is state custody."

Barron was not concerned with his own predicament. "What happened to Wendy?"

"Someone took her this morning. She's been missing now for over seven hours. I thought the picture had something to do with it, but that's not the case. I don't have a clue who took her or where she is." Rainey smiled at Barron. The little guy was visually distressed about Wendy. She asked him, "Got any ideas?"

Rainey worked on the laptop while listening to Barron's response.

"I stay here sometimes, out in the storage building. She put a heater and some blankets in there for me. Wendy doesn't want anyone to know. She said she'd get in trouble for not turning me over to state custody."

Rainey nodded. "She would."

"I only came here when I'd been cold so long I couldn't feel my toes. Wendy left peanut butter, crackers, and some bottled water out for me. Sometimes she left a few bucks. She put a heater in there when it turned cold."

Cane punched Barron playfully in the arm. "So this is where you disappear to. You said you had a date taking care of you."

Barron, head down and ashamed, replied, "I didn't want anybody to know I couldn't make it on my own, but I only do tricks when I got no other choice."

Cane laughed and wrapped his arm around his little friend's shoulder. "Connor goes home to get fed and get clothes once a week, more if his dad is gone. Get what you can where you can, little man. Street rules."

Barron smiled up at his friend and then turned back to Rainey. "Sometimes when Wendy knew I was here, she'd bring me hot chocolate or warm food. The last time I came by, the place was trashed. I cleaned it up and told her about it. I didn't want Wendy to think I did that to her stuff."

"Did she seem concerned?" Rainey asked, still occupied with Cane's phone.

Barron shook his head. "She said one of the other guys probably followed me. I try to be real careful. I only brought Cane because we were both running from that cop. He's a freak."

"You don't have to worry about him anymore. He was arrested about an hour ago for murdering your friends."

Cane and Barron exchanged fist bumps. Rainey finished loading the application onto Cane's phone. She unplugged it from her car and handed it and a charger to Cane.

"Here you go. Don't lose this one," she said. "I loaded an app on your phone. See that icon right there." Rainey pointed at the screen. "If you are in trouble and need help, hit that and it will send a signal to me and tell me where you are. On the flipside, I can find you whenever I need to."

"You lojacked my phone," Cane said, seeming unsure as to whether he liked that prospect.

"I wasn't lying to that officer. You are a material witness and I need to be able to find you later. I just don't have time to deal with you right now. I need to find my sister."

A ringtone announced the arrival of a text message on Rainey's phone. She pulled it from her coat pocket. Before stepping out of the car, she grabbed the wool wrap Katie had given her for Christmas. She used it to shield her head against the sleet that fell heavier as the afternoon skies turned a deeper gray. Time was running out for Wendy.

Rainey closed and locked the door as she read the message from Brooks. "The phone that sent the email is on and right there with you."

Rainey sent a return text. "I have him. Thanks. Any info on the Cashion family?"

Barron asked, "Is it about Wendy? Have they found her?"

Rainey could tell this kid really cared for her sister. She put a hand on Barron's shoulder. "No, she's still missing. I need to send you two somewhere safe. Will you wait right here for a man driving a black Escalade? He's ginormous, so you don't have to wonder if he's the right guy. His name is Mackie."

The boys nodded in agreement and Rainey made the call. Mackie would transport them to the Women's Center. They were still young enough to be allowed into the segregated section for women with teenage boys. Some of the women at the center were too traumatized to be around anything resembling a man.

"Mackie is five minutes away," she said as she tucked her phone into one of her coat pockets and then put on the black leather gloves she retrieved from the other. "Don't be assholes at the shelter. The people there will be trying to help you. No one is interested in putting you back into a bad situation. Okay? We're cool?"

Barron stared up at Wendy's house with flakes of ice in his long eyelashes. "I hope you find her. She's nice, you know?"

Rainey slipped an arm over the young man's shoulders. "Yeah, she is nice. I need to go look for her. Wait here for Mackie, okay?" She glanced over at Cane. "Don't rabbit. Get off the street. This is your chance."

Mrs. James approached, now wearing a heavy winter coat and hat. She carried two Styrofoam cups full of steaming liquid. "You young men look cold. I brought hot chocolate."

Rainey introduced the teens. "Mrs. James, this is Wendy's friend Barron and his friend, Cane. My associate is going to pick them up in a few minutes. Say thank you, boys."

Cane and Barron responded quickly and in unison, "Thank you, ma'am."

"You're very welcome. I've seen this one around," Rita said, pointing at Barron. "Wendy told me she allowed him on her property, so I wouldn't call the police."

"Ms. Bell," a voice from the yard called out.

227

Rainey turned to see an officer beckoning her to come.

Rita solved her dilemma. "Go on. I'll stay with the boys."

"You two behave. People are trying to help you," Rainey said as she backed away from the teens.

Barron spoke up before she could turn away. "When you find Wendy, tell her I said, 'It's a deal.' She'll know what I'm talking about."

Rainey smiled back at him. "I'll do that, Barron."

She turned her back on the boys and Rita James and hustled up the driveway, once again entering the last space in which her sister had been seen alive. One thought above all others rang in her ears.

Wendy is running out of time.

#

Rainey closed Wendy's front door and immediately noted the silence. The crime scene techs completed evidence collection hours ago. The search dogs were loaded up and taken away. Only two officers remained to guard the scene. They did so from the warm interior of their patrol units.

The sleet had turned to freezing rain soon after Mackie left with the boys. Rainey waved to him from the yard while listening to the team leader explain his reasoning for calling off the search.

"We pulled the dogs way out away from the house. They came right back here every time. The last traceable scent is at the back fence. Maybe he had an ATV or something back there. I can't explain it. She just vanished from the face of the earth."

"Did you look out here? Could she have been taken in a car from the driveway?"

"Anything is possible. Her scent is all over this property. What I can tell you is she crossed the trail into the woods, but the dogs say she returned to the fence. We're going to move down to the parking lot after this weather passes."

"Thanks," Rainey said.

Feeling dejected and at a loss as to what to do next, Rainey parted from the remaining law enforcement personnel and walked into Wendy's house alone, where she stood now waiting for the answer to her question to reveal itself. *Who took Wendy King?*

She pulled the wrap off and shook the ice loose before draping it around her neck. With her back against the front door, she closed her eyes and inhaled deeply. The aroma of cinnamon filled her nose from the potpourri scattered on the carpet. Rainey recognized the scent from Wendy's backpack along with a hint of her perfume. With her eyes closed, she could see Wendy grinning mischievously, coaxing her big sister into yet another adventure.

The ringing in her pocket broke the spell of silence.

She pulled out her phone and after checking the name on the screen said, "Okay, Brooks, make my day."

"Rainey Bell, little Wendy landed next door to the gold medal winner of the Fucked-Up Family Olympics. Gary Don Miller, the live-in boyfriend, is a convicted sex offender. He did time for having a sexual relationship with his last girlfriend's thirteen-year-old daughter. He found Jesus in prison. Has lived a stellar life since being released and works for the Towne Bakery."

"That explains his early morning leaving," Rainey interjected. "No parole violations, not even a traffic ticket?"

Brooks laughed. "No, he's squeaky clean. Like by the book, never missed a day of work, in the church pew every Sunday morning clean. Call me cynical, but you know what that usually means."

Rainey nodded though Brooks couldn't see her. "Yes, he's covering something up or fighting demons minute by minute. One misstep and he's back to his old tricks. He's either already violating or trying desperately not to."

"He met Juanita Baily Odom Cashion through the prison pen pal program sponsored by her church. She visited him a lot toward the end of his sentence. Talk about bad luck with men. Juanita's first husband, Barney, died tragically, but not before she 'fell down the stairs' a few times, or so say the ER reports, which the doctor thought was bullshit. Saved from her abuser by fate, Juanita then married John Cashion, Sr., who was medically discharged from the Army and deposited in a psychiatric hospital for several years, before he met and married Juanita. The medical profession provided him with every known treatment for schizophrenia and depression. Sadly, it was not enough."

Rainey interrupted the monologue. "I know about Senior. What happened to Junior? Where is Buddy Cashion?"

Brooks moved on to the son. "John 'Buddy' Cashion, Jr. spent his sixteenth birthday in the custody of the state and the next seven years in one psychiatric facility after another. He is a diagnosed schizophrenic. He lives in a halfway house and is able to hold a job as long as he takes his meds and stays monitored by house staff. The problem is, Buddy was not at breakfast. He did not go to work. A search of his room found a stash of his medications, untaken. Buddy Cashion is out of touch, figuratively and literally."

"How do you know all that?" Rainey asked.

"I might have mentioned I worked for the FBI when I called the halfway house to check on Buddy."

"I admire your initiative," Rainey said. "Do you have a description?"

"Buddy Cashion grew to be a big boy. He's six feet two inches tall and weighs two-eighty-five. Long, dark hair and beard in the last ID photo for the state. Hazel eyes. No tats. No scars."

"Well, he is certainly large enough to have done the damage in this house," Rainey commented. "What can you tell me about the Joanne Bonner case?"

"Not a lot. Joanne was a young nurse, age twenty-six. She bought the home six months prior to her disappearance. She spoke with her best friend on the phone before going to bed. She was discovered missing the next day after she did not show up for a lunch date with her mother. Joanne Bonner was never seen again."

"I'll see if Sheila can pull the case file locally. Maybe we can talk to the original investigators."

"There is a mention of Juanita Cashion in an article about Joanne Bonner's dog. It seems that the dog was repeatedly taken to Joanne's parents' home a few miles away but returned each time. Juanita Cashion is quoted as saying, 'I'm not a dog person, but that dog is determined to lay out by my back gate. I suppose we'll just let it stay here until it finishes grieving.' They built it a house and fed it. The dog stayed until it died two years later. That's so damn sad."

Rainey's attention turned to the blood stained baseboard. She could see the shape of the smear more clearly from her current angle, or was it what she wanted to see? It appeared to be an arrow pointing next door.

"What did Mack say?" Rainey raised the question aloud.

A confused Brooks asked, "What?"

"No, not you," Rainey answered. "I'm just thinking out loud."

"Okay, you keep thinking. I'm going to do some more digging."

"Yeah, do that. Find out if Buddy Cashion has a car. It might be in his mother's name or his brother's name, Travis Odom."

"I'll call you back if I find anything. Be safe, Rainey Bell."

"Always, my friend. Always."

Rainey put the phone back in her pocket and walked to the other side of Wendy's house. She looked out the window toward Juanita Cashion's home. The car Juanita had been standing by when Rainey arrived was no longer in the driveway. A tap on the front door drew her attention, as one of the patrol officers stepped into the house.

"Ms. Bell, we've been called back to street patrol," he said. "The sleet and freezing rain makes for a busy traffic accident day."

"I understand," Rainey said. "I'll lock up when I'm done. I'll let someone know they can seal the scene."

"Great. I hope they find Officer King," he said, on his way out the door.

"Hey," Rainey called to him, stopping him before he could leave. "Did anyone search the yards on either side of this house?"

"Yes, I'm sure they did. I personally checked the one over there, the Cashion place. The lady was really nice. Nothing back there, not even a dog—just a little workshop with a padlocked door. That lock had not been opened in years. Mrs. Cashion didn't even have a key."

231

"Okay, thanks. Be careful out there," Rainey offered with a forced smile.

"Yeah, you too," the officer said and then closed the door behind him.

Alone again, Rainey walked to the kitchen at the back of the house. The window looked into Juanita's backyard. The view was less than stellar, as Rainey could see very little other than the shared wooden fence between the properties.

Don't go alone, Rainey said to herself. She immediately argued with herself. *It would be too easy. No way she's been over there this whole time, right?*

Rainey turned her back to the window and leaned against the counter, talking to herself aloud, processing what she knew.

"Mack repeated what Wendy said, 'Go home.' Why would she have said that unless she knew where the UNSUB's home was? She knew this person. Why not just go next door and ask Juanita Cashion if Wendy knew her son?"

Rainey decided on that course of action before calling in another request that could amount to nothing.

#

Knocks and doorbell ringing brought no response from Juanita Cashion's home. Rainey checked the windows in the garage to find no cars present. The cold dripping rain froze on contact with anything not moving. The spring buddings glistened with the glazing. Winter appeared unwilling to release its hold on the Triangle. Rainey pulled the wool wrap up to shield her head. Even after two years, she missed her long mane of thick curls in winter.

She walked over to the gate leading to the backyard. A quick check of the latch revealed it was unlocked. Rainey paused before she began her planned trespass and called Sheila.

When she answered, Rainey asked, "Any news?"

"No, and they've called everyone in to work on the traffic problems. I'm sorry, Rainey. When the weather clears, we'll send the dogs back out."

"I understand. Hey, since Teague is in custody, my legal connections to the department are complete, correct?"

Sheila sounded a bit alarmed when she answered, "That is correct. You are no longer acting as an agent for the police. What are you up to?"

"I have a hunch and I'm about to enter unlawfully, but you didn't hear that," Rainey said, peeking into Juanita's backyard.

"Where are you? Just in case this doesn't end well for you, I need to know where to begin the search for your body."

"I'm at Wendy's neighbor's house. Did you know Joanne Bonner went missing from Wendy's house in 2005 and the teenage neighbor was a suspect? That same neighbor, John 'Buddy' Cashion, Jr., is now twenty-six, diagnosed with schizophrenia, and living in a halfway house that hasn't seen him since yesterday."

"No, I did not know that," Sheila responded. "I'll look into it right away. Don't do anything stupid, Rainey, like sneak around a suspect's home alone."

Rainey slid the Glock from its holster and closed the gate behind her. "I'm just going to have a look around. No one is home. Call me back if you find out anything."

Rainey hung up before Sheila could admonish her further.

Okay, Rainey, see them coming, she reminded herself.

The father she and Wendy shared would often say, "Always, always be aware. If you see them coming, you got a chance."

She began her reconnaissance awash in sadness that Wendy never met Billy Bell. There had been so little time to tell her about him. Both their lives were full to the brim. If this turned out well, Rainey vowed to introduce Wendy to their father more thoroughly. It was that father's survival instinct-laden DNA she was counting on to keep her sister's heart beating.

Juanita's backyard was well kept. A slab of concrete outside the sliding glass doors housed patio furniture and a grill wrapped in protective winter-weather coverings. The few warm days at the beginning of the month urged tiny green shoots of new grass and flower bud sprouts to peek at the sun. Ice began to encase the tender new growth, and the winter-dried grass crunched under

Rainey's shoes. Zeroing in on the workshop at the back of the property, she moved to the center of the yard to get a full view of the small building.

She guessed it to be a fifteen-by-ten-feet rectangle placed in the corner with only two sides exposed to the yard. The unseen short side butted up to Wendy's fence. The long backside hugged the rear fence. A gate, the one Rainey supposed the dog refused to leave, was near the other short side of the shop. A small window, the kind cranked open from the inside, looked out at the gate. The long exterior wall facing the house had a door and another larger window. All of the windows were curtained, preventing a view of the inside.

Rainey checked back toward the house, looking for signs she was not alone. Nothing moved. A cloud of steam followed each breath from her lips, as she slowed her heart rate and listened. She heard only the tinkle of tiny ice pellets falling around her.

There is only one way to find out if she's in there, Rainey thought, as she stared at the workshop.

"Wendy, this right here is the fine line I was talking about between criminal behavior and doing the right thing," she said under her breath to the sister who could not hear her.

Rainey crossed to the building, where she examined the padlock and hasp. It appeared to be old and rusty, unopened for many years, but a look at the ground below the door told a different story. Tall grass left to grow through winter was bent and pulled under the door.

Rainey gripped the Glock a bit tighter. She briefly thought of calling for backup, but then she heard the unmistakable clink of metal landing on a cement floor. The sound came from inside the workshop. Rainey flattened herself against the exterior wall, away from the window and door. Her eyes focused on the hasp and lock. Although the lock appeared rusted shut, the fact remained that the door had been opened recently, trapping long blades of untrimmed Johnson grass inside the door jamb.

While Rainey contemplated the rusted lock and the noise from inside, the door and its frame began to move. Someone had rigged the door to appear secure, and that someone was exiting the building. She ducked between the side of the building and the fence.

A broad and thick man a few inches taller than Rainey emerged from the workshop. His head was covered with a hoodie sticking out from under the collar of a worn, green, Army field jacket. He bent to drop a pin in the bottom of the frame before heading for the back gate. He did not notice Rainey in the shadows, nor did he appear in a hurry to scurry away. He seemed confident that no one knew he was there. Rainey saw no need to change that impression and let him leave.

All right, let's see what you're hiding in the workshop, Buddy, Rainey thought, assuming the man who just exited the gate was Juanita's troubled son. He fit the physical description, but it did not matter whether it was Buddy Cashion or not. What mattered was finding Wendy alive.

She bent and removed the pin, slipping it into her pocket. With the pistol gripped in her right hand, Rainey slowly pulled the door open with her left. A master craftsman must have hung the hinges that concealed the secret to the frame's movement. She paused to listen for signs of life. She pulled the keychain from her pocket to access the tiny LED flashlight, took a deep breath, and entered the dark interior.

Closing the door behind her, Rainey slid the wrap off her head and used the flashlight to find an identical pinhole on the interior side of the frame. She dropped the pen in place before looking around the mostly empty workshop. One chair stood under a noose slung over the center ceiling beam, a ghoulish recreation of John Cashion, Sr.'s last moments on earth.

This kid didn't have a chance at a normal life.

Large cardboard boxes lined the back wall, each labeled with the words "Buddy's Things". Juanita had moved her son out of the house permanently. The beam of Rainey's flashlight fell on what looked like a nest of blankets and newspapers, a makeshift bed of sorts. As she grew closer, it became apparent the blankets and papers were stretched across a low storage bench along the wall. Reaching out to uncover what was concealed, Rainey was glad she wore gloves. She had removed only one layer of thin blanket material when she heard the cardboard box scrape across the floor behind her.

She whipped around, shining her little flashlight into the darkness. A bearded Buddy Cashion stared back at her from under his slick bald head. He was sticking halfway out one of the cardboard boxes, which led to a concealed trapdoor in the back wall of the building.

Rainey knew this had to be Juanita's youngest son. The familial resemblance was clear. Along with cutting out his meds, Buddy had shaved his head and used a razorblade to slice a newly scabbed-over design of intersecting lines into his forehead. This guy was seriously gone.

"Stop right there," Rainey said, the Glock aimed at Buddy Cashion's face.

"You're not supposed to be here," he said, still on his hands and knees. He cocked his head to one side, processing the scene, and then broke into a smile. "Oh, wow. It's you. Your hair is different, and you're older, but it's definitely you." He had risen to a kneeling position in front of her before he bowed his head. "Protector, I welcome thee back to the past."

"Are you Buddy Cashion?" Rainey demanded.

He raised his eyes to hers. "I am in the vessel which was once Buddy Cashion. I have evolved into a deeper understanding than the entity Buddy could comprehend. I am the Shaman Gelaph. I descend from the Olympian Spirits, and the warlord and ruler over Mars, Phaleg, tutors me in my quest to become a superior warrior in the realm."

With words like spirit, warlord, and superior warrior peppering his conversation, Rainey had reason to think twice about her response. She decided to stick with the present and reality for now.

"Where is Wendy King?"

"You mean the present day Protector Wendy King," Buddy answered with a smile. "It's hard to keep up. There's the Protector now and then you in the future. I knew I was right about her, uh, I mean you. I had to save you so you could fulfill the prophecy. I couldn't save the first one, but I got it right this time because you are here from the future, so that means you survived, right?"

Buddy began to stand.

Rainey shouted, "Freeze!"

Buddy ignored the warning. Both her presence and that of the weapon in her hand were inconsequential to Buddy's delusion. He stood to his full height, reached for the window curtain, slid it back, and flooded the room with soft gray light. He smiled down at her, where she knelt near the pile of blankets and papers. With his size and the limited space they both occupied, Rainey thought she would need to kill him with the first shot if he made a move. She dropped the key chain in her coat pocket and used both hands to grip the Glock, aiming for the golden triangle between his nipples and throat.

He responded, "You don't need the gun. You need not fear me. I have been given the task of guardian of the Protectors from the Olympian Spirits. My sole purpose is to keep the chosen ones safe. What can I do for you, Wendy King of the future?"

Rainey could see dried blood on his Army jacket and watched as his cheek twitched. This tick repeated every few seconds, a telltale sign of long-term antipsychotic medication usage. Buddy was most definitely a paranoid schizophrenic off his meds, suffering with hallucinations and delusions. His speech was clear, and he appeared well groomed and healthy. If the recent skinned head and scarring were disregarded, Buddy Cashion looked like an average directionless twenty-something might appear after a weekend of gaming. Rainey decided to try to reach him by giving the Shaman story credence. She lowered the weapon but did not put it away.

"Shaman Gelaph, I need to see young Wendy King. It's important."

Rainey watched Buddy turn his head as if he listened to an unseen speaker.

This hunch was confirmed when he said, "The high priestess seeks assurances you are not a trickster. The evil one has many soldiers. Are you an imposter?"

In the split second Rainey had to decide how to answer the Shaman's question without disturbing the obviously unbalanced man further, the incoming call jingle she assigned Danny trilled from her pocket. The sound startled Buddy into a defensive stance.

He shouted, "That is the proximity alert. You are a shape-shifter. You are a trickster."

Buddy produced a knife from his jacket sleeve and waved it in Rainey's direction. She raised the Glock again. Though shooting him without knowing what he'd done with Wendy wouldn't be wise, wounding him was out of the question.

"You don't want an injured bear standing between you and the exit," her father used to say.

"It's my phone, not an alarm," Rainey said.

Before Buddy had a chance to react, she pulled the phone from her pocket and looked at the screen. She silenced the ringtone and in the same motion touched the personal alarm program icon, alerting everyone in her close circle to her location and that she needed help. The only complication would be the locator wasn't exactly precise. Whoever came looking would have to search within one hundred yards, and they would start with Wendy's house. Unless they thought to call Sheila, who Rainey decided at that moment was going on her emergency contact list.

Thinking the authority of the Bureau and the truth might be to her advantage, she said, "It's the FBI. They know I'm here. They want to keep younger Wendy safe, too. Can you take me to her?"

Buddy glanced out the window toward the house and then glared at Rainey. "He's here. That was the alarm. You lied."

Rainey stood from her crouch. Calmly, she said, "Look at me. Look in my eyes. Tell me you don't see Wendy King."

Buddy stared at her, focusing on the green eyes Billy Bell gave both his daughters.

"You see her, don't you?" Rainey prodded.

"Yes, the eyes are the same, but you're taller."

238

"It's my shoes," Rainey said, dismissing the difference and hoping he would, too. "I need to see the younger me. The prophecy depends on this meeting."

Buddy wasn't convinced, but he slid the knife back up into his sleeve. "Phaleg told me none of this."

Rainey gave his delusions validity, but also assumed the power role a time traveling "Protector" would have in Shaman Gelaph's world.

She chastised him, "Phaleg did not warn me of the injuries you inflicted on young Wendy. Where is she? She needs my help."

Buddy explained, "The demon had marked her for destruction."

Paranoid but lucid in his logic, Buddy listened to an unseen voice and then said to Rainey, "But you should know this. You survived to be you now, I mean then, I mean, you know, in the future, right?"

Rainey's mind flew through appropriate replies and settled on, "I was hit in the head. My blood is on your coat. If I remembered what happened, I wouldn't be here asking you where my body is, would I?"

"Okay, we believe you," he said, and then looked out the window again. "The demon is coming. You need to go. If he finds you here, my work will have been for nothing."

From her vantage point, Rainey could not see whether someone other than a figment of Buddy Cashion's imagination approached. What she could see did not matter. His facial expression confirmed his sincere belief someone was out there.

"We'll go together," she suggested. "Take me to Wendy."

"He knows I moved her. I saw him preparing to take her as he took the first Protector. I acted too fast for him. I'm better trained this time. The demon will not have Wendy King."

"Great, you saved her. Now, where is she?" Rainey asked again. She held the Glock up for him to see. "I can protect all of us."

Buddy offered another excuse for not taking Rainey to Wendy, "If she sees you, it will cause a paradox."

"You watch too many movies," Rainey said while attempting to contain her excitement. Buddy had indicated Wendy was still alive. "The paradox, if there were such a thing, would already exist. The moment I appeared here we started rewriting history for Wendy King."

Rainey thought her reasoning sound. Buddy either accepted her explanation or his worry about the approaching demon took his focus. He slid the curtain back over the window, plunging them into darkness except for the glow from Rainey's phone. He dropped to his knees and signaled to her to do the same.

"Shh. He's here. Cover the light," Buddy said.

Rainey had played along, but her patience was waning. She stuck the phone back into her pocket, knowing it was pinging her location to five people who would search for her and never stop. She contemplated taking Buddy Cashion into some form of custody, but lacking handcuffs and seeing how he'd beaten the crap out of her much younger and stronger little sister, she focused on finding Wendy. She could simply sit tight and wait for the cops to deal with him. Surely by now, at least one of the alert receivers—Katie, Ernie, Mackie, Danny, and Brooks—had notified the appropriate authorities.

As Rainey opened her mouth to once again ask Buddy where Wendy was, the door began to rattle with someone's efforts to enter.

"I know you're in there, Buddy. Open the fucking door," a male voice demanded.

The door rattled a few times more.

The man outside changed tactics and softened his tone. "Buddy, what did you do with the girl?"

Buddy stood abruptly. Rainey stumbled backward with his movement. She tripped over something and landed in the blanket and newspaper nest. Buddy, fixated on the "demon" outside, yanked the curtain open again. With the sudden burst of light came the realization she had fallen into skeletal remains. While Buddy bobbed up and down in front of the window, Rainey concentrated on the skull that rolled out of the nest and came to rest next to her foot.

The morning began so promisingly, with a plan to breakfast with family and be thankful for her blessings. That plan had rapidly gone to hell from the moment Wendy did not answer her cell phone. Rainey thought her current situation, trapped inside a small building with a paranoid schizophrenic, had deteriorated rather rapidly with the addition of the skull at her feet, not to mention the "demon" outside the door and the delusional shaman on the inside with her.

Rainey stood and moved away from the nest of remains. She looked down at the skull. "Joanne Bonner, I presume?"

Buddy didn't answer her but yelled at the "demon" through the window. "Fuck you. I'm not going to let you take this one. The prophecy will be fulfilled." He ducked below the window and began frantically giving hushed orders to Rainey, "Listen to me. Leave through the back. I'll hold him here."

"Who is this?" Rainey asked, pointing at the skull.

Buddy's reaction to the skull was that of reverence due holy relics. He gently lifted the skull from the floor and placed it back on the nest of bones.

"She was the Protector called Joanne sent to keep me from the demon's touch, but she wasn't strong enough."

The man outside grew more insistent. The door shook violently. Rainey watched the pin bounce and jiggle, but it held—for now.

Rainey pointed at the door. "Did that demon kill the Protector Joanne?"

"Yes," Buddy said, as he lovingly covered Joanne Bonner's remains with a threadbare, dirt-stained blanket. "When they let me come home again, I found her right where I knew he left her. I brought her here."

"Who is the demon? Who is out there?"

"Malphas, the Prince of Hell. He killed the King. He killed the Protector. He will kill the queen if I betray him. You must leave."

The man outside pounded on and kicked at the door. "Who are you talking to? Is she in there with you? Open the damn door, Buddy."

Rainey thought someone should be coming to find her soon. Even with an ice storm in progress and the weather-challenged drivers of the Triangle, surely at least one patrol car was in the area. Buddy thought the second in command to Satan was banging on the door, so she'd prefer law enforcement arrive sooner than later.

Buddy continued tucking the dirty blanket around his sacred pile of bones. The man at the door continued his ranting and banging.

In contrast to the chaos around him, Rainey spoke in a calm but direct voice to Buddy, "I'm not leaving without Wendy King, and if that is the Prince of Hell out there, a lock isn't going to stop him. Tell me where Wendy is so I can help save her."

Buddy, as paranoid schizophrenics tend to do, added a new element to continue his fantasy. "It's in the hands of the fates now. As long as I held the Protector's bones in secret, I had the power to keep him away. He'll destroy me now."

Oh, my god, you're killing me here, Rainey thought but remained quiet, listening to the sudden stillness.

The knocking and banging stopped. The voice on the other side of the door went silent. Rainey moved over to the window and peeked out. There were too many blind spots to know for sure he was gone, but she could see no one. A smile crept onto her lips when she heard the siren growing closer.

Rainey chuckled and said to Buddy, "It seems Satan's second is afraid of the police. I think he's gone."

Buddy jumped up. "The police can't see him. He tricks them. He wears a smiling face. I'll be blamed like before. I won't go back to the hospital."

Now Rainey had an agitated paranoid schizophrenic on her hands.

"Hang on. Don't panic," she said too late.

Buddy was already in full panic mode. He leaped into the chair in the center of the room and had the noose around his neck so fast she was sure he had practiced the move routinely. This was his exit strategy; the sins of the father were to repeat.

"Whoa, hey, that's not cool," Rainey said.

Buddy was no longer paying any attention to her. He mumbled prayers to the Olympians. At least that is what it sounded like to Rainey.

"Hey, Shaman Gelaph," she'd try anything at this point, "who is going to save the Protector if you're gone?"

"I have seen the prophecy. I am to martyr myself, in hopes that you will lead the others to safety."

Rainey had a hard time keeping up with Buddy's delusions. "What others? Where is Wendy? I can't lead them anywhere if I don't know where to find them."

Buddy looked down at Rainey. "Let me lie beneath the sacred bones with the Protector. Do not let the demon have my soul."

The disturbed man kicked the chair out of the way.

"Oh shit," Rainey said, as she jumped into action.

She grabbed his flailing legs and lifted, still holding the Glock in her hand. She could hear him gagging, feel his body spasm and jerk. The sirens grew nearer, but she doubted they would make it in time. If the noose had been tied correctly, it locked around Buddy's throat the instant it took his weight. At least the knot had not broken his neck as it was designed to do.

"Don't you fucking die on me," Rainey yelled.

She heard the sirens roll up and go silent. She had no time to waste. She pointed the Glock as best she could without dropping Buddy and fired a round toward the base of the door.

"Hang on, Buddy," she said, immediately regretting her choice of words.

Rainey heard shouting outside. "Come out with your hands up."

She yelled back, "I can't. I'm holding up a hanging man. Break the door. I need help."

Rainey saw a patrolman peek in the window.

"Help me. I can't hold him much longer," she shouted.

Seconds felt like hours before the door frame splintered and the patrol officers entered, assessed the situation, and began the rescue.

Rainey was glad to step aside once Buddy had been lowered to the floor and the noose cut from his neck. He wasn't moving, and Rainey feared, even with the faint heartbeat the patrol officer found, Buddy's brain had been deprived of oxygen for too long. Calls went out for emergency medical personnel for Buddy and detectives to deal with the skeletal remains. Rainey holstered her weapon and stood in the corner processing, remembering, and begging her brain to figure it out. *Where did Buddy put Wendy?*

Think it through, Rainey. She should call Katie and tell her the crisis had passed, but her brain wanted to process what it knew. The strong urge to pause and reflect was one she recognized from years of crime-scene analysis. Something here in this space caught the attention of her subconscious, and she needed to determine what it was.

One officer stabilized Buddy's neck while the other ran to direct the medical personnel to the patient's location. Rainey ran through her recent interaction with the Shaman.

"Let me lie beneath the sacred bones with the Protector. Do not let the demon have my soul."

The officer looked up at her. "What?"

Rainey did not look at him when she answered, "Buddy said that, 'Let me lie beneath the sacre—' "

The message clicked into place. Rainey crossed the workshop in two steps. She reached down and removed the nest of blankets, papers, and bones as carefully as she could, revealing a locked wooden storage bench below. She saw a shovel in the corner, lifted it high above the lock and crashed the blade against it. It took three hard blows to pop the lock open.

Throwing the shovel out of the way, Rainey leaned down to remove the dangling lock. One deep breath later, she lifted the bench lid and found what she'd been looking for—Wendy King, supine and unmoving, dried blood on her face, and her hands folded over her chest. It appeared her own underwear were scattered over her body. Rainey lowered herself to her knees.

"Wendy," she whispered as her heart began to break.

Rainey placed two fingers on her sister's neck, pressing in on the carotid artery, praying she would find a pulse. Wendy was warm to the touch, which was a good. Rainey pressed harder, searching for any sign of life—and then there it was. A shallow, almost undetectable breath and the faint, slow beat of Wendy's heart against her fingertips.

"Oh, thank God," Rainey said.

As she removed her coat and covered Wendy's body, she turned to the officer. "You get on that radio let them know we found Officer King. We need medical right now. I don't give a rat's ass about an ice storm. Get me some paramedics, ASAP."

Rainey pulled the phone from her pocket and hit redial.

Sheila answered on the first ring, "Robertson."

Nearly breathless from adrenalin, Rainey said, "I found her. We've called for medical. You need to step in here and make things happen. She's barely breathing, and I think she's probably been drugged with her schizophrenic neighbor's anti-psychotic meds, maybe Haldol. She needs help fast."

Sheila said, "I'm on it," and hung up with nothing further spoken between them.

Rainey pressed Katie's contact icon.

She, too, answered on the first ring, "Are you okay?"

"Yes. I've found Wendy. She's in bad shape. I can't talk. Just didn't want you to worry. I love you. I have to go."

"Okay, I'll let everyone know you are out of danger. Love you. See you at the hospital."

"Okay, see you."

It was kind of sad that she and Katie had been through so many crisis situations that the ending of another could seem so practiced. Rainey shoved the phone back into her pocket and then remembered someone else who should know. She pulled out the phone and looked through her contacts while she asked the officer, "How far out are they?"

"Two minutes tops," he replied.

Rainey looked down at her sister. She reached in to take her hand. She squeezed it tightly and said, "Hold on, Wendy. You're going to make it. Fight for me, sis. It takes a crap load of drugs to kill one of us. You have to fight."

Rainey remembered the light that beckoned her to come when JW shot her up with enough narcotics to kill her. She remembered how part of her wanted to float away, give up, and give in, to stay with her father who smiled back through a haze telling her it was not her time. Rainey recalled the doctors' comments on her astonishing will to live and knew they would never understand that it was Billy Bell who willed her back to life.

"You stay with me, Wendy."

She found and dialed the contact number she sought. He too had been waiting by his phone.

Rainey listened to his panicked hello before she said, "Rex, get to Memorial Hospital. I've found her. They'll be bringing her there."

"Is she—is she—"

Rainey answered the question he couldn't bring himself to ask, "She's alive. I think she's probably been drugged, and she looks like she took a few good shots to the head and face. I can't tell anymore until we get her out of this box. I just wanted you to know. See you at the hospital."

Rainey hung up rather than listen to the questions for which she had no answers. She slipped the phone into her trouser pocket and leaned over the box again.

"Come on, kid. Stay with me," she said, tucking the coat around Wendy's shoulders. "I've gotten used to having you around. I like having you as a little sister. I think I might even love you, you know. Thank you for saving my son."

Rainey saw the tear hit her arm. She hadn't realized she was crying. It startled her. While she'd grown fond of Wendy, she had not completely opened to the idea of sisterhood. At that moment, Rainey understood what Katie had told her—sisters are joined at the heart.

She heard the voice before she saw him, but the sound made the hair stand up on her arms. He was speaking to the officer holding Buddy's neck.

"Is he still alive?"

Rainey turned slowly and recognized the man immediately. All the crazy things Buddy said made sense in one glance. She stood and turned to face him. He saw her and reached into his jacket. Rainey pulled her weapon at the same time Travis Odom stuck the barrel of a forty-five semiautomatic to the officer's head.

Travis glanced back toward the house and then focused on Rainey. "I can tell by the expression on your face that you do recognize where you've seen me. I was surprised when Wendy did not seem to put it together the other day on the observation deck. I knew she would, though. I can't have that part of my life exposed."

Rainey smiled at the murderer in the door. "My, my, my. Travis, the way you deal with conflict is very unhealthy. First, your stepfather catches you molesting his son, so you hung him here in his workshop. Did Joanne Bonner discover you molesting Buddy? Is that why you killed her and made it look like your mentally ill brother did it? When you saw Wendy with those boys, you knew it was just a matter of time before she nailed you for your pedophilic tendencies, right?"

Handsome Travis smiled and took another glance toward the house. He bent to remove the officer's service weapon. The helpless officer stared at Rainey, pleading with his eyes for help. If she shot Travis, the slightest twitch of his finger could take the life of the terrified cop at his feet, but she knew time was running out. If Travis had an end game, it was about to be played as the ambulance siren whirred to a stop in front of the house.

"What are you going to do, Travis? You cannot possibly think you can kill us all and get away with it."

"Let's see," he said as his dark heart shaded his smile, "I'm shooting you with his gun and then I'll shoot him and Buddy with your gun. Then I'll tell everyone how Buddy shot you and how you got off two shots before falling dead."

Rainey didn't hesitate or waste one more second because as Travis glanced at the house again, she nodded to the cop and unloaded three shots to Travis's chest in rapid succession. The cop at his feet ducked away, but he really didn't have to. Travis Odom was dead before his body hit the floor.

Rainey heard a raspy whisper, "Nice shot, sis."

She turned to see Wendy trying to sit up.

"Hey, you," Rainey said, smiling. "Don't get up. You're going to be okay."

Wendy winced with pain and asked, "Mack?"

"He's safe. Thank you, Wendy."

Wendy's lips curled into a slight, and from the looks of it, painful grin. "Are you thankful enough not to kick my ass for leaving my weapon at your house?"

Rainey chuckled and said, "Today I am. We'll see how I feel when you heal up."

CHAPTER ELEVEN

3:30 PM, Friday, March 6, 2015
Memorial Hospital Emergency Room
Orange County, NC

Katie pulled the curtain back and stepped up beside the bed. The activity of the busy emergency room during an ice storm filled the air with the sounds crying children and overworked staff. A harried nurse had led her to the curtained bed and then hurried away.

Katie smiled at the patient, "I'm used to picking up a woman that looks a lot like you in this ward. How are you doing?"

Wendy smiled as best she could with her swollen lips. The cut above her eye had been closed and bandaged. A spot of dried blood remained on her cheek.

"I'm okay. I'm going to be sore, but the drugs are leaving my system as we speak." Wendy nodded to the IV bag. "Is Mack okay?"

"He will be when he knows you are all right. He asked me every hour if Nee Nee found you. He was very happy when I told him she had."

"I'm sorry, Katie. I know how hard you and Rainey work to keep your family from harm. Mack and I went out back to see if Barron was perhaps in my shed. I forgot to reset the alarm when we came back in. Travis Odom came in right after we walked into the office. I heard him. That's when I put Mack in the closet."

"Thank you," Katie said, patting Wendy's hand. "Rainey said you fought like hell for him."

Wendy smiled a little, but Katie could tell she was tired.

"Your mother called. She and your father are on the way. I told her we would stay with you until they arrived."

Wendy's eyelids flickered but then sprung open with her question, "Did Buddy make it? He saved me, sort of."

"He's in a coma. That's all I know," Katie answered.

With her eyelids at half-mast, Wendy said, "Travis knocked me out with a shot of Haldol, they tell me. He left me in the woods. I woke up a little bit when Buddy carried me into his workshop. I didn't wake up again until just before Rainey shot Travis."

"Where did he get Haldol?" Katie asked.

Sheila Robertson answered the question, as she opened the curtain to enter.

"He stole it from the half-way house. They reported it missing, but Travis was not a suspect—seeing as how he is or was an upstanding citizen just coming by to check on his little brother. He apparently went out the back of the house with Wendy just as Rainey arrived. I don't think he realized who he was dealing with."

"Why did he come after Wendy?" Katie asked.

Sheila walked to the other side of Wendy's bed and gave her a soft pat on the hand. It appeared she was aware of Wendy's badly bruised body and took care not to add to her pain.

She answered Katie's question. "Wendy had been looking into disappearances involving some homeless young men who used survival sex to subsist. After searching his home and computers, we've discovered he was a pedophile. Buddy was his first victim. Rainey told us she and Wendy saw Travis on the observation deck looking for a trick. He must have recognized Wendy as his mother's neighbor."

"Did he kill that other girl, the one that lived in my house?"

"Rainey's pretty sure he did. She thinks Joanne Bonner tried to help Buddy. Travis killed her to keep from being found out."

Katie had spoken with Rainey while she followed the ambulance to the hospital. She had agreed to an escort and surrendered her weapon, because for the first time in her life Rainey had actually killed someone.

Katie asked Sheila, "Rainey is clear on the shooting, right?"

Sheila smiled, "Oh, you have no worries. The cop she saved is singing her praises and thanking his lucky stars she's a hell of a shot."

Wendy tried to open her eyes wider, but Katie knew from her own experience that the effects of the drug would come and go for a few hours. She pushed a familiar Bell chestnut curl from Wendy's forehead.

"Close your eyes and rest. I'm glad Rainey found you, little sis. I'm so very thankful you are going to be all right."

Wendy's eyes closed slowly, as she said, "You know you're married to a badass, right?"

Katie chuckled. "I know that she will fight to the death for the ones she loves. It appears to be a family trait." As she turned to Sheila, Katie asked, "Where is she, anyway?"

From the curtained-off area next to Wendy's bed came the answer, "Bleccckkkk."

About the Author

2013 Rainbow Awards First Runner-up for Best Lesbian Novel, Out on the Panhandle, and three time Lambda Literary Award Finalist in Mystery with Rainey Nights (2012), Molly: House on Fire (2013), and The Rainey Season (2014), author R.E. Bradshaw began publishing in August of 2010. Before beginning a full-time writing career, she worked in professional theatre and also taught at both the university and high school level. A native of North Carolina and a proud Tar Heel, Bradshaw now makes her home in Oklahoma with her wife of 27 years. Writing in many genres, from the fun Southern romantic romps of the Adventures of Decky and Charlie series to the intensely bone-chilling Rainey Bell Thrillers, R.E. Bradshaw's books offer something for everyone.

Learn more at http://www.rebradshawbooks.com

Manufactured by Amazon.ca
Bolton, ON